The
Winter Gardeners

†HE
WIN†ER GARDENERS

DENNIS DENISOFF

COACH HOUSE BOOKS

copyright © Dennis Denisoff, 2003

first edition

Published with the assistance of the Canada Council for the Arts
and the Ontario Arts Council

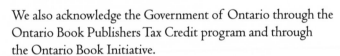

We also acknowledge the Government of Ontario through the
Ontario Book Publishers Tax Credit program and through
the Ontario Book Initiative.

NATIONAL LIBRARY OF CANADA
CATALOGUING IN PUBLICATION

Denisoff, Dennis
    The winter gardeners / Dennis Denisoff.

ISBN 1-55245-129-1

    I. Title.

PS8557.E484W56 2003   C813'.54   C2003-904962-0

This story is for Ivan,
who has taught me so much about
unconditional love without expecting
to learn anything from me in return.

A DAY IN THE HEARTLAND

They had been waiting for Constable Loch to come and remove the furniture from Giggy Andrewes's gazebo, when sleep had overtaken them. The air felt brittle in the hush of the afternoon and the peculiar bloomless plantings in the garden chafed against each other like shards of glass or weapons of soldiers eager for war. The blades glistened in the sunlight. So rarely did the breeze sigh through the tangle of Giggy's garden that any rustle from the exotics seemed less an act of appreciation than a mockery. The occasional cry of one of the peacocks pierced the air as if the creature were struggling to affirm its existence in the summer town of Lake Wachannabee. Each cry tinged Giggy's property, she recently conjectured as she introduced her nephew and his reticent friend to the garden such a short time ago, with an aura haunted by the history of Wachannabee Gorge and the indigenes that the British explorers first found among its caves and contours.

It was not until the gauzy sunlight began to spill over the rims of Jem's eyes and into his brain that the boy began to awaken. The nephew met the haze of the Ontario summer with the glazed indifference of an opossum, but eventually the pinkish blur of fleshly limbs strewn about the gazebo shed its aura and took on the bodily order of Giggy, Cora and himself. The mosquito netting undulated, paused, undulated again in the heat as it cast gentle whippings of shadow against the young man's cheeks. He hung lazy across the coffee table from his aunt, his slender candle-wax fingers furtively plucking the harp of soft threads worn through near the crotch of his cut-offs. The gesture belied his willingness to respond to his aunt's uncon-scious overtures for attention.

Cora's limbs remained sprawled across the cedar-slatted floor, shifting occasionally among the pages of the exploration narrative that Dr. Amicable was editing. The hairs on her left arm glowed like strings of honey. A drop of saliva fell from her bottom lip onto the top page of the manuscript.

Back, back and back again Giggy's eyes flickered to the last glazed scrap of strudel on the tray near her ankles. The gesture evoked the rhythmic sway of a ceiling fan and Jem found himself disturbed by its consistency. His aunt's mind was elsewhere, perhaps once again thinking over the Fafaist Manifesto or re-evaluating the decision she had made over a year ago to have the gazebo stuccoed. Caught trusting a Cubist, she now owned an extension that, in her view, was nothing more than an architec-tural goitre on the soft, solid facade of the Winter Garden. She would never again act against the advice of Miss Emily of Crew, who prided herself on clairvoyance ever since she had correctly forecasted Mavis von und Graf's death in a street fight in Niagara Falls. The architectural blight no longer made Giggy weep, no, but, combined with her recent infatuation with Russian melodrama, it did give her complexion a distinctly seedy pallor.

Her entropy was not aided by the fact that she had begun reading these Russian novels with no expectation of finishing them. Cora had more than once seen her hostess's tongue wrap about the sounds of a single line for four or five minutes or even more before finally lolling on to the next as hesitant as a rural virgin before the glory and might of the Sultan himself. It had been rumoured by Lady Bella Clasp, the veterinarian of the flaming hair who lived next door, that Giggy had spent weeks with one solitary finger piously retracing the opening line of *Anna Karenina* as her mind concocted permutations as evocative as the position of the Asian-American woman who at present rested at her powdered feet, the pages of Robert Shakely's exploration narrative nestling her body in an unearthly, phosphorescent glow.

Cora was sleeping with her arms akimbo and her smooth legs bent and overlapping like a pair of inebriated seagulls, their tone confirming her familiarity with the stationary rower in Giggy's basement. Even now, gazing at her, Jem could feel in the back of his brain the sensual, rhythmic pounding of the machine, its mechanisms whirring like a flock of rubber-band airplanes sent spinning by a cluster of knee-knocking school-boys into the heat of a white Italian sky. Had he been aware of her preference for consistency before inviting her north, things might have turned out differently for all of them. For him, muscle development – even the thought of muscle develop-ment – had always made his belly, nurtured for years on cocaine and the blackened seafood of the Louisiana bayou, *grrrr*. But now, since the 'murder,' all of his senses were benumbed.

Suspense is so stilted, he thought, so dishonest, and all people prefer to be trusted. Unfortunately, this veneration of clarity had in itself provoked some members of Lake Wachannabee to lie. Soon speculations were spilling from the lips of the townsfolk like seeds from poppy pods. In truth, nobody was sure yet that it would be deemed a murder but, for the sake of veracity in the long term, everybody was operating under that assumption. It was so much easier, really.

For Jem, the reaction was numbness. Just now, as he lay belly down, he was fully unaware of the trickle of sweat that was lurching its way along the moguls of his spine like a drunk meandering toward the lake's edge to wash away his sorrows.

'I do declare. Auntie?'

'Yes, dear?' Giggy loved her nephew's little bayou twang that, as rare as the burble of an albino catfish, caught the attention of all who heard it. Despite the fact that Jem had not been living at the Winter Garden for many months, she found herself often thinking of him as her son and had to struggle each time to cast the notion aside because of the limitations it implied for their relationship.

'No, it's nothing.' Since Jem's arrival, the two had begun to develop a system of communication that depended less and less on words. If language ever failed them, she would come to muse, it would be not because of their inability to converse but due to the inadequacy of the words they held in common. Their years apart seemed in fact to have made them more attuned to each other. The detritus of daily life, the responsibilities and irritations of raising a child or of being raised, had not corseted their relationship or cluttered the characteristics that they now valued so highly in each other.

'Everybody loves children,' Giggy had once tried to convince the PTA when presenting her closing arguments against a school field trip that required a brief but intimate sojourn on her property, 'more purely when from a distance, through that sort of impressionist haze that obscures their faces or at least their mediocrity or, shall we say, when the love is allowed enough irresponsibility to become more akin to the respect one gives friends or colleagues.' Then, to prove her gravity, she had turned in her summation to a Metaphysical. 'It was, I believe, John Donne,' she had offered, glancing at the smudged ink on the note card in her sweating hand (it might have read 'John Deere'), 'who made such adoration and its value obvious when in his sermon "Deaths Duell" he expounded all over the baby Jesus,

> 'About midnight he was *taken* and *bound with a kisse*, art thou not *too conformable* to him in that? ... There now hangs that *sacred Body* upon the *Crosse, rebaptized* in his owne *teares* and *sweat*, and *embalmed* in his *owne blood alive*. There are those *bowells of compassion*, which are so conspicuous, so manifested, as that you may *see them*

through his wounds. There those *glorious eyes* grew faint in their light: so as the *Sun ashamed* to survive them, *departed with his light too.*

'See here, how the baby Jesus, his forehead as smooth and round as a young girl's knee, is most venerated when he is viewed at some distance – as we do with portraits and monuments – there, on the cross, so tenderly, only a few yards away.' Giggy reached one arm out as if to touch a crucifix only she could see levitating above the sink in the Wachannabee Elementary teachers' lounge. 'And then, as Donne demonstrates, even further, as far away as the sun, with which he is one, verily.' The perspiration of her convictions had destroyed the remainder of her notes; there was nothing for it but to ad lib. 'This then is how best to view children, for it gives us patience and keeps us from punishing them too readily and from forgetting that they are not our possessions but our charges. That would explain why, legally, one must demand "custody" of a child, would it not? A type of ownership. One is encouraged to do so, as if it were a biological right to have this authority, verily, over somebody else.' Because Giggy had never wanted custody over Jem, it seemed obvious to the woman that he would gravitate toward her, just as most children gravitate away from the parents thrust upon them from birth.

Jem himself felt that he had not so much drifted away from his parents as been drawn by the kindness of strangers. The notion of personal agency had never entered his evaluation of the meanderings of his life. Absent-mindedly stroking the threads of his shorts, he recognized the boredom that characterized these wanderings – an apathy arising from a cultural familiarity with everything that had been invented or discovered since his birth, arising from the world being driven toward universalist essentialism despite being so far from the metaphysical. Rather than trying to understand it all, he conjectured, we assume that what we know is everything there is. Perhaps this new view had not only prepared him for his life of observation but also given him the patience and pacing that his recent sense of guilt and caution required.

So recently, he had felt no guilt at all, because of his unique love and lust for Robert. It had seemed as if he might always retain the lump of nervous passion in his gorge that he felt on first seeing the man there at the Winter Garden. None of the Winter Gardeners actually went in for the horticultural; that was why Giggy had had the landscape redesigned, planted entirely with vegetation requiring the least amount of maintenance. It was in this unnatural setting of plants free from human interference that Jem saw Rob standing among a contortion of raspberry brambles. Giggy was trying to steer her nephew and Chappy, the house whippet, in another direction, toward the fleshy leaves of rhubarb and Potter's hostas, and the boy's body obeyed. But his eyes, imagination and nerves clung with lust to Robert who, unaware of being watched, was picking overripe raspberries with only his lips, kissing them one by one off their branches, leaving behind a trail of naked nubs glowing white where the red berries had just been.

'I say,' Jem murmured as he relaxed across from his aunt, 'Passive observation.' He envisioned it as a career option. He knew some people who had careers.

He lifted his fingers off the hard-on that he had unintentionally coaxed to attention. Language did that to him. His mahogany-heavy eyes settled on the tool shed, as erect as a sentinel's station at the west flank of Auntie's mallows. Yet another of the gardener's garish constructions, it seemed to burn in the sunlight. 'Aloo-*minium*,' he chattered to himself, 'aloooo-*minium*.' There was something refreshing about the word. It sounded millennial, like spray paint or Swedish toiletries. Something cool slipping between his lips. But he was also using it as self-flagellation, to punish himself for the rodenticides that he may so recently have committed.

'Aloo*minium*.' So soothing a sound for a word marked by such pain. It was only yesterday that Jem had found the bundle of baby squirrels pasty-eyed and huddled in a corner of the tool shed. Upon discovery, he had latched shut the door to ensure that they would develop safe from the threat of predators. He'd then re-settled himself in the gazebo and consumed the last of his ginger ale and grenadine and had begun to fondle the edge of one of his aunt's novels. And it was then that his attention was drawn back to the shed – the squeals, the squeals. Another squirrel, one much larger, was trying to get into what Jem only at that moment realized was becoming a sweat box of death. The gardener's edifice was baking the babies alive.

'Shirley!' he squeaked in horror. The squirrel was one of Giggy's familiars. ('No, we don't know the creature's sex,' Giggy agreed, 'but it is the mother regardless.') Guilty, guilty, guilty – the word spun about the boy's head with the persistence of deer flies over roadkill. Yet he just watched, dumb-glazed, as Shirley scratched at the walls. Should he dare to interfere with nature again? The creature, its taut sinews soon torn and bleeding, continued to scrape at the barrier that kept her from her babies. All the while, she flayed her head back and forth as if unable to understand why nobody else was turning up to assist in the rescue. Even after her claws had begun to drip scarlet, she persisted in ramming her arms through the sliver of space she'd managed to scrape away beneath the door. Jem could just hear the infants, who must have recognized their parent's chatter, letting off faint hullabaloos of despair. And then, in frustration, in a final act of defiance against futility, Shirley began running circles of rage (as Jem himself had done on occasion), stopping only to throw her body against the siding with the dynamics of a percussionist before renewing the frantic dervish.

At last the boy, picking his moment, rushed to the structure, flung open the door and flopped backward onto the trimmed lawn as wafts of August heat poured forth. The waves hit him like Florida hits foreigners, but before he could even formulate a headline for the *Wachannabee Orderly* ('Heroic Youth Yanks ... '), the rodent lunged at him and clamped her dingy teeth onto the denim of his shorts. Jem stumbled backward crablike, trying to shake himself free. Shirley was flung headlong into the air. She must have made her decision before she had even landed to retreat to the security of the garden, for she did so in a bounce and an arc so smooth and art deco that it whiffed a touch too much of practice.

Jem escaped into the gazebo and, latching shut the door, watched the waves of heat flow up across the metal siding of the shed, wails of despair emanating even more strongly now from the heat of darkness. 'Hullabaloo! Hullabaloo!' the infants cried like impassioned extras in *South Pacific*. How many of their pelts had he parched with his thoughtlessness? How many might yet even die? It seemed hours before he caught sight of scarlet-eyed Shirley risking a return, scuttling through the sweet grass, darting from willow to willow to whortleberry as if she were a master of espionage.

He slipped behind a porch pillar and peered out furtively. Saliva flashed off yellow squirrel teeth. 'Yellower than the chaste moon,' Jem would soliloquize among the other Winter Gardeners later that evening, 'yellower than the roses that children place at the feet of the Queen of Araby.' The creature, upon reaching the heat-heady chamber, leapt into the darkness with nary a glance askance. Amid the chaos of chattering and rustling, the young man could only wonder who was scolding whom, and then the adult finally sprung Houdini-like into the daylight. In her teeth, she carried not one but two of the babies. Limbs abounding, the trio bumbled off toward the soothing darkness at the heart of the garden and the safety of its fronds. The evacuation continued until each of the infants was removed – eight in all, some so limp that Jem doubted that they had survived. 'Probably just snoozy,' Giggy would console him.

Today, a day later, the deathtrap stands once again as barren and silent as a women's public washroom, as barren as an ill-speculated condominium east of the Pickering nuclear plant, as silent as the Winter Garden itself ever since Giggy had discovered Rob's long, naked body unconscious on the Prussian blue rubber mat in the hallway near the weight room. No hair on his chest, or his legs, or his crotch, or even his armpits — just all that taut, glistening musculature highlighted, some of it even exposed. Rob had yet to speak to Jem since the event.

'Because, because, because, because, be-caaause,' Jem softly sang as tears welled up in his eyes for the umpteenth time. Chappy knew what the boy was lamenting but thought it wisest to stay silent rather than join in the grief. During his short career as a green racer, the dog had been muzzle-broken and had learnt well the rewards of silence. So, up against Cora's still sleeping torso he curled his body and under Giggy's feet he tucked his nose. Digging his claws into the floorboards of the gazebo, he cast a cautious eye at Jem's flat lashes as they trapped his salty tears and tangled together like a chorus line of spider legs. Giggy watched the shadow of her own body as, lengthening into the evening, it enwrapped her nephew.

✦

Despite the cooling air of the evening, Jem and Giggy continued to wilt at each other from across the coffee table as they watched a V of Canada geese pass over the lake and toward the evergreens that stood in the distance as sturdy as the obelisks of the West Nile and as flat as the black cardboard backdrop of *Dante's Inferno – The Musical* that Constable Loch kept in the storage room of the Lake Wachannabee Community Centre.

Upon his arrival at the Winter Garden, Jem's acts of affection toward his aunt had been fostered by a dutiful sense of reciprocity, but he was now simply pleased to see her happy. Love, he had learnt, did not always take the short and lusty route. This was the passage taken with Robert. His feelings for both his aunt and Robert – even the difference between his early love for Robert and the way that he missed him now – proved to Jem that 'love' was not broad enough a term to encompass the range of feelings.

Rob wasn't sure his feelings for Jem were love. He found the other exotic and affectionate and this, so far, was enough. If anything challenged the wounded man's fondness, it was Jem's inertia – no, his complacency regarding his inertia. He was rather young, Robert thought, to be facing his future with indifference, as if all that existed were the moment. Pleasure became gem-like only in comparison to less fulfilling moments. He had, of late, become far more sensitive to the heights of emotion and so much more appreciative. His lover, unfortunately, had not.

Jem's attention drifted off the V of geese and parachuted down to the dark surface of the lake, pierced here and there now and then by motley flips of fish snipping at the insects that always hovered over the water at sunset. Dr. Amicable's extremely long and slender canoe created another, more deceptive V cutting a silver slit in the water as it made its way from the public dock back to his cabin for the night. The man's editing of Shakely's exploration journals had made him something of a star in the community. The journals were the first extensive account of the Wachannabee region. Dr. Amicable's English, however, was too inelastic for work on the records of an eighteenth-century Hudson's Bay explorer, so he had accrued a cluster of eloquent assistants to help him, Rob among them. No doubt the only somewhat literate Robert Shakely never intended his words — 'No crapping today' and so on — for so many earnest eyes.

Jem twisted his torso and inhaled a serpentine of cocaine off the mirror tabletop, and then refilled his glass with the Canada Dry and crushed glacial ice that he kept in a small Styrofoam cooler near the divan. This mix had replaced cappuccino slushies as his *breuvage de la saison*. Living up here, he mused – lying on his back, eyes mesmerized by the golden effervescence in his glass – Auntie must often take pleasure in such exotic northern products. He took a sip, enjoying the cold dribble that ran down his chin and along one of the two grooves on the front of his neck. It inched its way into the slight indent of his chest and more slowly still down to the oxbow lake of his belly button where it pooled lazily and became still.

'I'm worried that you're drinking too much of that, dear. Anything habit-forming isn't worth experiencing twice. And you'll get to belching. You don't want that. I don't want that. Belching – who could say why – seems inevitably to lead to swaggering. And then, well, the slippery slope of slovenliness.'

'I don't know that I wouldn't mind a swagger. It has always added mystery to those who could pull it off. Val Kilmer, for example, or Huckleberry Hound.'

'Pull what off, dear?'

But this didn't interest him. 'I wonder if it looks like a V from directly above.' He coaxed a bluebottle off his soft left lid but let his lank black hair continue to hang heavy there.

'A swagger would no doubt work on you, dear — everything does seem to. Still, habits,' she cautioned maternally, scooping up some beer foam with a flake of her strudel.

'What do you say?'

'The flock?' Her lips pulled forcefully on a Cameo.

'The wake.'

She stared into the gloaming. 'Well, it's definitely a V from above, sweetest, but not from behind,' and yet, even as she spoke, Giggy realized that one V couldn't possibly set a standard for all Vs. What one saw from behind could simply be a different V.

'Oh, but it is from underneath.'

'Yes, possibly from underneath,' and then, hoping to help her nephew reach the same realization that she had regarding normativization, she added with forced casualness, 'it wouldn't be inappropriate, would it, dear, to consider David Hume at this point. "Skeptic," you know, needn't carry wholly negative connotations. I'm sure geese could make a V from behind if they tried. But then, that's assuming a fair amount of rationality for the fowl, yes? And yet who's to say that animals don't act rationally?'

Giggy took a swig of beer, burped sharply ('I must, for my condition') and imagined what the wake looked like from beneath, from underwater, her own billowful body naked in the cool night — a moment's respite from a summer of chafing along the length of her cleavage, under her full breasts, between the rolls on her belly and thighs. On especially hot days, when even the deodorant she smothered under her succulents did not seem to help, she tucked a couple of Cora's sanitary pads between her flesh and the wire support of her bra to ease the pressure.

Just now, Giggy found sufficient relief in her imaginings. She envisioned her submerged body borne by the black water, her kimono fluttering wet about her in the breezy current as fawn muskellunge and yellow perch flew past with flapping fins and Dr. Amicable's long and extremely slender canoe slipped over her like one half of a husked pea pod, casting a shadow in the moonlight such that, for a brief moment, her body became an aquatic image of yin and yang. Emerald was the pod and darkest ermine the water as her body bobbed like driftwood, just keeping itself from plunging into the masses of air. 'So too inspiring,' she murmured, lowering her torso in its chair as if submerging into a bath. This was not the first time the doctor had rested so comfortably on her mind. But a fraction Giggy's legs spread, the tips of her bare feet poking out from beneath her Balzacian kimono with the timidity of mice. Jem realized that she was having a vision from beneath the wake of the canoe.

I love her so much more than exotic Canadian products, he thought, more than René Simard's jumpsuits, more than maple syrup in tiny tin houses that Wachannabee children place in homage at the leathered boots of mounted police, more than the husky-skin culottes in which Québecois mothers swaddle and coddle their tender infants, more than the smoked salmon of ... oh so and so and so much more.

Recent discussions of murder had upset Jem's aunt immeasurably, and he hoped that these briefest suggestions of pleasure were spreading their reassuring warmth, like Tiger Balm on a twisted muscle, below the surface of her skin all the way down to her veins, her heart, the very marrow of her bones. Lost in imaginings, she stretched her feet even further out and stroked the curved leg of some furniture. The act itself was a gesture of reaffirmation, for Giggy was reclining on the very same chaise longue on which Constable Loch had so disdainfully refused to sit only one month ago, choosing instead to splay the girth of his khakied buttocks on a common footstool as he licked the lead of his working-man's pencil and mapped in only the thinnest trail of her eloquent defence: 5:15, sun setting in the west, flesh aglow as if illuminated from within.

His squatting macho had forced Giggy to admire his chiselled ass despite the fact that his hackneyed shorthand irritated her. That day, she had decided to wax especially baroque for his sake, guessing that the others' reports – Jem's, Cora's, the professor's, Robert's (although one might forgive his unwillingness to speak, what with the facial wounds virtually ensuring that his lips were sealed) – had probably all been made mundane by each of their futile struggles for objectivity. Oh, she thought now, gently rubbing the last, succulent memories of her nocturnal swim out from between the sweet-smelling rolls of her belly, I'll have to give the constable Dr. Amicable's manuscript of Shakely's journal just so that, even if he never discovers the truth of the crime, he will at least have a hint of how such a thing might be inspired.

She meditated on Dr. Amicable's words, her admiration for his passion unlikely to become anything venerary, it having reached a level beyond the erotic. But there was something about Shakely's artlessness that she was finding more and more appealing, more visceral, the longer she allowed herself to live within the over-wrought aestheticism of her own mind. Giggy gulped some more beer and ran the long nail of her left pinky along the edge of the chaise longue, surprised to find it snag on a slit in the material. This lazy sew struck the matriarch as not simply unfortunate but embarrassing, even peculiar. The whippet's effort to steal her attention failed. The chaise longue, like much of her furniture, had come from her deceased mother's long-since-demolished-but-once-five-star hotel in Zurich, the Ambassador's Arms. *Home Away from Home, for Ambassadors and Kings*. A tear in the fabric of the furniture was a tear in the fabric of her memory.

Giggy's concerns about the material were rooted in the images that she recalled of herself as a pert thing curled up on the chaise while Mama played the piano in her eccentric way — charming, really, with a pained anxiety coming through in the brief silence that foreshadowed each sudden poke of Mama's only index finger. Watching her play, one could not help but think of a chicken learning to type — an impassioned chicken, unquestionably, but still … These fond, formative memories made it all the more troublesome to imagine that the piano and the chaise longue, which had all this time remained as united as wealthy Siamese twins, might soon be separated. They were all she had left of her childhood and now she was giving one of them up to the constable's charity bazaar. She could still hear Mama, in a continental English as reassuring as a receding thunderstorm, proudly inform the baronets who sojourned every season on their way to the Black Forest mineral baths, of the refinement of the hotel. 'Five stars, five of them, dahrlinggs,' she would zsazsa. 'It takes talent to whip up a hotel like this one. A bucket of talent. And I've got a bucket.' The memory brought back to Giggy her mother's last years of pain, of waning hope — not pride, as the daughter had once thought, but desperation. One recurring image, only one, as Giggy left in search of her destiny — that of Mama standing as glorious as a Rhode Island Red next to the piano, wagging the pointed nail of a finger in warning. The sun ricocheted off the mother's aurora of auburn hair. It was the brilliance of the locks, Giggy later lied, that caused her to tear. Oh yes, Giggy had her own bucket, a bucket full of painful memories. If only she could sell *them*, she thought, instead of the furniture.

'You're right,' volleyed Jem, tugging absent-mindedly on a lone chest hair. 'Those big old geese *could* make a V from behind, and they could also make an R. Or an O. Or a B.' A single tear as plump as the central diamond in the tiara of the Infanta of Paraguay squeezed itself from the duct tucked into the boy's lower left lid. 'I do believe they could probably make just about any letter under the heavens and still make a V from below.' Now he stretched his coltish legs into a V as a visual aid, remembering his childhood swims in Catahoula Lake under the full Louisiana moon, the way in which the sweet, muddy waters pulled him forward as he stepped gingerly along the soft, grey depths shifting below, the way in which the mud-blind fish and weedy banners caressed his calves and thighs. Waist-deep, he would turn like Salomé to face the white virgin moon, the summer air warm yet chilling his skin, the orb's beams piercing his body like a promise, his then hairless chest breaking into goosebumps while his scrotum receded into his body like a bashful snail into its shell. Silver swamp daffodils, their petals stiff-shut, swayed over the jet waters, each stem holding a perfect whiplash curve.

The young man's eyes focused on the drapes of mosquito netting that clung around the front of the house like a giant hairnet. The bugs had begun to bother, all spindly and aggressive — blackflies, deer flies, gnats, an everglade's worth of mosquitoes, all incessantly spinning tangles of anxiety and illness in the dustless air.

'No, not any letter. I can't imagine an O,' said Giggy.

'Oh well, dear, if you can't imagine it . . . ,' half-attentive.

'Well I can't, love, or an X for example. It would take a lot of Canada geese to make an X in the sky, yes? I wonder how many geese it would take to spell FOX. And with their heads and legs, because you'd have to view them from behind for that, wouldn't they look more like asterisks? Animals are so self-serving; they'd only do it if it suited them. But humans . . . well, humans aren't much different.'

If a V, thought Jem, then why not an X? Wasn't it just two hip-joined Vs?

It had been all Giggy could do to convince Constable Loch that the Queen Anne chaise longue had no part in the crime —

even though, since Cora had been staying in the Winter Garden for some time now, Giggy was herself unsure, although unadmittedly so. It was that smear of scarlet, the size of a small palm print, but which she clearly recalled as pomegranate juice she had spilt herself years and years ago, that had made Queen Anne suspect. Province states had crumbled for less, she mused concernedly, Bethgoz-Lisotania, to name what for Giggy was but the most obvious example.

Not that she would ever join the community in its defamation of Cora. Indeed she couldn't imagine any one person, let alone the toned but tiny Cora, having the strength or agility to remove all those rectangular strips of flesh from a body in protest. And who would have cleaned up all the mess, the spills of blood that had to have been left behind? There were no traces of cleaning supplies to be found and there must have been so much blood on those craggy stones. And Cora was, well, brittle, wasn't she? Is 'brittle' not the kindest word in this case? She was young only in years, that one. Her maturity pressed down upon *joie* like a stack of encyclopedias on a maple leaf.

Giggy was not guilty of assuming that Cora's earnestness and caution (she avoided calling it conservatism) were the visitor's fault. It was something arising through Cora's interaction with the rest of society or, more precisely, arising from the pressures it forced on her. As such, these traits of respectability and precision did not belong to Cora, but existed in a space between her and society. Their contours could be read on the surface of her body but they were nevertheless the product of external influences, like body paint or a second skin.

Giggy was correct in deducing that Cora wore her wounds with pride, and that this was necessary if she were to protect her sense of identity. The girl had been travelling with Jem for who knew how long, in the United States and now here in Canada. She looked only a few years older than him, but she was definitely the chaperone. Giggy could see that many would feel that her nephew was both feeble and egotistical. But Cora, she saw in him the kind of person that she was destined to support – such a one as she herself might have become had she not been queer *and* a woman. And so Giggy recognized her younger self in Cora's overreliance on melancholy as a form of joy, on contentment as fulfilment. The matriarch could only hope that Cora's growing love for Jem (for she truly believed that all must eventually love him) would allow her to shed some defences. He may not teach her to swim through the onslaught of vindictiveness and malice as he did, as if it were only the exhaust and whine of a Sea-Doo. But for now, Cora could at least manoeuvre in his wake and learn that indifference was at times the most effective form of self-defence.

Cora's high valuation of responsibility, Giggy felt, meant that she had the patience, but not the adventurousness, to have peeled the strips of skin off Robert. The older woman could not help but wonder, as well, how patient Robert had to have been to have let himself be so ensnared. It almost frustrated her, the sense that his point of view, the unique materiality of his experience, was just beyond the grasp of her clumsy fingers. Giggy had once watched Lady Clasp, who lived across the east field, use a pair of tweezers to strip the skin from boiled tomatoes. After the roiling water had inflamed the pieces of fruit, their tissued skin puckered, seeming to beg to be pulled back. The veterinarian, her flaming locks hairnetted, had approached each of the orbs with a tenderness verging on a perfectionism almost Catholic in its ceremony, Futurist in its faith. There was a symbiosis, a sort of conspiracy, it seemed, between the woman and the glowing orange-red globes. The recent crime, however, must have required more than a Kmart kitchen utensil and the skills of the village vet. Robert, it had been conjectured, must have been peeled with something like a scalpel or an Xacto knife. Despite signs of restraints, it was felt the delicacy of the procedure had required that he had been coerced somehow into participating. The lab had found no substances in the young man's system that would have knocked him unconscious, nor signs of severe restraints. Oh, a body in protest, ruminated Giggy, that might be the title of my memoirs. And she began kneading her chafing flesh once more.

The lack of evidence either in favour of or against Cora had gnawed on Giggy's already stressed mind so persistently that she'd finally decided to donate it, the chaise longue on which Constable Loch had discovered the red stain, to the Lake Wachannabee Bazaar. Since they had yet to attain confirmation of a crime and nobody had pressed charges, there was no basis for taking evidence, but Giggy felt it best to let the furniture go regardless. She'd never expected that her humble gift would attract much attention, but the townsfolk began to gobble the fruits of speculation from each other's baskets as if starved for gossip. At first, she was most perturbed to find so many pronouncing her name with a soft 'G,' but soon this gaucherie was surpassed by the one declaration consistent in all their accusations: the wealthy lacked morals. 'It is at times even too easy to conceal,' bewailed the matriarch in language decadent in its convolutions, 'the actual poverty from which I, like the black grapes of Sicily, have grown.'

Giggy's eyes focused on the point at which the geese had disappeared, and she began to worry again about her decision to give the furniture away. An exploratory nail had revealed the slit to be almost five inches long. She could slide her hand into it as if it were a pocket. Giggy saw the slice symbolizing the monetary sacrifices that poorly clothed her life, the vulgarity that she had otherwise been able to hide from the social classes against which she still humiliatingly defined herself. It was like playing Patience without wearing underwear, a habit she had picked up in the 1980s from the maid of a Moroccan civil servant and which she hesitated to break because it was now one of the traits by which she was defined.

The tear in the fabric seemed especially uncouth to her because she had never noticed it before. Might have somebody else? Might have the constable? Why had she ever brought the thing up from the basement? Could Constable Loch have construed her desire to get rid of this furniture now as an admission of guilt? She didn't want to admit any guilt, but for some reason everything in her house had become guilty by association. The accusation of murder had spread like skunk scent off the Prussian blue mat and into the nooks, crannies and wainscotting of the many-chambered house. She had initially thought that buying new furniture would clean her home of the moral taint but then realized that this would only reinforce the suspicions of the town, ultimately positioning her as a flying buttress for the hate-mongering pillars of the community. She now couldn't understand why the constable had suggested she give the piece to the bazaar in the first place. Perhaps this was his way of provoking her to plead guilty. But if she had no intention, could she make the plea? Where does the legal system draw its own little pencil marks of ethics?

Presently, the community belched its fumes of suspicion almost solely upon Cora, although the information Jem received from the gossips on grocery day was clearly skewed by odium. Giggy herself had never known Cora to spend a night outside the villa, and the two women shared a bedroom. One morning the family had found the word 'OMDALISK' spray-painted across the limestone wall of the Cubist gazebo, and they assumed it to be a reference to Cora's Asian ancestry, her jet black hair and eyes. It was Jem who had been able to define the misspelt word, for he had himself once been compared to an Oriental concubine, albeit for purposes purely cordial. Giggy had suggested to the younger woman that if she wanted her reputation to change she should wear more makeup and start riding a girl's bicycle, but Cora, who grew up in Las Vegas, had never adequately considered the concept of gendered machinery, and Giggy herself could not explain. She knew it had something to do with skirts and scrotums, and so she said. Maybe it was a difference in the metal V connecting the handle-bars to the seat. Or the number of tassels on the handlebars or how long they dangled. She'd proposed that it had something to do with pedal-pushers, and so Jem began wearing a pair just to prove her wrong. That had only been for one day, after which he switched back to his cut-offs, the same pair he wore now as he lay asleep yet stroking the frayed threads of the denim.

'Darling, wake up. It's almost nighttime.'

'Mmmmm. You know, when you whisper, you sound like Eva Gabor.'

'You knew Eva?'

✦

And still, despite the night verging on taking over, nowhere to be seen was Constable Loch. 'No, they wouldn't look like asterisks,' Jem chuckled. 'I'm quite sure that geese when flying tuck their old legs away for protection from high wires. I'm sure *I* would.' And then, after a pause, 'Not FOX but maybe FAX; I don't think a flock of geese can make circular letters and still make a V from below. They can't spell C-O- ... COAX, for example.'

Jem could not come to tell his aunt, who had been so gracious in offering him a job as chef in the Winter Garden in order to keep him from becoming, as she put it, 'a tendered loin of the New Orleans streets' ... he couldn't come to tell her, who had paid for his Greyhound fare all the way from Louisiana and had complimented his drawl and had even let him bring Cora along ... he couldn't come to tell her that it was he, yes, he, who had suggested that the posters that created such a patchwork over so many of the telephone poles in Wachannabee County, that were taped helter-skelter to community mailboxes, even tacked next to the 'Pets for Free' section of the bulletin board in the post office (kittens, rabbits, kittens, kittens, rabbits), that it was he who had suggested that the posters carry the boldly blazoned phrasing 'INCLUDING QUEEN ANNE' and nothing more. Everybody knew what Queen Anne was:

'Who else in Lake Wachannabee would have such a thing?'

'What is a chaise longue, really?'

'It means long house.'

'Who in the twenty-first century would buy a long house?'

'I couldn't trust whoever it is.'

'What is a long house?'

'Don't you mean log house?'

'?'

'I think, actually, it's "long *shirt*."'

Well, maybe everybody didn't know what it was exactly, but they were all sure that this *objet d'approvisionnement* had to be singled out for a reason, and they decided without convening that it had to do with murder. There was a crime and now there was a piece of evidence. Somebody cobbled together an auction website – www.giggy.com – and, despite confusion over what a chaise longue was, the bidding had begun. Jem, meanwhile, lived with a constant trace-fear that one day his aunt would discover these posters and confirm the rumours that Dr. Amicable had already passed on to her, and his career as the cook of the Winter Garden would crumple down about his slim, pale feet like a sarong secured too hastily.

Giggy slugged back the last of her beer, rolled her torso gently to the left, then to the right, and then – taking advantage of the momentum – back to the left and slipped the empty into the cardboard case next to the chaise longue. In the same flow of motion, she grasped her Cameos off the table and eased her body back into the sag of the furniture. Eyes heavily linered with affection gazed over at her nephew, who seemed a touch on edge as he sprawled calf-like on the divan which, in order to not break up the set, Giggy had decided to donate to the bazaar as well.

And still unheard was the rumble that Constable Loch's truck, as it approached, would send over the fields of grain and sunflowers, and so there was nothing for it but to continue spending time in wait. Even the night seemed late this evening.

Aloo*mi*nium, aloo*mi*nium.

Kittens, rabbits, kittens, kittens, rabbits.

'You may be right about the O,' said Giggy, 'but the C is a wily mistress.' She arched her eyebrows and bided a moment before wondering what it was with the youth of today, that they never laughed, but then admitted to herself how insensitive it was to categorize an entire generation with a single mood. And disdainful ennui, of all things. How Dostoevsky, how Ablomov, how Camus. 'It may appear circular from below (on the page, that is, not the sky) but if you turn it on its side, love, and you have enough geese, you could spell a C. Maybe even an O, though I just can't imagine … Oh, I guess if you have enough geese you could do just about anything.' Tilting her head sideways to assist with the mental image, it was only the clatter of her hearing aid (not age, dear, but an overextended encounter with the younger members of a Swiss funtwelscht ensemble) hitting the floor that kept Giggy from tipping out of her seat. She crawled out of her chair quickly to recover the aid before her whippet gobbled it up.

'I bet Coca-Cola is training geese over northern Montana right now to spell their name,' Jem contributed. Ah, my little luftmensch, Giggy thought proudly as she poked her nose beneath the Panamanian end table.

Jem was sure that the popularity of the chaise had something to do with the crime committed against Robert. Beautiful Robert, he revived, insouciant Robert, his brackenberry slip of a tongue, his pale smooth flesh like the cream of Holsteins, his eyelids as if brushed by the deepest of Libyan pollen. Soon a veritable diadem of tears began to drip silently onto Jem's lap. Before Robert had become a victim, Giggy had nicknamed him 'le petit communiste,' after the photo by Pierre et Gilles of the milk-skinned Slav with false eyebrows. But this connection had become impossible to maintain ever since rectangles of the young man's taut flesh had been so meticulously stripped off his body — sections of thighs, ass, chest, arms, neck, even face: primarily the cheeks, chin and forehead, but also a bit of one ear.

The sado-masochistic enactment of a blazon. His healthiest pieces of new flesh, those that were not bandaged, ran in rough patches across his thighs and lower abdomen. They reminded Giggy of winter sunburn, smoked salmon, the luminescent apricot chiffon so popular at Midwestern weddings in the 1970s. Initially she had found herself hesitant to tend to these wounds. Jem, conversely, remained committed, inspired by the sensitivity of his partner's torso. He wanted to take pictures of the damage with Robert's camera, but he recognized that the passion carried the risk of being psychologically abusive. Mental relaxation was still as important as physical relaxation for the man – not that there was any worry about the latter, thought Jem, since he was almost fully immobilized.

Giggy had taken on the responsibility of turning her nephew's lover from back to belly or belly to back three times a day, and this new intimacy had been enough to increase her attachment to him, although she dared not nickname her little pumpkin again. There was something in these actions, she realized, that supported a force greater than she could articulate. The regularity and repetition of the assistance created a habit of giving in Giggy's life that she had not experienced before. It felt to her like a sort of primordial nurturing that lifted her beyond any daily woes. It was as if helping a person with his sorrows, not simply lightening his pain but sharing in it, experiencing the pain felt by another as if for a moment it were one's own, worked to lessen the discomforts of one's selfish life. It was, she conjectured, perhaps most akin to what soldiers felt when nursing their companions in battle – a love not only sanctioned but heightened through pain. Spartan.

When she helped Robert shift off his back onto his side, and then let him rest for a moment before turning him onto his belly, her seeing his discomfort was also her participating in it and thus making it something less extreme and lonely than it otherwise would have been. At these moments, Robert's agony became a shared experience that allowed Giggy to step out of her own identity as the matriarch of the Winter Garden and into a softer role that gave her character roundness. Just as it is that fleeting emotions first attract saints to their calling, so, too, did this experience introduce Giggy into a community that pulsated beyond the patterns and conceits of her town or even those of society in general. It was no less than what the Victorian philosopher Violet Paget had described, as she tended her ailing brother, as the transhistorical empathy that allowed one to feel comfortable in being companioned by the past.

Many called the crime 'murder' even though Robert was not dead because, in one of those startling coincidences that so disconcert movie executives, a news story had recently made the rounds describing a murder case in which the methods used were similar to those practiced on Robert, down to the suspected scalpels, the absence of anaesthetic and even the size of the fleshly strips, which ranged in thickness from that of onion skin to a quarter of an inch on the juicier parts of the body. Based on this information and the fact that the victim in the article had died a quick death, the doctors who looked at Robert's patchwork anatomy claimed that he too was bound to die, unless one could grow back skin, layers and layers and layers of skin. 'And there isn't enough time for that, is there?' the community had chirped into their phones with the harmony of crickets, 'There just isn't enough time.' Cora, who had become understandably defensive in recent weeks as she was more and more frequently murmured to be the prime suspect, had also grown infuriated by this habit among locals of turning every statement they made, every insinuation, every accusation, into a question. It was as if their incessant use of the interrogative somehow emptied their accusations of responsibility, the question mark becoming an upturned ladle out of which poured all the bilious pleasure they found in another's discomfort, leaving nothing but the empty wooden spoon of a question mark. But this could still be painful enough if rapped against the widow's peak or at that softer rise of flesh just behind the ear.

Having massaged their conclusions into unanimity, the doctors eventually accepted that the patient would at least die more sympathetically at the Winter Garden than if he were kept in the hospital, and so they asked him if he wished Giggy to take him home. One blink – yes; two blinks – no. The family made its procession from the hospital to the villa: first the ambulance with Robert and Jem in the back, then Giggy and Chappy in the Bricklin – the gangly whippet rather more twitchy than usual – and finally Cora pedalling furiously in their dusty wake. She was soon passed by a clutch of reporters who caught up with Giggy and the whippet just before they entered their home. Unwilling to carry on a lengthy conversation while Robert had yet to be comfortably set up, she agreed to make a statement. The whippet, true to his hunting ancestors, remained silent but frenetic. The breed may be admired for covering a maximum of distance with an economy of energy but, when not racing, Chappy used his excess in any way he could.

'He's alive,' Giggy pronounced with regard to Robert, after some thought, 'but, as Théophile Gautier might have said, he's not living.' They all understood what she meant of course, but this did not stop them from misconstruing the epigram in a way that encouraged false speculations: '"Not Living" Reports Close Friend.'

'If Coca-Cola *is* in northern Montana,' the woman interrupted her memorial self, 'I bet they wish their name was Vova-Vola. So much easier to spell with geese.' She found her hearing aid behind the *corydalis lutea*, screwed it back where it belonged, and then snatched a drag of her menthol to show how seriously she was thinking. The final distant hints of daylight glimmered off the long and extremely slender canoe that the professor and his assistants, almost invisible in the offing, were tugging into the pines. The sky had donned a blue so deep that Giggy knew that, should she turn away for even a moment, the night would rise up and steal in to replace it. The moment — despite being imbued with her love for Jem and the maternal altruism she had discovered through the pleasure of Robert's pain — was as ephemeral as the colour of time. The deep blue survived only through her most recent memory, her will. With this realization of power, she felt herself destined to blink, and so she did ... and five stars the colour of bluebells surfaced above the untroubled lake. A black velvet curtain had fallen on the day.

The constable would not be arriving today. Jem rose to prepare the barbecue for supper. He had promised himself that this week he would master the rotary grill. As her nephew teetered across the gazebo under the weight of a can of lighter fluid, Giggy made her way inside to rotate the victim. Without surfacing from her somnolence, Cora had formed a pillow out of the journal entries that Dr. Amicable had given the household to read. Robert Shakely, poor boy, had died here on Lake Wachannabee, and part of the professor's project involved his search for the factory foundation. He would include an appendix, he explained excitedly, with a map of the structure and its location. But, for now, all that he had produced, with the help of Rob and the other assistants, was the bed Cora had fashioned from a few edited pages and an introduction written less by the professor than by his helpers. Cora opened her eyes and stretched her torso, leaning her golden shoulders in toward the stars, which seemed to brighten in response.

✦

The Journal of Robert Shakely

edited by
Dr. J. C. Amicable

We who study history are always delighted to locate any text recording our past, whether it be the smallest of pictographs ripe for the rubbing or an original manuscript such as the one reproduced, annotated and indexed here. These texts are as much crystal balls shedding prisms of light on images of previously unknown worlds as they are precious hints to our own passions, the mechanics of our world, and the private activities within it. 'The heart of the Wachana tribe,' as Shakely refers to it, may still beat within these pages, and I present here the entirety of what remains of the manuscript because, as the now infamous manuscripts of Peter Fidler and Edgar Christian have shown us, even the most seemingly banal pieces of documentation can prove fruitful, either for what they casually include or for what they intentionally avoid mentioning.

My own desire, however, is not to enter into the rich and ambiguous realm of empiricist intentionality at this time, but simply to present the work along with some pieces of information that I have recognized as being related. Nor would I wish to belittle the historical and anthropological value of this document, but I would be delighted to know that in some instances it will be the pure and innocent quest for adventure that has driven others to finger the pages as it drove mine to finger the original. There is a passion, a vitality, within the annals of history that is often lost in their reconstruction and it is my hope that, in this instance, I have managed to bring forward a view of life and a system of values that may exist in contemporary society even if these values have no voice of their own. I am speaking here of the bravery, spirit, individualism and quest for adventure that seems to have run through the blood of these traders and explorers.

The following journal was located in its original form at the New York Municipal Archives by myself in the summer of 2003 while I conducted research on the Hudson's Bay Company's inland explorations of the late eighteenth century. It is recorded as arriving in Montréal, Canada, in 1902 from the London archives of the Royal Trade Company records. At some point it was transferred to New York, where it has until now remained in storage. It would appear that a first transference would have to have occurred prior to the fire at the Montréal Archives in 1932, though three random leaves of the document bear French-language date stamps of 7 August 1937 (to be referred to in future as the French Random Leaves, or the FRL), suggesting that these fragments of the document had not left Montréal prior to that date. Furthermore, the only date stamp I have been able to locate with an insignia matching that found on two of the three random stamps are those used by customs guards between Canada and the United States in Québec and possibly in the province of New Brunswick. But these latter stamps are traditionally accompanied by a signature stamp, of which there are none on the FRL.

It is certain that the document has spent time in storage in the United States soon after 1937, because there are seven random leaves bearing English date stamps of 6 January 1938 (to be referred to in future as the English Random Leaves, or the ERL), strongly suggesting that the French stampage was part of a customs export shipment procedure (though the style of stampage does not correlate to the style on other manuscripts exported to the United States at this time) and that the English stampage was part of a customs import shipment procedure (the style of stampage, in this case, correlating adequately [that is consistent with at least 75 per cent of Assumed Basic Customs Records Procedures (ABCRP)] with the style on other manuscripts imported by the United States from Canada at this time).

However, the New York Archives record the manuscript as arriving on 12 March 1953 and the date stamps on the storage leaves, signed by O. M. Weakan, corroborate this date. Calligraphy verifies that Weakan was also the person who placed the entry in the Archive records, thereby undermining the validity of this date somewhat. Furthermore, my assistant (may I take this moment to acknowledge my five star-quality assistants, who have helped in every aspect of my inspections and uncoverings), Brix McConnell, has located an entry in the National Archives of Canada in Ottawa, Ontario, stating that the manuscript, or the unlikely possibility of another manuscript carrying the title 'Journal of the most remarkable Transactions and Occurrences at Prisom Factory Commencing 3d April 1775 and ending March 1776,' was entered as in possession on 1 July 1938. This information would suggest that the document had, after entering the United States in 1937, passed back into Canada in 1938, possibly for further archival documentation, and then lay forgotten until March 1953, when it would have been delivered to the New York Archives, where it has remained until now. However, the Ottawa possession date, which is sharply and clearly inscribed, is dubious, since that is Canada's national holiday and, while certain civic workers would be expected to work to maintain the regularity of the nation, archival researchers, my assistant has discovered, would not in all likelihood have been among them.

The Montréal fire may be a false concern if the manuscript was simply not in storage at the central building. Similarly, it cannot be definite that an archivist was not working on Canada's national holiday. In summary, the manuscript seems to have been written for the Hudson's Bay Company by Robert Shakely and later delivered by someone to his shareholders in London. It then passed through Montréal on its way to New York, returning to Canada for an extended visit at the National Archives before returning to New York in 1953.

The text itself has been deemed legitimate, as the signature of Clairy Prundt on the inside cover of the original corresponds with his signature elsewhere in the company's records and the dates in the text correspond with dated references made by other company employees and employees of the North West Company and the Hudson's Bay Company in their records. As Robert Shakely's journal is itself the only record of the completion date of the document, historians are left to conjecture on the validity of its claim. Occasional statements suggest that sections of the journal consisting of more than one day were probably written during single sittings. It is definite, though, that the journal was completed at some time between 16 December 1775, when William Pond refers to his visit to Prisom Factory via Wachannabee Gorge, and 1 April 1776, when Pond returned to the central storage post by the same route, in response to requests made by the Home-Guard Cree.

Shakely's history, prior to his joining the Royal Trade Company, is unrecorded. Company records state that Shakely was hired on 12 August 1775 as Governor of Prisom Factory (named after Lord Ashley Prisom, Principal Shareholder) to oversee twelve men, with 'that number increasing substantially the following year if trade proves lucrative' (*Records: 1775, 36*). Shakely's journal implies that he was fairly well educated in surveying and had been trained in commerce. He also seems to have been somewhat read and was learning astronomy from Peter Post, the factory surveyor, during the autumn, before their situation became more dire.

The original of Shakely's journal can be viewed at the Royal Trade Company Archives (Archives of the Province of Ontario, 212 Glasshall Avenue, Ottawa, Ontario, K2K 4A2). For an analysis of Shakely's incorporation of astronomy into his company duties, see my article 'Robert Shakely and Astronomic Narrativity,' *Studies in Navigational History* 3.II: 54–69. The influence of subordinates on Shakely's management is analyzed in my article '"The Heart of the Wachana": Robert Shakely and Hegemonic Despondency,' *Journal of Exploration Discourse* 5:IV: 12–27. A comparison of Shakely's text to the records of William Pond is forthcoming in *Journal of Exploration Discourse* 7:I.

Dr. J. C. Amicable

Jem met the simmering scent that now permeated the gazebo with the dazed apathy of a periwinkle in a crab trap as the fleshy links skewered on the rotary grill began to take on a golden beige like that of the brisket and sprung ribs of Giggy's whippet. While the novelty of the links' spit and sizzle consumed his attention, the breeze seemed to coax the moonlight through the wrinkles of the mosquito netting and cast painless, luminescent strips across the dog's stifles and well-bent hocks. Chappy lay inattentive to the concerns of Jem, whose potato-pale fingers fondled the barbecue's operating manual as ineffectually as they might a string of pearls. Cora had risen and descended into the basement as if carried on a wave. She found comforting the moist channels that for others were simply perverse in their awkwardness as they wound hither and thither below Giggy's home. The matriarch herself, on first purchasing the house, felt their convolutions distasteful: 'There was no need for such a maze unless it was to assist in something ... incorrigible. The air, it could only be noxious. Try not to breathe the air.' Jem could now hear the whir of the stationary rower as Cora flexed her limbs taut and loose, taut and loose, working for maximum extension, watching the speedometer gradually rise as if it were measuring not speed but effort, perseverance, patience.

Giggy had heard of the 'American Heartland' and recollected something in the national anthem of Pellami Pellami regarding the weeping hearts of the Caldomi, but this did not make having the heart of the Wachana so near her own villa any less exotic. Originally, she had been the least interested of the household in reading Dr. Amicable's manuscript, and this made her all the more grateful, as she entered Robert's room, to have recognized the pagan ambience that the text had cast over her perception of the day.

After coaxing the convalescent onto his belly and dabbing Polysporin onto his gold-leaf buttocks, thighs and lower back, Giggy used a dishtowel to pat the spills of watery blood and pus that had seeped from his wounds and trickled down the sides of his body. A pink aura of secretions, like the illumination around a saint, had spread out from his body and stained the sheets. Giggy ever so gently touched the blond down that was returning to parts of his ass and softening the lines that marked out his muscles like an illustration in a textbook for high school gym instructors. She felt a sense of nurture in pressing the welts to allow some fluid to be released, although she did so hesitantly, realizing that there was also a purpose to the liquids being there. She stared about the silence of the room that she did not want just yet to leave.

As if themselves in need of something more to do, her hands latched onto Robert's camera. She spit on the tuck of her blouse and swirled it over the lens. She could sense that he was watching her, but she could not determine whether it was appreciatively or otherwise. Nor could she make herself turn to check. It didn't really matter; she wouldn't be taking any pictures for she had no idea how to work the thing. But the silence of the past days demanded to be filled with something and, if she did not try to continue to derive pleasure from her family, it would be filled by the odium of the townspeople who continued to hover like insects waiting for blood. Giggy was slightly put out by the sense that nobody else in the house (Rob understandably) was attempting to fill the void, although it was clear that everybody felt it. They were like B actors on a lifeboat, waiting for the director's instructions, knowing from the music that another calamity was pending but nevertheless feeling uninspired to fear. They were relying on the ambience – the noise from outside – for their own sense of agency.

Perhaps, Giggy thought diplomatically, it was the strain that had made Jem's affections for Robert wane. As if on cue, the breeze carried her nephew's voice into the room as he whispered, as gently as if he hadn't noticed that she'd left the gazebo, 'Do you really think that one can grow so darn much skin back?' The tears that gathered in the cradles beneath Giggy's eyes took time to flow over her lids and slide down the moguls of her cheeks to her chins before dripping down and mingling with the vulnerable surface of Robert's neck. The saline stung and the patient winced, but Giggy – so emotionally touched by her nephew's query – couldn't notice. And Robert, who in fact felt so little now, could not say he was displeased to know that at least some of his nerve ends had survived.

It's not that I don't appreciate her dolorous concerns, he thought as he observed one of Giggy's tears zoom toward his face, but that they have become so small in relation to this new set of sentiments to which I have been exposed. He knew that, despite emotionalism, her actual feelings were, dare he say, common. Of this, he felt sure. Less certain was he that she could not appreciate, as others he knew did, the pleasure of emotional excess itself, emotion distilled until it led you like a scent to action rather than it arising only in response to how you or others had acted. Jem, he thought, might yet be enough of a willow to bend to such a set of sentiments, but would he be willing to sacrifice pose, image, surface as Rob himself had?

Jem's perspective had been damaged by the crime. The stripping of Robert's body had given Robert a greater presence, a formidability that everybody had to address. All those within the constellation of the Winter Garden found their positions altered by the event. As marbles in a jar shift when even the smallest is removed, each relationship changed, however slightly. And each change would be the catalyst for other changes. While Giggy took to it gratefully and Cora found herself forced into self-defence, Jem felt displaced to the background of the scene, a foot-maiden to the people whom he had once loved in a way that was more inclusive. His confidence that the dynamic was temporary did not appease his anxiety because Jem was in fact not consciously recognizing or evaluating these changes so much as catching them in the silences that Robert and Cora were both using to protect themselves. He was sure all would be rectified once Robert was healed and Cora exonerated.

The accusation of murder, however illogical, tinged everybody's emotions as if it were a sort of truth. The stain would never fully fade, just as Robert's skin would never grow back to the translucent tint over which Jem had so often dragged his eyes, the tips of his fingers, his hair. Ah, but if the man grew it back to the damask of roses, or even the swarthy ochre of a sun-dulled nectarine, could Cora still be sent to jail? My lover's skin is nothing like the sun, he paraphrased. If only Robert could speak, he thought. How Jem now wished that Cora had never slept with the man that one fateful day, that he himself had never agreed to spend that afternoon helping Lady Clasp weed the spraugwart out of Giggy's herb wheel – for that matter, that they had never decided to come to the Winter Garden at all. It astounded him the way in which one heterosexual tryst could, with such ease, conceptually overwhelm the myriad other affections in which it appeared – just as a single diamond, when garishly cut, could overwhelm the cast of rubies on a brooch. In his moments of greatest despondency, Jem couldn't help feeling that the affair was his fault, that he was in some way responsible for the lives of all these people.

'Well, you are responsible, love, you are.' It was Giggy, her voice as smooth as Marilyn singing to JF. She turned from

46

Robert to smile at Jem who had by now somnambulated into the bedroom. Her balances and counterbalances of love – for Jem, for Chappy (at the moment, drawn out and wheezing on the gazebo floor), for Robert and, sure, even Cora – rocked like a buoy in the wakes of her emotions. The straps of her bra cutting into her shoulders seemed to reify the poignancy of her sympathies. 'Oh, discomfort.'

'Sorry, Auntie, I'm being a big old narcissist, aren't I?'

'Yes dear, a smidge. My pain runs through me always, you see. I think I may have to get out of these straps and have a lie-down.'

'Auntie, do you think that the sailing will simply never come smooth?'

She tried to envision Dr. Amicable's canoe on rough waters, but to no use.

'Life, the sailing of life,' Jem elaborated.

'Ah, it is especially rough just now, yes? But we're managing okay, dearest. Robert will be better soon. And anyway ... You know, Jem, if you ever want to talk about something, if something was bothering you, you can always let Robert know. He can hear. Not that I'm not available, should you ever need ... but just now, dear, the pain.'

'No, I don't need to talk.'

Walking down the hallway to the gazebo, Giggy struggling to remove her undergarments, the two could hear Cora outside slipping onto her bicycle, the tires along the gravel road crackling in the darkness and then turning right, toward the lake. Jem could imagine her towel and bathing suit, as always, bouncing limp and gangly in the basket. The silences of Cora that he once admired – assuming they were a sign of wisdom – now struck him more frequently as depressing, as if they were accusations directed at him. Giggy, conversely, found them perhaps not suspect but at least curious. Because she couldn't help but retain affection for the young woman as well, this curiousness came to

47

her senses more as a sense of loving pity, akin to the pity a father has for a son who doesn't take to hockey. It was Cora, after all, who had taught Giggy that, in a pinch, tampon wrappers can be used as a supply of rolling paper. A woman's secret, she thought fondly to herself, flashing back to some of her bonding experiences in the 1970s. She missed the womanly warmth of a feminism stoked by hope alone, and it was this that she had wished to revive through her acquaintance with Cora and that she now lamented as Jem's friend drew further into herself.

Giggy finally managed to unhook the straps of her bra and release the pressure on her shoulders. She straightened up and then, slowly bending over for the first time that day, chucked Chappy under the chin as the dog twisted onto his back to expose the narrowest pink belly. 'Pretty bones, pretty bones,' she cooed as if flattering a skeletal parrot.

The dog in fact was pretty – something that had been officially established early in his life, which he had begun as a show dog simply for being a descendent of stock from the Meander Kennels, back when they were still under the control of Miss Julia and Miss Shearer, back in the glory days of whippetry. One of the sisters' earliest dogs, Slag, had set the standard in so many ways for the American style and, while the women continued to breed and show well into the 1970s, the pet's ancestry traced back to this early male. Chappy's credentials showed classically – the solid colouring of his firm coat (in his case fawn, although ochre and yellow would do as well), eyes the darkest of hazel, and that crisp black nose. As an individual, Slag had stood out not for the barrel of his brisket or the subtlety of his stop, but for the deco linearity of the back of his neck – a crest that some mused might finally become a standard measure of quality when they saw how perfectly Chappy repeated it. Giggy's dog was, to put it plainly, 'straight Meander.' Among fanciers, no more needed to be said.

With such pedigree and beauty, it was outstanding that Giggy had retrieved him from a shelter. The fortune that saved the whippet from a life of posing and daily baths lay in the fickleness of beauty. As a racer, he might have had a fine career, for he got along well with his chucker and even seemed to enjoy the potential of flight when the man would pitch him in stride toward his owner at the end of the run. He was a clear shot, many whispered, for breaking the record of ten lengths' theft. It is true, of course, that races take place exclusively on circular tracks now with a mechanical lead, but the youths of Meander are still first trained in the old-fashioned way, with a straight track and the trainer ragging his charge forward. Despite Chappy's racing potential, however, the purity of his line, colouring and facial features saw him — like slender Soviets selected at six years for lifetimes of ballet — funnelled into a career as a show dog. And all might have gone as planned, had it not been for that ear, the left one.

Chappy had a brilliant head — lean and slender with virtually no stop. The width between the ears wasn't remarkable but it was established with no sign of corpus cleavage. His underjaw was strong and, while some saw a risk of undershot, a certain degree of reserve in this regard had just gained fashion. His eyes were rich and deep but still confidently hazel with no risk of yellowing. Even the ears appeared fine at first — they had the malleable texture of a clutch purse and a sharp but not rigid forward turn on the conch, and they were appropriately semi-pricked when alert. Then, one morning, the owners noticed that the whippet's left ear was gay — that is, fully pricked. With minimal coaxing, they were able to work it back into the proper position but, next day, there it was, jabbing skyward, gay as ever. And the next, alas, and the next. Oh, a soft ear might be faulty but, since the 1944 Standards of the Breed, one fully pricked has been recognized as warranting severe punishment in judgment. Even the more lenient standards of 1930 recognized a gay ear as 'incorrect.' Chappy's left ear seemed, once it had tried it a couple of times, to go gay on a whim, whether the whippet was at attention or not.

Good dogs have been put down for less, and thankfully these owners chose only to disown their little anomaly.

Thankful, indeed, was Chappy, for now he was destined for a life of chasing squirrels and chewing rawhide. Truth be known, his left ear was in fact pricked only when the dog was listening. The confusion arose from the fact that he had more of the hunter's spirit than most whippets, although they were all, from their early Northern English origins and terrier blood, 'snap dogs' in the hunt for rabbits and such. Poachers first began developing the breed, admiring their stealth and silence, and so the breed itself was the product of subterfuge and deception. But Chappy did not love simply chasing; he loved the concept of the hunt. 'The taste of blood,' as only Dr. Amicable loved to joke, 'is in his blood.' The hunt was, for Chappy, conceptual and pure such that he found it as much a reward to be alive to the possibilities of a hunt within his environment as the actual chase itself. By being aware but not actually hunting, the dog found he could prolong the emotional tension that had been bred into his very sense of pleasure. Even in apparent sleep, the sinews of his musculature would shift about beneath his solid coat, as if on the alert. His eyes moved slowly, steadily recording data. His ears, in particular the left, remained attentive to the conversation and the position of all things animate. And it was this virtual permanence of an ear pointing heavenward that set the youth's gypsy trajectory from Meander Kennels to the shelter and eventually to the more accepting arms of the Winter Garden.

Giggy slipped a doggy treat from a pocket of her kimono and ran it under Chappy's nose like a cigar before jimmying it between his teeth. She jostled it back and forth playfully while the whippet held on, emitting a growl that could not be heard but only conjectured from the thrumming of his throat. She finally let go and the snack disappeared into his ochre maw.

'You are responsible for them, you know, dear,' she whispered, this time to herself, as she gave Chappy a closing pat pat

pat on his belly. Giggy stretched back up and looked over at Jem, finding herself yearning ever so slightly to take part in the sexual aura that always draped over him like a Spanish veil. 'Not in any guilty way. You've done fine by them all. But one must always be responsible, you know, if one is to be loved … unless of course the object of your desire is an artist or a gardener. Nobody should get emotionally involved with either.' Jem assumed that his aunt was trying to get his mind off his worries, although Giggy really only wanted his attention – the flip side of the same coin perhaps. 'I speak from experience. I, who have been burnt by Cubism.'

She picked a scab off one of the scraps of strudel and settled into the chaise longue while Jem, throwing aside the operating manual that he'd been using absent-mindedly to fan himself, slumped back into the divan which had not forgotten his contours. Barbecuing could be such a chore, and now all the sausages had vanished. Chappy stretched, opened his eyes and stared with disconcerting force at Jem (who was gazing into the darkness), then flopped onto his back, his limbs scattering into random bends, the collective effect of which resembled a sinuous swastika. Notwithstanding the fact that he was soon snoring the snores of the satiated, his eyes remained open. Chappy, his mistress and her nephew waited together in the crystal stillness – for what, none of them knew, perhaps for Cora's return. The moonlight sparkled off the lake, the glass of Canada Dry, the five tiny fangs caught over Chappy's black lower lip. And even though the wait was so long that the dog had tracked the full arc of a satellite across the sky until it dipped behind the curtain of pines on the western edge of the porch and still Cora had not returned, the saliva that sparkled on his incisors continued to glitter as moist as dew.

✦

The constable had given them an excuse, should they ever have considered needing one, for spending the day in the gazebo and now, despite the night having fallen some time ago, they continued to assume its viability. Jem had heard them all before, the complaints about the garden, and he was not especially keen to be the ear for them yet again so late on this long, lonely night. The catacombs of foliage in which the Winter Garden nestled were a confused testament to Giggy's ongoing efforts to fuse aesthetics with her own version of utopian socialism. When she had envisioned her Cubist Eden, she hadn't been aware of the pretentiousness of artists or, more particularly, Belgian avant-gardists. But, to be fair, she did now appreciate, after all her reading, why a Cubist at the end of the last century might have been disenchanted by both the direction of aesthetic theorists and some of their ongoing claims to innovation or, with equal pride, conformity.

'No, no, not Cubism alone,' continued Giggy, beer and hash beginning to work in harmony. 'Not Cubism alone … I have been burnt by *Art*. I say it that way so you know the A is capitalized. The institution of *Art* has altered my sense of touch permanently.' Lightly did she smile now, fixing her focus beyond the insect veil. More tightly did she fit her body into the chaise longue, having for the moment put Robert out of her mind.

How too tiring, thought Jem, who could never get into the spirit of his aunt's diatribes. Yet he knew how much she enjoyed them and often felt it was his fault that she was strapped for intellectual parlance. He imagined that he could take pleasure in her discussions, if only she would make room for him to participate. In conversations with his aunt, he more often felt like the useless waif with the gentle limp who'd failed to keep up with the piper, or like someone who, reading some story or other, suddenly realized that the author had never wanted him to get the point, and, with this new-found knowledge, saw the process making sense, the responsibility of the story being cast on nobody's shoulders because there were no expectations to fulfill, no assumptions to assimilate. There are no ugly sentences, he reflected, only ugly readers. This would have been fine with Jem if his aunt used the same model, but she preferred having her authority acknowledged. Thus their conversations held frequent silences which she mistook as understanding.

Despite being slight and soft-spoken, Jem often felt crowded psychologically by his aunt. She consumed his affection desperately, like a locust, reading any image of love or sexuality that he presented — regardless of whom or what it was directed at, or whether (which was more often the case) it was directed at a hundred and one random targets — into a sign of their mutual fondness. This is not to say that Jem's devotion lacked but that, as he was realizing, all of his energy was being sucked into his aunt's black hole of affection. But for Jem, the polymorphousness of his erotic energy was the very root of his identity — a queerness not camouflaged by indirection but liberated and emboldened by multiple possibilities. Queerness has made coming out, reasoned Jem, so much more difficult for kids today. Oh, the closet still exists, but now it's denied in favour of a sexual identity resembling some sort of sixties open-concept bungalow. 'Eventually we're all queer,' Christopher Isherwood had once said to Jem's aunt over an especially aggressive game of croquet marked by too much cheating. He had meant it as a joke, but she could tell he was a bit ticked that he wasn't winning.

Since then, Giggy had found the quote most useful for explaining her unique method of poaching eggs.

'You see, I have lost my sense of touch.' Giggy lightly pressed her nephew's forehead with her fingertips before realizing that the visuals were misleading. 'I have new feelings that aren't my own. They belong to foreign artists. Everybody who looks at *Art* thinks they understand the artist's intentions, even if it's just a step toward realizing that the artist doesn't care either way. It's a suspension of disbelief; the viewer takes on the persona of the artist. How can you understand something if you don't put yourself into the axis that allows its comprehension, yes? Don't look at me that way, precious. Oh, I admit, I read that somewhere, but I shall yet make it my own.

'Historically there hasn't really been any audience, only intentional artists – some making better *Starburst*s than others (I refer to that famous painting by Van Gogh that he never got around to starting), better because their *Starburst*s are understood by more of the other artists. Or let's say the better artist is the one whose talents are most varied, the one who can create the widest variety of *Art*; this is really just aesthetic open-mindedness in a strapless. Yes?

'No,' and here Giggy shook her loose face, casting about for the right words, 'this is really just the emulation of the lowest common denominator. My dear mother had always felt that emulation bespoke a lack of confidence. It's not in my makeup.' Giggy's words poured into the night like so many spores cast upon the wind for unknown lodgings, while a million disembodied ears hovered less than half-attentive just beyond the deep tangle of shrubs and bushes that drew the villa into the landscape.

Jem, having lost early on the logic of her speech, had begun instead to think about Cora, whose swims usually took only an hour or so unless some kids punctured her tires or tethered her bicycle to the rusty belly of the ferry. In honesty, the latter had not happened yet; in a community as small as Lake Wachannabee, no local would steal anything except, perhaps, for the occasional carrot or, by mistake in the darkness, turnip from Lady Clasp's garden. But ever since Constable Loch had insinuated that she, as Robert's lover, was the prime suspect, it had become closer to acceptable among the members of the community to pester Cora. 'As if little old Cora even knew how to hold a scalpel,' argued Jem, 'or a cock.' Jem and Robert's longer love had simply not entered the constable's mind, and this made the Texan feel overlooked. All the residents of the Winter Garden knew that he, not Cora, should be the prime suspect. This was why Cora had chilled to him. 'To that man Loch,' growled Jem, 'Robert and I are like lesbians to Queen Victoria — inconceivable, like unicorns or shepherds. But when he is finally forced to recognize us, I *will* become the suspect.'

He followed Chappy's glance to the chaise longue on which Giggy was seated. The index finger of her right hand was rubbing absent-mindedly along the cut in the cushion. Chappy's eyes swayed back and forth, back and forth. A few mosquitoes continued to whiz with effrontery just on the other side of the netting that surrounded the gazebo. The soft camel moths shook as they clung to the threads of the material like mountain climbers, prodding about for the slightest tear in the fabric that might give them access to the light and its promise.

'It's the notion of the artist itself that stifles *Art*, really,' Giggy mumbled into a fresh beer. '*Art* is always free from the artist, it's always found, despite being so dear. What I mean is *Art* is out there,' she flailed feebly at the clematis blooming near the west window, but we feel that we have to catch it and pin it in our little collections before we acknowledge ... That's all that artists are, you know — collectors, not creators.' She cast an arm into the air as if encouraging her camel to charge. 'We all want to find the five greatest *Starburst*s. Ah Minou, we must start a new movement. Here, at Lake Wachannabee.'

'But Auntie Sugar, you know, you have no paints.' Jem spoke half-heartedly. He could tell by Giggy's language that she'd already thought the notion through, had even come up with slogans. He could imagine the black lettering on the xxxl T-shirts:

ART MUST BE FREE FROM THE ARTIST
FOUND ART IS FREE ART

'Yes, you're right about that, dear.' And then, 'Is that a problem?'

'Something to work around, at least,' Jem offered with a coddling smile. All their stomachs growled simultaneously, a barbershop trio.

'Why are men at the top of the food chain?'

'?'

'I mean "people."'

'Are they? I would have thought, oh, the falcon or the eagle. They're on the top of the totem pole. But that's art, and people find art so unnatural.'

'No, the food chain has men at the top. The chain of art? I don't know. Painting, I guess. Or poetry. Or film now.'

'That's not a chain at all. That's a hierarchy. Don't you find this porch light queasy-making?' Three large grasshoppers had jumped onto the netting and begun to swing as gracefully as Lebanese street urchins who had been raised from infancy to become trapeze artists for a potentate. Their vigour disturbed a gang of mosquitoes, which let go and hovered inches from the barrier like shoppers on Boxing Day. Reminiscent of the boys in von Plüschow's photographs, the insects' smooth empty bellies had begun to sag. If they did not eat by morning, more than a few of them would surely die. The moths, meanwhile, clung in earnest as their numbers increased. The last of the mosquitoes eventually withdrew to the veterinarian's, resigned to the notion that they would have to settle for cow's blood yet again.

'But Fafaism, *ma petite chose*, doesn't want paint, doesn't want paintings, doesn't want to catch *Art* in its little nets and pin it in its silly little collections.' Giggy had begun arranging a Chinese paper shade over a bulb above the door. No explanation presented itself for the elbow-length gardening gloves that graced her arms. Jem felt relieved that she had finally lifted herself off the chaise longue, although the indentation left behind still marked the furniture as hers. 'All it wants is strapping young artists and strapping young ideas, but not to use them. It must free itself from already established aesthetics. Pass me the pliers, love, to twist the wire. Fafaism wants to free *Art* from the artists.' Free Art From the Artists, Jem realized. 'No, no, needle-nose.'

As often happened when Giggy had excited herself with her own thoughts, she began to speak in English as if French were her *langue maternelle*. She had never lost her sense of fraudulence for occasionally using the title 'Madame' without being able to carry on a conversation in French. She would have gone for 'Duchess,' but when she had the title included in her entry in the phone book, Constable Loch informed her — somewhat too effervescently, she felt — that it was illegal to use that title in North America if she had never lived with a Duke. She'd then ordered a dog from a shelter in the city, with the full intention of naming it Duke, but when the whippet arrived, well, it was obvious to everybody living at the villa at the time that the canine was not a Duke at all, but a Chappy. She tried, she really did, to refrain from nicknaming the pet 'Pretty Bones'; the words seemed to her contrived, like the title of a poetry collection trying to have it both ways, to be acceptably dangerous — like getting a tattoo but a tiny one, and somewhere inconspicuous.

Her own tattoo was planted high and proud upon her left breast. A butterfly, it fluttered colourful and sincere up toward her collarbone. Oh, would the glorious insect always force her

57

to recollect that unpleasant summer of 1986 when she agreed to be the spokesperson for the Greenery Diet Camp? Yes, the weight came off, and yes, the food was tasty. And yes, she became thinner and her flesh retracted; her buttocks, her thighs, her breasts all shrunk to more common dimensions. The little butterfly, it alone seemed not to rejoice in her new-forming figure as the skin tightened and the insect shrank until it looked more like a dried bean or, in kindness, perhaps a dangerously French birthmark. Then the decade progressed to its decadent end and everything grew again – the size of hamburgers, the cost of housing, the national debt and, joy, Giggy grew too, back to the seductive contours that so mercifully accepted her upon her return. The butterfly plumped up as well, slowly regaining a familiar silhouette as the black ink stretched into deep purples, reds, greens, until even the lighter shades were visible – yellow, pink, even spaces of the matriarch's own flesh tone. As if in thanks to Giggy's corpulence, the insect grew larger than it had ever been before, stretching its light-tinged wings beyond the believable, turning the woman's chest into a veritable celebration of confidence and sensibility.

'So, lovey, you've thought about this before, then?' said Jem, searching lazily on the coffee table for the hash. 'With the name Fafaism?' The mirrored tabletop distended Giggy's face.

'Why, definitely. You know me – think, think, think. But I can never get from this notion of a collective aesthetic to a non-aesthetic, sweetie, from the idea that there's a social benefit to an inclusive aesthetic. Collective aesthetic – that's an oxymoron, I'm sure of it. It seems to me that with an analytic paradigm, where the aesthetic is itself structural – not just analytic terms, mind you – we get through that net. We even have a name. It might be that the concept is much the same as Dadaism but that alas has passed, has been destroyed for us, crushed like an orphaned duckling on the freeway.'

'Oh, why a duckling?'

'I hope I haven't turned you off with my theorizing. You'll be a member of this movement, yes? Oh, say you will, love. It would mean so much to Auntie. What it needs now is members; an art movement is like a family. As long as there are members, you've got movement. But one member is never enough.'

'What'll I have to do?' Unable to find the hash, Jem considered bumping some K and visiting Robert. But it was too soon. The skinned man had told Jem that nobody else knew that he could speak – well, rasp monosyllables – and this was an advantage to Jem, one that he might risk exposing if he were too high. Moreover, it is perhaps too obvious to be an axiom to live by that one should never take K after inviting the police to one's gazebo.

'Well, I don't know. Cook, I guess. Same as always. Suppose you attend the meetings?'

'I wouldn't say no.' Jem dipped an index finger into his glass of Canada Dry and traced a line along the length of his leg. Luminescent enough in this oriental glow, he flattered himself, for a youth of nineteen. 'I really did rather hope I'd paint, though.'

'Well, honey, I suppose you may. But paint with something that doesn't make a mark.'

'That doesn't sound much worth the effort. I guess I might paint with Canada Dry.'

'Perfect. *Parfait.* A paint that's always dry. I don't imagine that we'll need too many actual works. Maybe, darling, just keep doing the same one over and over again. I suppose I'll – we'll – have to explain that in the manifesto.'

Jem could hear Cora pedalling up the gravel driveway and then a car's tires crunching along behind. For some reason the vehicle's lights were off. In the darkness, nothing was visible beyond the gauzy veil. Indeed, the insects themselves were no longer visible in the orange glow of the paper shade and, as Giggy suspected, most of them had gone home to their swamps soon after the sun had sunk into the pines.

59

'Turn on the light, honey,' Giggy said, returning to her seat. 'I can't see anything.'

'It is on.'

'Well, turn it off then, lovey. I want to see who's coming. Oh look, I believe it's, oh, your friend.' She cracked another beer. Jem, still sitting, let his fingers scurry along the wall until they found the switch. He clicked it off and his arm slipped back to his side, the fresh rush of blood tingling in his veal-tender biceps. Cora's bicycle clattered against the steps to the gazebo as she swung open the screen door and rushed into the protection of the netting. The door bounced twice before slamming shut in the needle-nosed faces of the few remaining zombie-desperate insects. Jem shivered. Chappy pricked an ear. 'The colonel has returned from his duties,' announced Giggy, which was what she always said – in echo of her mother – when she had decided to end a conversation.

They could still hear the vehicle sneaking down the drive and vague hope remained in Giggy's brain, if nobody else's, that it was the bazaar movers at last. Jem could make out a large car, a four-door it seemed, probably white. His aunt saw nothing at all. 'Are you sure about that trick with the lights? That vehicle is blinding me to death. I see spots.' A touch drunk, Giggy turned to the wall for support, imagining herself as Joan Crawford in one of the later scenes from *What Ever Happened to Baby Jane?*. Chappy lay supine, canvassing, canvassing.

'Oh angel,' Jem drawled, gazing at Cora from a safe distance as she stood, bent over, catching her breath, 'are you going to make it?'

'Hurry,' returned Cora, 'let's go inside,' through gasps, 'I'm being terrorized.' She motioned ineffectually in the direction of the vehicle. Her skin glistened like brandy over dried apricots.

'Do you need some medicine? I have pills upstairs. Or maybe just tea? Jem, I think an iced infusion, or maybe chai would be the thing just now. I don't know. Do I?' Giggy had spent all summer waiting for chai to become the thing. In this, she hoped, at least, to be ahead of the curve. 'Cora? Would you like anything?' and a pause and 'Can it be she's ruptured her eardrums? I understand the very same thing happens in Spain at the midnight anniversary mass for St. Teresa of Avila. Always to the pearl divers. All those poor little pearl divers with nothing to hear. Cora, dear, were you diving?'

'So deaf,' agreed Jem, imagining the divers, for some reason, as eternally youthful, 'so underappreciated,' imagining himself as one of them. He took Cora by the arm and the trio shuffled into the house, Chappy having already scuttled upstairs to get a better view of the intruder from his bedroom window. Giggy could not help but notice how snugly Cora's buoyant, heaving breasts fit into her ribbed T-shirt. The directions toward which they pointed were simply unnatural. She knew she was jealous, threatened by the young woman's cast-off sexuality. As emotionally refined as she was, Giggy nevertheless was quick to be intimidated by the commonplace. At present, she felt Cora's silent pride was unjustified but couldn't decide whether the pheromones in the air were those of vanity or of barbecued carcinogens. She had only recently realized that her own breasts grew heavier during the summer, as if the moisture of her flesh accumulated in the lowest sections, as if she would at any moment burst out lactating (albeit not exactly from her nipples), as if Jem's arrival had brought out instincts. And yet the skin along the underside of her chafed breasts remained so dry that often she couldn't wear a wire-support bra at all, and with a bosom as full as hers, well, any other strap of cloth was symbolic at best. Wearing a brassiere was the main thing she regretted having to do for tomorrow's bazaar.

Jem handed Cora a glass of ginger ale while the two women leaned into the night and peered out the window, each into her own separate darkness.

'That isn't an iced infusion, Jem dear. It should have ice in it. Would you like a pill or something, Cora? That's what they're there for. Are you certain they were after *you*, dear? How about some of that E that everybody's lollipopping these days? Or is there another piece of the alphabet that's fashionable now?' Trapped in solitude, Rob could only wonder what had happened and strain to hear their voices.

From the moment Cora had first entered the Winter Garden and Giggy felt obliged to stare her into submission, the matriarch had concluded that the youth was someone who assumed too readily that any signs of attention were meant for her. She knew the woman had intelligence and conviction, the two characteristics that she found most admirable in anybody, but something flirtatious suggested to the aunt that Jem's friend lacked self-confidence. 'I think a mild sedative is in order, Jem darling.' Giggy was well aware that the best way to boost one's confidence was to flirt. During her own youthful flings with the local boys on Pellami Pellami, she had developed a tactic of flirtation requiring only a ceiling fan and a couple of strips of rice paper. 'What do you say, Cora, would you like a sedative? You don't speak. Oh, this is too difficult. Try and co-operate, dear. It's Barcelona all over again.' The colonel, her father, had threatened to restrain young Giggy's activities there, but fortunately her dear mother interceded by transporting her daughter to Macedonia. Giggy thanked her stars daily that Jem's homosexuality had released him from such intrusions. She had not yet calculated what she would do if he turned out to be polysexual. At present, the steady sound of gravel crunching under the slowest of cars kept her focus on the immediate crisis and her desire that it would end so that she could retrieve her cigarettes from the gazebo. 'Cora, angel, take a seat. That seems to be the best thing. This nasty tryst has begun to drag out. Would you like a cushion?' Jem's attention was equally focused on the gazebo and the furniture that the constable had still not come to remove. Even now he could not establish whether he would feel more at ease if the authorities took it off their hands or if it were simply left there to be worn away by Giggy's corpulence.

No sooner had the sound of tires on gravel stopped than angry car lights snapped on – the two on the ends large and round, the three on the inside small and spangled. This unique arrangement, Jem noted, could prove a useful bit of information in the future. His practice of passive detection – waiting for the clues to come to him – was turning up little evidence, so such peculiarities were precious to him. He should find a pen. As he stared back with languor, Giggy and Cora slid into the shadows of the giant chiaroscus flopping its scented leaves over the archway. Chappy, meanwhile, let out a silent whine that, had they heard it, would have spoken most honestly for all of them. The dog maintained his post of surveillance at his bedroom window.

Everybody was frozen – Chappy, Rob, Giggy, Cora, Jem (mesmerized again by the bubbles of his ginger ale, something eternally beautiful there – aloo*minium*, aloo*minium*) – until suddenly, as if startled, the vehicle sped backward out of the drive, turned around and screeched down the road, leaving a scriptive V of black rubber sizzling on the pavement. Cora tried to memorize the sound of the engine but it faded so quickly, making her fear that the car hadn't driven far away at all. Giggy closed her eyes to appreciate the pattern of veins that its five lights had left sweeping across her lids.

'Jem, sneak out onto the gazebo and get my cigarettes. And, dearest, I fear you'll have to start dinner anew. The sausages have gone missing.' Chappy had come down and begun to gnaw on the tasselled corner of an Alsatian pillow. Jem made his way onto the gazebo and turned on the light, the glow of the Chinese shade suggesting a shift into a reality between the tension of the house and the driveway and yet separate from both. Chappy's eyes, meanwhile, two gems in the dark, watched the women move into the security of the study.

✦

THE BAZAAR

Giggy sat at her vanity. In the mirror she could see Cora sleeping in the early morning light emanating from the open window. Cora's cheeks glowed so against her pillow that Giggy was convinced the other woman had been accosted in the night by a perversion of rouge. An extension of skepticism to Cora's image as victim was, in the matriarch's view, inevitable. Giggy wiped the moisture of sleep from her face and shoulders and began to apply her talcum with a duster bearing a disturbing resemblance to the tail of a bull calf. Glistening with oils and pins, her perm seemed to be enjoying these moments of liberty before Giggy tucked it away under a summer wig. Today, most likely, it would be the amber bob; it gave her the pert look of having just lighted from a Derby clipper – an appropriate look, Giggy felt, at a bazaar, what with all the heat, open-toed sandals and pogo dogs (what she as a child on the island of Pellami Pellami had been taught at Sunday school to call 'Jesus on a stick,' the Sisters of Perpetual Dolour just managing to squirt the mustard out in the shape of a cross).

It remained a wonder to Giggy that, year after year, Constable Loch made enough money from this bazaar to keep the children's summer camp in operation. She knew that the community depended on it for funding and this, she convinced herself, was why the constable had been so desirous of her chaise longue. A few years back she had heard that the children's excursion would be a scavenger hunt through Wachannabee Gorge, which marked the southern boundary of her estate, and she felt she just *had* to donate whatever it took to have those youngsters shipped off to a petting zoo or prehistoric silt deposit further down the road. That first year she had sacrificed her entire collection of gilded insects.

She couldn't understand why the notion of free-range children had fallen from popularity. So much literature depended on that culture. Tom Sawyer and Huck Finn. Peter and the wolf. Heidi and the ... deer, was it? It had been the way in which she herself had been raised, and even young adults like Jem had developed well when left to their own devices for exercise, entertainment and socializing. As a free-range child, Giggy told herself, one's character had an easier influence on the community one developed. The recent buggy-bashing competitions for 'best' schools and communication-building sports seemed to be producing high-strung, over-pumped children whose values could never seep to any philosophical or emotional depth because they were forced, like run-off, to rush across the surface where their signification was most apparent. There was a time, she recalled wistfully, when being high-strung was considered an eccentricity marking pedigree. Oh, set your children free, she advised nobody but the visage in her vanity.

Children are over-packaged now, she reflected, dabbing foundation onto her cheeks. Too many adults are treating them as a species of lapdog. A miniature whippet was of course a delight, but an infestation of the nerve-edgy beasts was rather too suggestive of a virus. She preferred to treat the undeveloped members of the species as adults whose rawness demanded affection, attention and education, but not admiration. Why admiration? Charm had never found a bower in the quotidian. Giggy adored the notion of family, simply adored it, but she saw no reason why children should be a part of hers, even if that particular domestic model seemed to have worked for the disturbingly homogeneous von Trapps. Maybe if they hadn't all had the same hairdresser?

'It would upset the peacocks' nerves,' she had explained to the civic planning committee, 'to have the children rummaging through their terrain, and goodness knows if I don't own that chunk of forest anyway.' Nobody had wanted to bother getting a land review organized, had there been enough time for it. So they'd accepted Giggy's eventual offer of cash as a sign of civic humanism and bussed the children to U-PICK-M Orchard in the neighbouring county of Appleby. The parents were so pleased with the exercise and localized cultural sensitivity offered by the event (as described in the program pamphlet and website) that they had even begun discussing an Apple Fest, a way of obscuring the proletarian strain of the children's adventure through liberalist celebration. 'The Appleby Apple Bee,' they would call it, suggesting a harmony of communal labour. There would be floats in the shapes of pies and people with giant beehive hairdos, and the mayor of Wachannabee with a squirt gun full of apple juice, and contests where children would scurry to consume as many tarts as possible in some allotted time (say thirty seconds) and to pick as many apples as possible (say in three weeks). Unfortunately, the plans had gone the way of good intentions, never making it much beyond a supportive editorial couched among the classified ads of the *Wachannabee Orderly*.

The Apple Bee was not to be, and the revived interest in foraging in the gorge had spurred Dr. Amicable to make known the exploits of the fur traders and indigenes of Wachannabee, as recorded in various Jesuit diaries and explorer journals. After a quick read of the doctor's report, the recreation manager had become sufficiently nervous about letting her brood waddle off into the bowels of that cavernous maw. As if the cannibals might still be alive, wasted to the bone but waiting, all the more hungry for that. False? The manager doubted that. Had she herself as a child of Puget Sound on the west coast of the continent not been taught about the encounters between Chief Maquinna and Captain Cook, and the massacres of sailors for no other reason apparently than the consumption of their thigh meat? Yes, she had, and so she was quick to side with Giggy's suggestion for an alternate plan.

'Strange bedfellows.'

'Whatever gives the closest shave.'

And nobody cared to disagree, for although none of them understood what the metaphor meant, it seemed concise and thus true. Every Thanksgiving since then, Giggy reaffirmed her union with the recreation manager by sending her a block of chocolate in the shape of the *Deutsche Nonne Ertrinken* (the habit moulded out of marzipan, the mottled flesh signified by the meticulous pricks of a labourer's pin). When the company in the Québec townships that made this spiritual treat stopped its mass production, she went so far as to have just the one treat made specially for her. Regardless of the resolution, even now, whenever she thought of a dozen sticky children plucking at her verdure, Giggy would let off a shiver that extended from her deepest marrow to every fold of her flesh and even to the whippet, if he happened to be on her lap at the time. And so she saw herself shiver now, seated as she was at her vanity.

'Cold?' asked Cora, stretching as she sat up in bed.

'No, amiable by nature. It's just that today's children are so pre-fab. So Stepford.' Cora's quizzical response went unnoticed, for Giggy had suddenly decided to talc her feet as well. She would, after all, be using them today. Her dusting complete, she pushed aside her powders to make room for her scents. It was remarkably early for Giggy to be busying herself with anything, but she was hurrying in the hopes of finishing before Cora began. She needed to prepare her voice for breakfast. They were to hold the first meeting of the Fafaists. In addition, while Giggy never had seen what the other woman dabbed behind her ears, there was always a seductively excretive smell about her that, through its suggestion of vigour, evoked in Giggy lethargy. It reminded her of Rhumbaba, that gaudy starlet of perfumes with which only Miss Budge continued to bother. It might have been attar of tuberose or storax that was Cora's culprit; Giggy was unsure. Whatever it was, she feared being caught in the same room with an open bottle of the stuff.

Giggy uncorked her decanter of patchouli (twelve drops mixed with a tablespoon of almond oil in anything but a plastic container) even though she'd ceased wearing it ever since Jem had begun. Her love for her nephew had made the scent too meaningful for her own use. So, she just let a few wafts loose into the warming dawn and replaced the avocado-shaped stopper, gently sliding the bottle aside among the rest of her crystal menagerie as if it contained the ashes of her nephew himself. Perhaps, she mused with the fondness of a grandmother, one day it shall. She glanced out the open window to check the weather, and then chose tiger lily rounded out by clove and rose extract. Teal were the clouds, terra cotta the cologne and lily the woman's complexion, the latter two blending to create a blush that was quickly absorbed by the flesh of her already heat-damp neck.

'Not a fine thing to be followed home, is it?' she asked sympathetically. 'That is, without an invitation being proffered.' Cora never cared for the other woman's discussions, but it was Giggy's villa and Yin-yin had raised her daughter to be a thankful guest. Even as a child, she had made an effective conversationalist, developing ways to sustain discussions among forest rangers even after they had become inebriated and without them really noticing her involvement. So she found it easy now to persevere, waiting patiently for Jem to bore so that they could continue their undirected pilgrimage about the continent. 'You know, I used to be followed home all the time, back in Pell Pell. And, angel, do I empathize. They stick like flypaper, the buggers.' Cora had hoped that Robert's wounds (for this, she felt, was a nonaccusatory way of referring to the damage) would have a disconcerting effect on Jem that would eventually stir him toward departure, but the pain, it turned out, had made him want to stay all the more. 'Not totally insulting, though, eh?' Giggy pressed on. 'Give it that, won't we?' How could Cora have gauged Jem's affections? Then the community began demanding suspects, and then they'd spensered Cora, and now the two friends couldn't leave, regardless of their wishes. 'So, who are they? Boys, I guess. Girls don't go in for that sort of wooing. How I was wooed back on Pell Pell. Ah, to woo … and to be wooed.'

Every morning, Cora entered Robert's room and asked him something – anything, really. Her intention was simply to get him to speak so that his words, his warm language, could even momentarily overcome the stream of accusations against her and replace it with the balm of his Canadian accent. But as the day that Giggy found poor Robert bleeding and unconscious on the exercise mat in the basement sank deeper into memory, even Cora grew anxious about what, if anything, would ultimately come from the man's mouth. 'Cora?' What will he remember, what will he imagine, and what will his motivations be? 'Hello? Angel, are we talking? Ring ring?'

Meanwhile, day by day, Cora found Giggy's proximity more aggravating. She could not understand why Jem's aunt insisted on sharing a bedroom with her, especially since there were so many unused rooms in the villa. It wasn't sex; she was sure of that. 'God, Cora. Come to, girl; do you want a drink?' Giggy poured a brandy. 'Here, have a bit of this, and loosen your tongue.' She admitted that it was entertaining going to bed at the same time as Giggy, who cleansed and primped for hours before finally scenting the room and tucking in with her stack of melo-dramas or, more recently, sheaves of Dr. Amicable's manuscript. Today, the bedroom exuded the tangy fragrances of cajeput leaves, juniper berry and clove – nothing like the acidic lilac air freshener that Yin-yin used to spray around the rec room after one of those evenings with all the other forest wardens smoking cigarettes and sloshing vodka over the carpet until dawn and then skinny-dipping in Crystal Creek and spewing bad jokes about something fishy getting away. 'You aren't going to tell me, are you, angel? Well, I don't need to know, but then nor need you go stirring up the household with your dalliances.' Usually Giggy's room was scented with rosewater and frangipani, or a morbid mixture she brewed from a faded yellow book of perfume formulas. On cool days she let the sappy scent of black spruce linger over the villa like steamed ether under splinters of winter pine. The scent was especially soothing in combination with Giggy's catechistic murmur as she made her way through Robert Shakely's journal. The chain of her glasses hung as useless as a worn-out rosary while the lenses – unsupported by the arms of the glasses hanging lank as the limbs of Aubrey Beardsley – pinched down on her nose. Her curls, held in place by a spider's web of netting, seemed like so many contented snails sucking a stone, bobby pins glittering like the corn-yellow diamonds in the tiara Lady Clasp had worn to last year's Appleby Bob Ball. 'I think we won't engage in this chatting business so much in the future, don't you agree, angel? Would it be too much to ask you to rub some lemon balm along my vertebrae? I find it so eases the pain of being seated. That's it. Yes. Really press it in, right up against the bone. It's going to be a long day.'

At first Cora had asked Giggy to read louder so that she could listen but, despite the other woman's efforts, the words always eventually tumbled into the loose passages of her throat and burbled forth at best only as rumblings. So Cora began to borrow sections of the manuscript, and this sharing was enough to establish a camaraderie that, albeit more difficult to maintain during day-lit hours, re-anchored in the harbour of each night. The hope for just such an affection had been the initial reason that Giggy had asked Cora to share a room. But Cora noted, without offence, that Giggy's interest in her was incomparable to the devotion that the matriarch had for her nephew. This other love seemed Aristophanic — as if Giggy had found her other half, one who not only completed but also reflected her such that she became whole in herself.

Her love for Jem seemed not to bubble up like sporadic effervescence from an unplumbed well, nor to gambol rough and ready like glacial waters down a Rocky Mountain spring, nor even simply to cascade and glisten like a waterfall or a sheet of sunlight in a Kurdish sky; it seemed not to froth forth like a fleet of whales or rumble over like a herd of wild horses, nor to split apart like the smile of a freshly cracked watermelon, nor to slither as gently as a baby ermine making its silent way back to the warm belly of its mother; it seemed nothing like the sudden turn of a flock of black-capped chickadees as their flight comes close to a barbed fence, or the herd instinct of death-ignorant lemmings or that of a community of penguins as they slide wet-bellied into the glacial breaks, or that of a mesmerized flock of flamingos suddenly blessed with a frothy wave of freshly born sea vermin; and nor did her love for Jem seem anything like the blessing cast upon the wave of vermin suddenly caught in a backdraft that sucked them away from the ridiculous gaping maws of pink flamingos, the blessing cast upon the hundreds of salmon never drawn to swim into the channels of hungry penguins, that cast upon the thousands of insects (moths, mosquitoes, cicadas) whose instincts allowed them to back away and avoid the pummel of a community of lemmings, the snap of spastic-shifting chickadees, the trammel of a stampede, the slap of ermine, the gash of melon, crush of whale, splash of water, blaze of light . . .

No, Cora well knew that Giggy's love for her nephew was like a sharp pierce to the quick, a Sebastian quiver-stab so pure that its clarity would end Cora's own quavers of disdain for

Giggy, a woman whose affection seemed both unbound and boundless, unquenched and unquenchable, whose kindness Cora herself could not question. It was Sebastian not only in its purity but also in its self-sacrifice, a full offering of herself as both a reflection and completion of her nephew's being, his own quest for identity.

The degree of the woman's devotion to Jem, Cora realized, would always leave the least amount of room for her own affections and, in this small community, to whom else could Cora turn? Robert, she had once thought, but now he had become more untouchable for her than for anybody else only because she had been known to have touched him. The political potency of flesh to flesh. Although Cora's solitude was painful, the poignancy of Jem's friendship and Giggy's unarmed charity was as clear as the morning light breaking in upon them now.

Giggy's primping had finally begun to show signs of winding down. She applied the last touches of her eyeshadow *pièce a pièce* and considered wearing lashes, but chose instead to present herself *au naturel*. She stroked the growling belly nestled on her lap as she made some final considerations. In the end, she did choose the amber bob. It never fit too snugly and was equipped with a layer of padding designed to absorb perspiration. She noticed that the hands of her clock were showing past eight and hoped that Jem had remembered to feed Chappy, who had now entered the bedroom and begun expounding his silent, spitty yaps, a bit of pillow stuffing cutely skewered on one of his incisors.

Cora showered and, when she returned to the bedroom, was happy to find Giggy gone. At the vanity, she combed her long, blonde hair and set it down to her right. She hadn't worn it since they'd arrived at Lake Wachannabee. There seemed to be no reason. So much became irrelevant, she thought, just through a change of space. Beliefs, desires, identities rise and descend, appear and fade with the shifting contours of one's geography.

She ran the brush through her short black hair, tied it back with a red kerchief, decided she looked comically suburban, and pulled the kerchief off and cast it on the bed.

There it was again, something gnawing inside her – a loneliness, and yet more pleasurable. A sense of melancholy so true that at first she mistook it for her period settling in, but that had never been so pleasing a sorrow. Then she thought of New Orleans, and tried to formulate her emotional pain as a sense of dislocation, but she knew that this wasn't the case either. She thought that maybe it was the impending investigation, that here she was in foreign territory, a suspect, and nobody seemed really to care except to harass and torment her. This explanation convinced her until she detected the smell of coffee and smelts on toast, the voices riding the steam up the staircase, the clickety-click of Chappy's excited toes. Only then did she realize that what she missed was Jem.

✦

Cora had met Jem in Louisiana.

'That's M-i-ss-I-ss-I-pp-I. M-i-ss-I-ss-I-pp-I. M-i-ss-I-ss-I-pp-I.' This was the memory that the incessant pound-pound-pound brought to Cora's mind — a pound-pound-pound that she had expected to sense in a gay bar at a Mardi Gras, but which was now so constant, so virtually innate, that she found it frightening rather than soothing, which was how she imagined the pound-pound-pound of her mother's heart had been as it pumped blood down deep into the womb where Cora had once sat, Buddha-like, waiting, not tensely, not hurriedly (i.e., what a lineup!), like the time her mother had gone in to pick up the nacho fixins for Friday supper and Cora was left sitting on the yellow scruff of lawn edging the parking lot of the Food-Mart in the sunshine of a Las Vegas spring.

As a child, Cora had come to the unfortunate conclusion that her reserve and patience were unique, virtually talents, and so there on the asphalt she waited, even as she saw what appeared to be her mother's Datsun glinting like a ruby as it pulled out of the parking lot, waited because she was eleven and not nervous and the national park in which they lived was only five miles away, but, in honesty, primarily because she was eleven and unsure whether it might be acceptable behaviour for her, at this age, to run into the mall screaming her mother's name, 'Yin-yin, Yin-yin!' just so somebody else would take charge, or whether she was supposed to find the manager all by herself and ask to use a phone, or what. Cora never wanted to lose control and so she waited what seemed to be a very long time, a good half hour, watching the shadows of the trees lengthening, creeping toward her home as perhaps she herself should do, until finally the Datsun returned, screeching around the corner into the half-empty parking lot and barrelling toward her. Cora, as she recalled, could see her mother's set jaw from over a hundred yards away and she remembered Yin-yin's blue-black hair blown back and shifting in spastic jerks, although the family Datsun had never been a convertible. Cora's therapist had proposed that the jerks of hair were a manifestation of the mother's ire. And Yin-yin was angry — angry with the child's patience, her control and emotional conservatism being interpreted as passive antagonism rather than the fear and vulnerability that the child was in fact experiencing.

While Cora didn't remember waiting in the womb in the same Tao-like manner as she had that afternoon at the mall, she did get frightened whenever she realized that a pounding, any pounding, has been going on for some time, for such a long time that it risked never stopping, which was how she felt just then, flat on her back on a pool table in Rawhide, one of those famous bars at the cross-roads of the New Orleans French Quarter with the not-so-secret room upstairs (if it was really supposed to be secret, Cora thought, they wouldn't let any fool with ten bucks go up there), with baroque wrought-iron balcony railings that everybody hung over to throw their strings of beads down at the men shaking their floppy cocks so unspectacularly down below. She was testing herself yet again, hoping to let herself get lost in a collective pleasure, but doing so too zealously to allow herself to blend fully into the experience. Like one rosy glint, she imagines, amid the fluorescent colours and cheap beads of the city's moist night.

'Th-row me somethin', mistah,' they called, really throwing the second half of that first syllable out into the collective air space, 'Th-row me somethin'', even the tourists taking up the intoxicating Louisiana drawl. Earlier that afternoon, Cora had caught a 'throw' cast aside by a greasy-haired crooner who was born in New Orleans and was the king of that, the twenty-fifth, Bacchus parade. Just then his string of beads was beginning to choke her as it ground against her vertebrae, feeling like those mats of wooden balls that taxi drivers strap over their seats. Cora knew then that she should not have agreed to have sex so soon after getting the tattoo. Even if it was a small one. But then she hadn't known when this type of opportunity would arise again. Cora wasn't regretting the pain of this latest attempt at a sense of community, trying instead to make it a part of the erotics. But she realized that a lot of what was going on was just dumb, awkward pain. It had been her hope that Louisiana would help with her ongoing efforts to release herself from the constrictions with which she was raised and it was only at this moment – a little too late – that she realized such an effort was itself too calculated.

In the distance, the calls continued to beckon, 'Th-row me somethin', th-row me somethin'', and she imagined limp penis, which didn't do it for her. The weight of the beads on her chest was affecting her breathing. Even the men calling from the street below knew that the pleasure was not in the plastic baubles but in whipping out your cock, and they weren't really concerned about getting anything thrown at them at all, except for compliments – a clutch of chubby Kowalskis screaming 'Stella!' into the humid night air. So this Mardi Gras subversion, this material excess, this symbolic casting away of monetary wealth like so many stars is itself subsumed, reflected Cora, because in New Orleans during Mardi Gras even money, money, money can't get you anything that anybody else can't get. This became clear to her at the opening parade of Mardi Gras week, as the strings of beads began filling up the gutters. First, people discarded only the small necklaces, the ones without clasps, those that didn't fit over even Cora's head (which was still scraping painfully against the turf of the pool table), or the necklaces with cracked beads in ugly colours, or those that had plastic profiles of Bacchus or Apollo dangling from them, and the opaque necklaces with the tacky beads shaped like molars. But soon other necklaces were cast aside, even the ones with various size beads in aqua and tangerine, opalescent jewels, and even the metallic necklaces (once the metal had begun to rub off). Cora clenched her teeth, her lips, her eyes, so she would feel, more than see, the people standing about nursing their beers and gazing at her. How she wished she hadn't consented to this; she was going to be late for a date she had made with a curious guy she had met at her motel. Oh, and the woman with the dildo was proceeding so inefficiently, thought Cora. Does she even really expect me to orgasm?

Cora felt the necklaces landing on her chest and her thighs, rolling down her uplifted legs and grouping around her crotch. Ironically, ABBA singing 'Money, Money, Money' sounded innocent in this opulent yet seedy back room, and she realized that she hadn't heard any blues since she'd arrived, or seen Spanish moss, or gone to Paul Prudhomme's restaurant with its chicken gumbo and blackened redfish – black 'n' blue fish, Jem called it, 'Jem Waferly' being the name by which the gaunt Texan that she'd found swooning in the hallway of her motel introduced himself.

'See that man?' he had moaned as he, with a cigarette between his lips, pointed down the hall at a rubber plant. Cora tried to heave his cat-limp torso aside with her leg so that she could pry open the door to her room. 'How he does give me the vapours,' the Dallasian drawled as he fluttered an imaginary fan in front of his long, pale neck. Cora thought she could even see a sort of glow on his skin, although it was too tepid this time of year for that real down-south humidity to take effect, the ravages of which were visible on the faded and mildew-tented outer walls of the old mansions and shotgun shanties lining the streets. 'You just go ahead and feel my little palpitations,' Jem coaxed, taking her hand in his mannerist own and pulling it down so that he could place it on the crotch of his shorts. She let it rest there as if checking the pulse of a gecko until he seemed satisfied, and then invited him in for a Bloody Mary. 'Sounds to have stimulatin' possibilities,' he replied, although she figured he would have accepted any offer.

So, she hadn't done any of these uniquely Louisianian things and here she was getting fucked on a pool table, something that one could do almost anywhere in the world, really. She remembered the ABBA song from when she was a kid, like three or less, at their home in the park where Yin-yin and her husband, Cora's father, both worked as forest wardens, making careers out of putting order into nature. To have it playing here at Mardi Gras made sex seem just a little cheap and maybe slightly immoral, even for an ethical relativist like Cora, especially compared to all those fulfilling natural attractions in the park – Saffron Falls, all those brook trout splashing around in Cobbler's Creek (or was it a brook?), and, we can't forget, the world-famous ...

'Money, Money, Money' suddenly started up again. The other woman, if Cora could see correctly through her lashes (one of which had come loose and lay diagonally over her eye), was slurping a beer even as they fucked. She could see the silver and blue label shimmering in front of the woman's face as she swilled a Blackened Voodoo. 'A local brew with the perfect amount of malt bitters to counter the heat of that Creole cookin'': a waiter had actually said this to her. She didn't care for the taste but loved the name and had decided to make Blackened Voodoo the unofficial brand of her own private Mardi Gras. And now she realized that the woman who was still poking her was also drinking her beer. Cora recollected her father saying that there were only two ways to win over the tourists. The first was to lie about the size of the fish.

Cora needed to get out of this town. She knew either she had to push the woman away and make a run for it or she had to fake orgasm (or orgasm, but that didn't seem likely) and then everybody would understand that the show was over. The beads kept pouring onto her chest and thighs and face, so much so that she had to turn her head from side to side to keep it from getting buried, and this tore her wig. Amid the rainbow shower of plastic jewellery, she suddenly realized that her glasses were missing, and all she could think about (besides 'ouch') was making sure they were all right.

Her mother had instilled this concern in her at an early age. Cora even recalled when she'd lost her glasses once as a child, the trauma. On a field trip to the mountains, she and her friends had been tobogganing down a hill that ended when it reached a river. Just before the toboggan shot into the icy water, she and all her friends would jump off. But once, Cora hadn't, and found herself actually on top of the toboggan, floating, but also slowly sinking, as it made its way toward the white water in the distance, pounding, pounding. 'Give me something to grab on to!' she shouted, but her gaggle of friends just ran along the shoreline flailing their arms in the air. One of them had begun to run back to the houses to get an adult or simply out of fear. Her glasses were missing, and Cora could see nothing but the ice-cold water bursting against her face and hair in the winter sunshine – brilliant purples, greens, ambers. She felt muzzled. She was drowning. It was getting impossible to breathe. The colours of light and water now barely overwhelmed the darkness that was overtaking her. She struggled to get her head above water.

When she finally surfaced, she realized that she had just relived the entire experience again, there in the back room of a New Orleans bar. She was covered in necklaces. Some guy in a euphoric paroxysm had smashed an empty beer bottle on the pool table and was signalling for another. Cora shoved the beads from her chest just as she orgasmed. Oh yes, the other thing that sells the tourists, her father had said, was Old Faithful. She pushed aside her partner, who looked sort of relieved but noncommittal, jostled down her skirt and started to march away until somebody yelled, 'Hey, you forgot your glasses.' Cora turned to see the crowd, which smiled at her as if they had just assisted in an intervention. Projecting from it, there was one arm, pale white, clad only in a rolled-up denim sleeve. The veins were well-defined and a cheap little maple leaf or dog was tattooed navy blue on the soft underbelly of the wrist. For a moment, the lanky, masculine fingers with a white moon covering half of each fingernail, mesmerized Cora. They were the most beautiful fingers in the world. She took her glasses.

'Thanks.'

'They're busted,' he said.

'Yeah, well,' she returned, taken by the warmth of his gesture, but then wondering how she could be talking to somebody so soon after her public spectacle. She let the crowd suck the arm back into itself as it surged in two streams — one up to the baroque balconies and the other toward the bar. She worked her way down the staircase, her reputation preceding her like the foamy ridge of a wave, the crowd parting as if for a queen or a leper.

The air outside, although muggy, was comparatively cool. She got to Canal Street, went up to Rampart and followed it along to Louis Armstrong Park where a remnant of New Agers was painting faces and telling fortunes. She didn't have to go here to get to the Café du Monde where she was to meet Jem, but it was the only place from which she knew how to orient herself. She bought a joint and lit it, walked past the park and turned back down on St. Ursuline Avenue which was not too crowded until she got back to Bourbon Street. She made her way through the crowd to the Mississippi River. 'M-i-ss-I-ss-I-pp-I.' She wondered if her mind was always going to do that whenever she thought of that rank, industrial flow. Her knapsack was heavy on her shoulder but she couldn't switch it over because of her new tattoo.

When she got to the café there was a lineup. The patio was full of tourists wearing yellow, green and purple T-shirts and drinking warm beer in plastic cups. So she went to the diner just across the street and took a seat by the window to watch for Jem. She ordered a coffee, just a regular coffee, and cleaned her nails with an Xacto knife she carried in her purse for protection. The tour brochure lying on the counter had a picture of a lobster crawling out of a saxophone. Inside were descriptions of tourist experiences:

Our Lady of Guadalupe Chapel, 411 N. Rampart St., New Orleans. Built in 1826 during a devastating yellow fever epidemic.

Is there any other kind, she said to herself. She had been honing her bitterness, trying to make it more 'bitchiness,' more functional as a form of sympathetic irony. Jem, she had found, was impressively precise in his bitterness. She wanted to spend more time with him, develop his kind of elusiveness.

Papa Joe Ordogne's Cajun Bayou Cruise, Bowie Swamp, New Orleans departures. Stop over at Toppy's for 'gator soup lunch. 583-8775 (cell).

St. Frances Xavier Cabrini Shrine, 1400 Moss St., New Orleans. Tour: historic building, chapel, shrine where Mother Cabrini, first U.S. citizen saint and patroness of immigrants, lived and educated city orphans.

Cora just knew Jem, whom she saw crossing over to the diner, would have a hundred witty things to say about that, but she couldn't think of one. 'Hey, listen to this,' she said, and read Mother Cabrini's description.

'That's just shallow, n'est tea?' Jem offered nasally, as he slipped his Liza-like figure onto the stool beside hers. 'Coffee, just regular coffee.' The boy's eyes were consciously undirected. His hands picked at the white threads dangling from the hem of his cut-offs. 'Shallow,' she repeated, realizing that he'd failed her. Jem, she concluded, had taken a bit too much coke again, but it had made his skin as pale and smooth as bathroom tissue and it was a perfect contrast to his wit. Wit is, she noted, first and foremost something one wears. And she'd been clashing. Either she'd have to start dressing like Saki (did photos of him exist?) or move somewhere where the lack of sun would pale her complexion. Meanwhile, Jem had begun to strip because, once again, he didn't have the buck twenty-five to pay for the coffee. It may have worked somewhere else, but the waitress's hand-on-hip glare made it clear that she was not going to have any of it. The five quarters that Cora spilled onto the counter to pay for her own coffee glittered in the Louisiana sun like silverfish. Fat Tuesday.

'I gotta get out of this place,' Jem mumbled.

'Not until you've paid, hon.'

'Where to?' asked Cora.

'I have an aunt up in Canada.'

✦

Cora froze at the honk. She had until recently felt confident that her decision to come to the Winter Garden with Jem would be a remedy for the boredom she felt with herself. Since the scandal, however, she'd begun to question whether she might not have bitten off more than she could chew. This morning she had intended to try to regain some calm but Giggy was so eager to hold the first meeting of the Fafaists that they had to do so before Cora had a chance even to breakfast. The Las Vegan took the minutes, which was more like dictation, since Giggy was really the only one talking, with Jem and Cora offering only occasional hmms of support. Cora had promised that, as soon as she'd had something to eat, she would transcribe the notes on the computer and distribute copies to all the members. She'd only begun her breakfast when the frighteningly familiar sound of a horn made her hurry out of the room.

It was clear to Jem that her nerves were weakening and, in the context of his newly developed skill of passive surveillance (or at least observation), he knew this meant something. It was a clue. But really, where could he file it? Her tension seemed so physical as it surged toward him that he felt a compulsion to leap aside. 'So too anxious-looking,' Jem sighed as she rushed past even as he too made his way toward the gazebo to see who had arrived. Constable Loch and two of his assistants. At last the wait was over.

'Mercy, if I'm not happy as sugar. Constable, you have arrived, and gosh, you do *look*,' Jem complimented, still catching his breath. Cora had moved past the visitors with only a nod and was busily inspecting the vehicle's lights. The constable, Reginald, was a crisp specimen: six feet tall with taut haunches riding sharp into the depths of his shorts, fleshing out symmetrically just before the crotch. The rest of his body – the broad shoulders, the feet solidly planted apart – seemed to flare from this centre like a supporting cast. The man exuded the aura of a superhero, an image his assistants dreamed of attaining but so far had not managed even to emulate.

'Look?' His milk-white hair was cut straight and short like a monk's and his close-cropped beard, despite being mussed, came to a point as refined as that of a paintbrush. Despite the harsh reality of summer, the man maintained an overall impression of being the product of a medieval mannerist.

'Oh, it's just so nice these days,' Jem explained, 'to come upon somebody who's doing it without trying.' The sparse black hairs gathered in greater profusion among their white counterparts at the tip of his beard, as if it had been dipped in ink. Jem regretted his first efforts at casualness, not simply because they seemed to have been lost on the guests but because they risked being interpreted as irritants.

'Yes, well,' mumbled the constable in an attempt to regain the authority that he always assumed, 'we're here … for the furniture.' Speaking with hesitancy was his habit, as if always prepared to be misunderstood, as if he were jotting notes to himself and throwing them into the air. This speech pattern, however, did not diminish the man's beauty. Something by El Greco in his last phase. Jem could only pray that someday he himself would be as handsome.

'Of course, how nice you all are for helping Auntie so. Just this way – follow me, chums.' In contrast to Reginald, the two assistants, with their toned, adolescent stomachs, tussle-blond hair, and lobes as fleshy and common as eggplants, were indistinguishable drones. The female had somewhat perkier breasts but otherwise they were both off the rack. 'There's the one and there's the other. Mind, try and sell them together; they'll fetch more that way.'

'We'll have to take what we can ... '

'That's it. Just don't be crude in your sale, constable, if you needn't be. Auntie, you understand, was extremely fond of the furniture. She doted, doted heavily on it. You can still see the indentations of her recent doting. It would snap her heart to see the chaise longue treated as, well ... I don't want to put down any of the other furniture for sale but, you know, treated as some second-hand trash from the nineties.' He was sure he was insulting somebody but couldn't stop himself. 'Not all nineties furniture. Just the aseptic stuff – black and camel, retro-Eames, you know the sort. You wouldn't want to belittle a Queen Anne with something like that.'

'No ... no,' returned the constable, confused but embarrassed to say so. 'We'll get what we can.'

'Natch. Get what you can, as long as it's a big old cheque for the children, right? You seem a little agitated. Need a rub?'

'Um, well, no, I mean ... '

'I'm the naïf in this scene, Mr. Constable.'

'Reginald.'

'Right. Oh, look who's come. It's Auntie. And you've met Cora. Cora, look who's here. I was just telling the constable, Mr. Reg, how he does just ...'

'Oh, Jem, not now.' Cora couldn't help but feel anxious in the constable's presence. For her to play dumb would only agitate him and she could do without that. She had been unable to determine whether the lights had the same arrangement as those on the vehicle from the previous night and, sometime during her inspection, she realized the desperation in even hoping for similarities. This was a truck and the night visitors had definitely been in a car.

'Sorry we're late, darling,' said Giggy. 'Who might those youths be?'

'I believe they're movers.'

'Movers and shakers,' laughed Giggy, trying to act social in preparation for the day's outing. The awkwardness of being casual was a learned trait.

'They helped with the Queen Anne.'

'Nothing for us to move, then? A little cushion perhaps? No, I assume not. Oh well.' She buffed one of her nails with an imaginary file. How she wished she hadn't mentioned the chaise's cushion, which she'd removed after noticing that some rodent had torn open one corner.

With the furniture securely strapped into the vehicle, the cluster of acquaintances stood in the front yard attempting amicability. Only Cora found herself leaning the other way, sitting on the steps to the gazebo and stabbing at a plate of egg substitute. Giggy eventually took a hoe out of the shed and began poking about the margin of the garden. She couldn't quite figure out how to use it. Her main objective, really, was to attract the peacocks for the constable's amusement without dipping any of her toes into the fertile earth. 'I'm sinking! I'm sinking!' she laughed as her weight pushed the heels of her shoes into the soil. Jem ran over to play, while Reginald and his helpers took the opportunity to exit the scene.

'Did you remember to feed the peacocks this morning?' she asked, stroking her nephew's lanky, chernozem hair.

'I put out the food but I didn't wait for them to show. I did hear them over by the Fountain of Blind Eros, though. Would you like me to check if they've eaten?'

'Yes, why don't you?' replied Giggy, feeling especially beautiful today and thus especially doting. She stooped down and picked a trident of bluebells, which she tucked into her nephew's pocket while her free hand demurely checked a rash.

'Cor,' Jem shouted, 'want to join?'

'No, I'm going to fix my flat.' Giggy refused to admit to herself that the woman's reply had cajoled a bubble of joy into her heart, for she cherished the idea of strolling over to the peacocks' roost alone with her nephew. A person can only dote on one individual at a time; anything more would be grandstanding verging either on the saintly or the sacrilegious. Daycare workers were trained to suffer from this fault. The moss was as soft as lilies beneath the foot, the sweet scent of ptomaine gentle in the air. Giggy could easily have spent another day wilting innocent in the August heat of their property, doing much what everybody else does on such a day: drinking beer and cocktails, chasing peacocks and hosing down Chappy, whose mouth had become foamy from the heat. Her constitution had always been pastoral; in this at least she was constant. Although remnants of the morning's cool lingered, the faded denim of the sky promised this day would offer another ten hours of extreme heat. Giggy had already had to ignore a couple of trickles of sweat that had crept down the ridge behind one ear and soaked into the padding of her wig, a helmet of gold against the elements and aging.

Cautiously, then, she set herself in the shade of the weeping willow to watch her nephew wander off in search of the peacocks, who hadn't been roosting. In the haze, he appeared to her as an indigenous warrior on the hunt, or perhaps one of the handsome, taut-skinned men in Dr. Amicable's manuscript. There was nothing to prove that they were taut-skinned, but in Giggy's mind everybody who lived in North America back then had to be, men and women alike. The crystalline clarity of an explorer's life, while not for her, seemed to turn young men into determined demigods whose strength lay in not only their fortitude, but also their resilience, codependence and beauty. Without each other, they were nothing. And so Jem too, she felt, would lose his beauty if it were not for her admiration and the love he shared with herself, with Rob. Days later, revisiting her deification, she felt the image that returned to her was only made all the more precise because of what happened next.

It could not have been guessed but poor Jem, rather than discovering the peacocks, found instead the whippet vomiting behind the tool shed. Giving the scamp a sympathetic pat on the back, the boy carried him over to Giggy who, upon being informed, reacted less calmly. 'Poisoned! Oh, my littlest one has been poisoned.' And this would have become the unsubstantiated conclusion with which all three of them proceeded, if Jem's pats of affection had not led the dog to cough birdseed across the youth's hairless lap. The whippet's grin quickly convinced the matriarch that it had at worst been an issue of windpipes.

Canine changing hands, the three rested, bowered by relief, before returning to the front of the villa where Cora, having finished patching her tire, sat in the shade of the gazebo sipping iced tea, the glow of the liquid gilding her neck and chin as buttercups do. The glorification of Jem combined with the recuperation of Chappy encouraged Giggy's affections to spread beyond them to Cora as well. I really do like this girl, she thought, as the brood arranged itself in the Bricklin, the matriarch slipping her mauve dogskin driving gloves over her plump fingers, careful not to damage her nails. Such a typical Sunday drive, she mused, having no clue what day of the week it really was. The concept of weekends, her mother had instilled in her from the moment at which she had taught young Giggy the days of the week, reeked a touch of the bourgeois.

Rob heard the vehicle leave and thought he could even taste the dust of its departure. He had understood that the constable had been there this morning, and that the man had finally succeeded in getting the chaise longue into his hands. But perhaps this meant nothing. Indeed, perhaps it would just be sold and allowed to disappear from history. But Rob felt sure this would not be the case. The constable knew something, something of which only Rob, of all the Winter Gardeners, was aware. But how much Reginald knew remained to be seen from his actions. The fact that Rob himself could not understand the furniture's real relevance to the scandal made him worry that it was he himself, and not the constable, who was dog-paddling in unknown waters.

✦

The reek of foie gras emanating from Giggy's picnic basket could not compete with the sensory overload of the bazaar spread out hodge-podge and higgledy-piggledy over the wrap of lawn that hung off the shoulders of the community centre. Despite the vivacity of the participants, the affair appeared at best mediocre – so much so, in fact, that Jem wondered whether the constable had not aimed it low, much as he seemed to surround himself with assistants whose inadequacies high-lighted his own beauty. Jem felt no guilt in his infatuation with the man, for it was a love only on the level of eros, not once rising to an echo of the marriage of two like minds that Plato so favoured. To call his attraction to Reg 'love' was an unfortunate limitation of lazy language, 'lust' being equally inadequate. It was a form of admiration for beauty that stimulated a response, but it did not encourage immediate sexual release any more than it drew him toward any sort of long-term investment of emotion, or even conversation for that matter. As such, it was for Jem distinct from what he felt for Rob, a love that persisted even when physical attraction might be put to a challenge.

Jem's enchantment with the constable was, in this sense, as banal as the bazaar. There was little besides Giggy's furniture to attract either attention or adequate funding. Private stalls sell-ing Creamsicles and third-world jewellery had clustered around the outer edges like barnacles, while the SPCA, AIDS Society and

West Nile Information Centre had set up booths under the shade of a Siberian elm.

'Jem, darling, be a dear and buy things.' Giggy handed her nephew a fifty-dollar bill so crisp that he was sure she'd slept on it.

'Anything special, Auntie?'

'Something that will make you swoon, dear. Or something for the motor car. Better yet, something that nobody else will buy. If Constable Loch meets his goal, we'll have some champagne afterwards. What do you say?'

'Who's your daddy?'

'That's all a mother can ask. Oh my, more trouble for Cora, I fear.' Giggy took up a position on the chaise longue, which she had not yet psychologically disowned, that gave her a view of Jem's friend, who was again suffering the scornful ogle of the community. Sir Clasp, veterinarian's father, seemed to be dripping at the lips as he muttered expletives in her direction. 'Poor little Cora.' Some locals were even following her around whispering gibberish to each other. 'Must she be so forthright in her values, Jem darling? Couldn't you tell her to don a tinge of obscurity? Give her my sunglasses; I'll make the sacrifice.'

Cora did not hear Giggy's recommendation directly, but she had heard something like it from others. Many times. It seemed a cliché to discourage lesbians (which was how Cora was now self-defining) from displaying the same confidence as men. It wasn't a politics of sexuality, but one of gender, boldness being her deviancy. And then, like twin beacons of salvation for the young woman's rattled nerves, two rolled-up T-shirt sleeves flashed from the shade of the beer tent. Bella Clasp and her compatriots did prove amicable, even though they must have known who Cora was and of what she'd been accused. Bella's participation no doubt encouraged Sir Clasp's foaming rants from the margins. The whispering of the crowd, meanwhile, had risen to a whizzing of effrontery, but none of the taunters would dare cross the barrier of a beer tent so early in the afternoon. They gradually began to disperse in search of second-hand treasure. 'If only the burden,' lamented Giggy aloud to nobody in particular, 'could shift from the poor dear to me, even for a moment.' With a hankie the size of a playing card she dabbed at her face. 'Oh, don't cry,' she advised herself. And indeed, there was no need to shed a tear for Cora, who was not in the worst of spirits. She was finding it refreshing to hear, for the first time since her arrival in Wachannabee, the topic turning to tattoos.

Jem found a painting of two enamoured unicorns covered in white glue and rainbow sparkles. If Fafaism, he pondered, was supposed to work against an already established aesthetic, as Auntie had claimed that morning, then maybe Fafaists, rather than painting nothing, should strip the medium off already existing works. The problem would be getting Giggy to accept this without realizing that it wasn't her idea. He also bought a pair of flip-flops, a few kittens that he dispersed among the children and, for his aunt, a lazy daisy cake which he had the seller cut into slices on the spot. The remaining forty dollars he gave to an old married couple knitting penis puppets in the AIDS booth. The size made it easier than finger puppets on their eyes, the two men explained. They handed him a little red ribbon in thanks and Jem pinned it to his shorts and gave them five dollars more, so they offered him some condoms, but he showed them that he was well supplied, so they offered him another ribbon, which he pinned onto a passing MP who, appreciative, dropped ten dollars into the cash box. A breeze brushed in from the lake, distracting the couple long enough for Jem to slip into the crowd.

Giggy was dozing on the chaise longue, her bangs hanging askew over her right eye. Constable Loch, hovering in the middle distance, was concerned that having her corpulence cast across the piece would make it more difficult to sell. Jem shaded his aunt's eyes with the cake, and she stretched as languorous as a well-fed panda before straightening up. 'Oh, lazy daisy cake,' she whispered as softly as if her name were Tina Louise, 'how perfect for a bazaar. You and Chappy must have some of it as well. Sit yourself down.' She knew that Jem would refuse the food; he prided himself on his hipless line, an aesthetic which he accentuated by avoiding socks and by letting his hair grow long down his narrow back. Like a self-conscious goatherd, at the feet of his aunt he draped himself, hoping that his pose might lead others to muse about the transition of focus in Wang Dynasty murals from the emperor to the reclining concubine. It was a transition, he well knew, that had maintained its influence on the arts to the current day, most noticeably in such popular works as *Farewell My Concubine, The White-Haired Girl* and *Beauty and the Beast*.

'Here, have a taste, no song and dance now,' Giggy cooed, beginning to nibble on the first in what she expected would become a series of slices.

'You know I can't eat coconut. But don't you worry yourself, dear; I just had a hot dog,' he lied, and they both laughed in the sunshine. In retrospect, the perfection of the day should have been the warning of its own downfall. Jem could see Reg weaving toward them from across the lot, his cock outlined like a baby monkey being smuggled into the country. 'Are you sure it's okay for us to be using the merchandise?' he asked his aunt.

'Why?' In what appeared to be a gesture of self-defence, Giggy shifted her breasts further into the support of her brassiere.

'Constable Loch is moving in our direction.' The man's sexuality was so overwhelming that Jem found himself suddenly wishing he were at home alone with Rob. He was embarrassed of the fact that his lover's plight seemed to keep fading from his attention; he was not yet prepared to acknowledge that his affections were waning simply from boredom. Love was still there, but it expected so much less from its experience. The presence of the constable had the effect of making Jem's apathy shift into a sense of guilt.

'Are we really using it, darling?' She glanced from one side of the chaise to the other, as if she had just realized it was beneath her. 'I mean technically ... '

'I'm afraid we are.'

'I suppose you're right, dearest, but the constable wouldn't cause a fuss about that. Where is he? Where are my sunglasses? I think I forgot my sunglasses in the car. Where is the car?'

'It doesn't matter, Auntie, the jig's up.' By the time Jem was able to finish his sentence, by the time he was able to make sure his own cock wasn't nudging out from his shorts, was able to tuck his undershirt in and push his hair back, able to help his aunt into a locked, upright position, to cast a glance across the crowd to spot Cora chatting with the patch of pierced and tattooed women and men who'd taken over the beer tent (and felt a mild pang of separation, and another echoic pang for Rob), by the time he could make sure that Chappy was still at the end of his leash, which Giggy had tied to one of the legs of their furniture, by the time he could remember as much as possible of what he had said to Reg when the constable had arrived unannounced weeks ago and asked the Texan and everybody else who lived in the Winter Garden what they had been doing on that fateful day when Robert was found stripped of his skin, and remember everything in what he had said that was not exactly the truth (who needed to know that he moisturized his elbows?) – by the time he'd done all this and quickly fantasized once more about his injured love, Reginald already towered before them, blocking out the sun as completely as sudden waves of sea urchins washed up and covered the shores of western Mexico, as formidable as the pillars and policemen that encircled Tess in the final pages of Hardy's novel, as dark and looming as the shadow of heaven itself through which fewer than half a dozen desperate stars might glint.

'The jig? Where *did* that word come from?' How was it, Giggy thought, that everything sped up so suddenly, and in such a way that the word 'jig' led her to think of nothing but wrangling dancers yanked by puppet strings. There was no dance – if anything, the locals were moving even more slowly through the humidity than they had been upon arriving. They wandered about, in fact, like a satiated pack of the living dead. Something in the tone of Jem's language had nevertheless disrupted the rhythm of the day. Something in the sharp angle of the constable's gaze projecting down to her own eyes, the sun glaring despite being fully behind his torso, left her feeling as if she might tip off the chair, which she clutched as if it were a raft. Even in the seconds before the action that, in retrospect, seemed inevitable, all three could feel the tension in their positions and the sudden shift in the current of the day, a shift so harsh that at least one of them had to have sensed its possibility, however weakly, when they had met at the Winter Garden earlier that day.

'Lazy daisy cake?' How could he refuse, thought Giggy. He's obviously not aiming to be the sinuous type.

'How much ... are they asking for it?'

'Oh, be my guest, Constable. You wouldn't happen to have any champagne to wash it down with in that office of yours?'

'No, the furniture. I'd like to buy it.'

'Well, I don't know. You're the one who's selling it.' Giggy turned to Jem, uncertain and embarrassed.

'Don't be looking at little old me. I'm as in the dark as a canary in a coal mine,' responded Jem, shrugging and letting his knees bash together lightly. Reg practically glared. 'Cheep cheep,' Jem responded, as if a canary could care to be sarcastic.

Giggy's culottes were almost visibly chafing and she could feel the sweat forming where her breasts lay against her belly. 'Oh, to stretch naked on this mossy knoll,' she murmured, 'and have you sprinkle talcum over my raw flesh.' She was flirting with the masses, but there was nothing new in that. Constable Loch pretended not to hear, as if transfixed by a small twig that he had stripped bare and was now twirling between a thumb and forefinger.

'I'll take them both then, yes ... both, the chaise and the, the other thing.'

'Divan.'

'Have to do my share, right? The children ... Help me carry them into the office,' he said, turning to Jem. Giggy huffed, aghast that anybody would ask her nephew to move furniture. The slightest exertion could force his body to begin to bulge in (shudder) indescribable ways, contrary to the aesthetic he so encouraged in his limbs. She even felt twinges of guilt at times when she saw him handling a cast-iron pan. On those nights when she remembered, she made sure to fill the kettle and place it on the stove herself, just so he wouldn't have to lift such a weight for next morning's tea.

'But he's only nineteen,' she blurted, unable to control herself and yet able to follow the nephew's lies about his age. Despite her subtlety, the constable frowned, as if her reduction of Jem's age was in fact an increase. 'That kind of exertion is going to create muscles,' she tried again. He admired her voluptuousness, sure, but Constable Loch had never understood the woman and, at this moment, was not about to try. As far as he could see, her words didn't only fail to make sense, they failed to connect to the topic at hand. He pushed his sleeves up to show that nothing was about to stop him. The curved silhouettes of his biceps led her yet again to reconsider her nephew's carnal aesthetic. Jem, who had risen, stepped demurely behind his aunt, pinning his bangs back with some bobby pins he had fished out of the loose pocket of his cut-offs.

'It's okay, Auntie,' he assured her through pin-clenching teeth, 'Mr. Constable, I'll soon be ready.' Giggy let out a few more huffs, placed the cake on a crate next to the chaise longue, and heaved herself out of the furniture. Bobby pins set, the men lifted the piece off the ground, but they took no more than three steps before two sharp harks shattered the fragile beauty of the day.

It would be hard to say which cry came first, but it seemed to be the one let loose by Giggy, who had fallen on her knees. The other, the second yelp, had been offered by Chappy. It was to be the only sound that the whippet would ever make. His beautifully long throat stretched by his collar, the canine lay on his side, slender but too large regardless to fit between a dot-matrix printer and a Belgian pfluge. His body, like some ill-directed anchor, was crammed into an unflattering contortion while the constable, not noticing the exact cause of the commotion, continued to try to remove the collar from the leg of the furniture by yanking on the latter. 'Oh, oh, oh,' cried Giggy, spasmodic, with each of the constable's yanks, 'Oh, oh, oh, oh,' sincerely distressed and prepared not to sell the furniture to Reg or to anybody if this was the treatment she was to expect. 'Oh, oh, OH, oh, oh. Constable, this spells ruin.' The cake had fallen in among a pile of compact discs and a clatter of last year's cell phones that began beeping a record of their slow deaths as the icing seeped into the circuitry. With a rather becoming dexterity, Giggy began disentangling the wheezing creature even as she hugged him to her. His tense legs paddled wildly, as if each had a mind of its own, scratching Giggy's belly and breasts until lines of blood began to flow over the gentle folds of her chemise. It's the Ambassador's Arms all over again, she thought, throwing the dog aside. 'Help me, somebody. This isn't novel.' The sight of the blood seemed to send the whippet into a greater frenzy, reviving perhaps the hunting instincts of its North England ancestors. Although only briefly trained as a racer, the frenetic scrabbling of his limbs made it apparent that he could have made his mark. Constable Loch dropped his end of the furniture, catapulting Jem into the distended belly of an unsuspecting Caucasian.

'Ooof!'

'I'm so sorry,' said the constable to Giggy, 'Let me help you,' and he tore open his shirt, exposing the massive expanse of his chest and a coat of hair as thick as steel wool. Chappy coughed up a bit more birdseed. Jem swooned, and the Caucasian caught him. Giggy would later admit that she was unsure whether her palpitations had been caused by the event itself or by the vision of the constable's exposed chest, which was but a part of the experience. The charge that the man took, she would add after she'd finished reading Dr. Amicable's manuscript, conjured up nothing less than the expectations placed by the Hudson's Bay Company back in London on the adventurers sent to secure pelts for the shareholders' wives. Loch yanked loose the tail of his shirt and spat on it. He dabbed feverishly at the fresh sprigs of blood and Chappy danced about the scene as if anxiously waiting his turn.

'Is this all really necessary?' the Caucasian asked.

'Let the man be, honey,' replied Jem. 'Auntie already looks more revived than she has all summer.'

'The dog is rather energized as well,' noted the Caucasian.

Reg acted with such furiousness, shifting the cloth from lips to breast to lips to breast, that it was difficult to tell whether he was cleaning away the blood or tasting it. Ivory was her breast and coral the blood as the officer wiped the woman clean in gentle, arabesque swirls that stiffened more than one nipple at the scene. Jem had risen to his feet but still held the edge of the Caucasian for balance. The crowd that had gathered felt a responsibility to applaud. Chappy licked his mistress with relief while her heartbeat returned to the pace of the enervated.

Only four thin lines in the shape of a W remained on her left breast to tell of the incident. Such a perfect letter, and yet it symbolized nothing, even there, next to the butterfly. Jem, all a-dote, helped Giggy to a chair and then checked on Chappy who, now kicking under Cora's arm, regretted having ever come to the bazaar. He chewed anxiously on the corner of her lapel and she let him. Constable Loch, seeing that there was nothing more that he could do to calm the family, had the Caucasian help him with the chaise longue, which they carried into the station, this time without incident. When the two returned, Giggy was sitting between Cora and Jem on the divan, a lopsided lazy daisy cake on her lap. The family rose briskly, clutching Chappy to their collective bosom. The dog flailed uselessly and Giggy, not stopping to find out what price was being paid for the furniture or whether it would be enough to keep the innocents out of her backyard, declared that her family was departing.

High were the spirits of Cora. She had found a group of people who had nothing against her and who too had had their tires and belly buttons punctured. One woman had even had her Jetta pushed off the loading dock. Giggy, meanwhile, couldn't decide whether the day had been ultimately a worthy experience or a nightmare. She had rid her home of the guilt-ridden furniture – a relief – but at the expense of these scratches – which were painful – and yet had eaten lazy daisy cake – a good thing – that had cost fifty dollars – neither here nor there – but then she had seen Constable Loch's beautiful chest – a pleasure, albeit in a disturbing sort of way, in part because she realized that Jem also fancied the man, and in familial conflicts the parent is so often expected to concede. Ah, but it was all at the expense of Chappy being choked between a pfluge and a dot-matrix – so incomparably, inexcusably horrible and traumatic. Yes, that was the proper emotion for this situation – tempered trauma.

So how could this Las Vegan vegan, wondered Giggy, keep up her rant about these fantastic new friends of hers? Were they preferable to the Winter Gardeners? Why then doesn't she go sleep with *them*? As if Chappy had not suffered enough, having also to put up with her yattering, Giggy's mind went on, as if she were not aggravating his post-traumatic syndrome (or whatever), as if he would ever commence to happy lapping again. How could this Cora girl proceed to coerce even her nephew away from cajoling the little one into at least a cautious assurance of normalcy? She glanced over at the whippet, busily cleaning himself in the most awkward of places despite his seatbelt. As

Giggy rushed the Bricklin along the gentle winds of the road, clipping the occasional turn as a means of clipping her own jagged nerves, her state of agitation morphed into a controllable aggression toward Cora, a woman whom she had so recently appreciated but whom she now, as she pulled into the driveway, chose to define as a self-centred, home-wrecking egoist.

'*Égoïste*,' shouted Giggy, '*égoïste!*' throwing off her dogskins, slamming the car door and marching toward the house, tears welling up in her eyes, the remains of the daisy cake balanced on one plump hand like a waiter's tray. She stormed into the gazebo without looking back. None of the others understood what she'd said, but the effect was the same as if they had. Nor did any of them know who Giggy's attack was directed toward, but they all agreed that the best thing to do was skinny-dip until the woman cooled down. From the camouflage of the mosquito netting, the matriarch watched the trio walk down the road until they disappeared among Lady Clasp's sunflowers, their petals like tepid flames paying homage to the waves of summer heat. Giggy turned on the open toe of her sandal and stepped not like the trio into a floral glory, but into a bloody splay of glass shards.

Dozens, hundreds, thousands of painful fragments all with an angular beauty that the domestic context kept Giggy from appreciating. Among the brittle petals of glass strewn across the hardwood floor also lay a knotted kerchief the colour of raw leather. It was only on closer inspection that Giggy discerned – '*Quel horreur!*' – that the cloth was in fact stained with blood. She had enough presence of mind and strength of curiosity to postpone fainting until she had cut open the material with a pair of scissors and gently coaxed it apart, revealing a scrap of paper and the remains of a rodent with its head crushed in. It was no ermine, Giggy could tell, but otherwise, who knows one rodent from another? It may have been a flying squirrel. My God, not Shirley! It was definitely mortal, for the paper was soaked with the blood of the animal and Giggy could make out only what appeared to be part of her own name. It took some moments before any ideas for action formed in her mind.

She first checked on Robert, whose slumber appeared not to have been shaken by her yelps of anxiety. Nothing else in the house seemed to have been disturbed either. She called the constable to report the scene and he was eager to come over, despite the fact that the bazaar was in as full a swing as it could expect to reach. The freshness of the evidence, he seemed to imply, was of importance, but Giggy was not so sure he wasn't flirting and this led her, as she seated herself on the piano stool, to question her own reasons for calling him. She played a little something on the keys, not really attentive. How odd that this intrusion into her home had become, in her view, a reason to tally the day as ending on the plus side after all. The shattered glass offered for the first time a clear sign that the criminal who had peeled Robert raw was not from her family. They had all been at the bazaar when this had happened.

She felt sorry now for her outburst at Cora and made her way to the gazebo to watch for her family's return. Off over the heavy heads of the sunflowers, she could just make out one of Lady Clasp's graduate trainees sliding a gloved arm up the behind of someone's Holstein, four others waiting patiently in line. Ah, Bella Clasp, Giggy mused. There was some sort of beauty in the woman's virility. The combination of vigour and open-mindedness made her seem like one of those resilient provincial matrons in British serial dramas. Even freshly bathed, the veterinarian seemed to exude a sheen of dirt: a coppery tinge to the skin and hair; a dryness to the face that left wrinkles at the corners of her eyes, as if she were always laughing at the world; a roughness to the hands, the fingers, the nails, that implied an excess of philanthropy. The gentleness she extended to others, to the animals for which she cared, permeated even her home, with its floppy hollyhocks and irregular patches of day lilies, and its room after room of overstuffed chairs against which were piled various books and magazines like shells shored up against rocks. Everything inside the house seemed to have a healthy layer of dust. If the shortest route from one point on her property to another was through the house itself, this was the route Bella Clasp took, and this same philosophy of ease defined her character. It left the woman looking more often than not like a painting, nature always glistening like a supportive backdrop to her own voluptuous silhouette.

The matriarch of the Winter Garden could hear Robert shifting in the shadows and the sharp particularity of his presence brought on a loneliness. The gazebo felt airless, the villa empty, like a military hospital after the war has ended and the soldiers have been sent home. Was the person who threw the missile out there perhaps, watching from among the rhododendrons, from behind the aluminum shed? She turned her back on the structure and, for distraction while she waited for the constable's arrival, picked up Robert Shakely's exploration narrative. She made her way down the stairs to the basement and the passageways that meandered damp and cool beneath her home. Here she always found it easier to breathe and, today, it made Robert's presence seemed less oppressive.

✦

Journal
of the most remarkable Transactions
and Occurrences at Prisom Factory
Commencing 3d April 1775 and ending March 1776,
kept by Mr. Robert Shakely, Governor;
containing a Full Description of that Settlement,
and the Adjacent Country;
and Likewise of the Feasibility of Trade
with Suggestions of Consideration &c. &c.;
and Likewise of the Feasibility of Expansion
Further Inland with Particular Attention to
Trade Potential West and Southwest
with Suggestions of Consideration &c. &c.

Remarks in April – May 1775

[April] Sunday the 2nd

Fine pleasent weather. Arrived two days a go and find Factory in order although needing heavy mending Darling Garret surveyor, Peter Post and Sebastian Orley arrive with me. Set to putting house in order tomorrow. Low on provisions, Post and Orley have been ahunting. Others and further supplies expected to arrive within a month. As instructed by your honours had Garret begin surveying the area upon arrival. Checked for damage Roof of main house, storage shed damaged probably by fallen tree though tree has been removed. Most walls require rechinking. Today at late noon met Six Canoes of Wachanas[1] in the Lake, which Mr. Harris had recorded as Trout Lake but which the Wachanas tell us is Wachannabee Lake of which Trout Lake is but a small bay round the isthmus at the south end, we being situated on an inlet at the north end much as per the map offered your honours by Mr. Harris.[2] The Wachanas speak some English and Post likewise some Wachana but is unable to fully understand their dialect.[3] He says they lisp or slur which suggests they are from a further western tribe which is promising for expansion toward that area though why they are in this territory is unclear and bodes not well.

They had no pelts to trade but said that they would bring their trade here if we would guarantee them rifles and brandy which I said we would. They were most concerned about the brandy as they say the Canadians offered them brandy but they do not trust them that

---

1. The name 'Wachana' also appears in other records as 'Wachanna,' 'Wachawna,' and 'Achwana.' In neither exploration journals nor Jesuit diaries do other tribes make even a single reference to this tribe by any of these names. The possibility exists, therefore, that there are other derivations of the name that have not yet been connected to these or that this tribe, for some strategic purpose, gave a false name to Europeans.

2. No extant version of this map remains. Shakely's description appears relatively accurate.

3. The Wachana tribe is now categorized as a minor branch of the Hurons, with some strong linguistic correlations. Lack of cultural or religious echoes, however, suggest an earlier ancestry for the Wachanas followed by an adaptation of Huron language either for business or simply communication, as occurred with English.

makes me sure that the Pedlors[4] are also in this area though I have not seen them.

Wednesday the 5th

Fine pleasant weather. Continues clear. Strong eastern wind. Busied men last few days gathering moss and clay for rechinking and clearing area of roof and shed from damage. Peter Post and Sebastian Orley returned with three large sturgeon and two smaller white type fish much like trout but less flavour.[5] Garret surveying. Post further employed shingling wood to patch roof as posts were not broken in damage and only minor repairs appear necessary. Good strong stonework around base and chimney fortunately not damaged as area seems void of rocks consisting mostly of deep red soil or mud and humus implying high iron content though unlikely as Wachanas suggest desirous of iron tools.[6]

I take this moment to request in future that exceptional surveyors, mappers, &c. be included in any first

---

4. 'Pedlors' is a common term among Hudson's Bay employees and other English speakers for referring to the French-based explorers and trappers working for other companies.

5. After this point, Shakely refers elsewhere in his records simply to 'white fish.' The reference is probably to the species now defined as whitefish, which are indigenous to the region. If this is the case, then this would constitute the first use of the word 'whitefish' to define the species. The fact undermines Dr. Max Williams' argument that the 'Renaissance,' as he refers to it, of Canadian piscatory classification did not begin until 1807.

6. Shakely's naïveté here is rather surprising. Neither Wachanas nor Hurons have any history of making goods from iron. Knowledge of and access to the material cannot, of course, guarantee its functionalization or utilization. Moreover, as the journals of Peter Post and Samuel Hearne both suggest (See Pladarodnaya: 1988b), indigenous tribes have used the same word for both metal tools and metal jewellery. Shakely appears in his accounts not to recognize the possibility.

expedition team. Even slight confusions regarding names, locations, directions, &c. lead to major delays, even of weeks, and possible injury. One week can lead to weather changes that hide animals tracks and other signs of food, leading to starvation and possible deaths. We thank God have not encountered such tests of our fortitude but only because of working together and checking and rechecking directions often to ensure our direction is correct. Even then we are days later than future traders with clear instructions will be. Exceptional supply of fish and meat in area — various rodents, beaver, deer and various fishes. Fowl not as abundant but not necessary. But this makes reliance on good weather all the stronger and risk of starvation and deaths too.

Sunday the 9th

Rainy weather. Easterly. Seven tents arrive at Factory over night. No furs to trade. Ask for brandy as assurance of future supply which I deny as we have only one keg. Spend day inside working on structure of building, setting up stone stove pit in centre of main room, Post involved in rechinking. Some supply of useful stone found but without signs of iron deposits.

Observation of Wachanas not informative. Today they spend the day mostly in tents, some men go ahunting or fishing return later that day with many supplies. In early evening two Wachanas found in fort stealing liquor stored in cellar. Have consumed some liquor and taking more. Say they are not stealing because of side entrance and show us entrance to cellar previously unknown. We allow them to take the liquor that they have already removed from keg (As per your honours' instructions, hope to develop allegiance.) Wachanas say

9

their stay is for short period only, intent on moving southwestward to territory monitored by French Pedlors who more readily supply necessities for trade. I assure all necessities available with us but they sound discouraged due to refusal to supply liquor. But they now know we have little to supply. Evening ends with cloud covering, rains briefly and stopping.

Monday the 17th

Fine pleasant weather all week Continues cloud over [cover?] Strong eastern wind

Post discoursing with Wachanas proved to be local but separated from other Wachanas due to difficulties. Conflict unclear but recent. My concern with retributtion for favouritism. Post encouraged to continue socializing with Wachanas, developing favour and establishing information on trade flow, supplies, &c. Other access to cellar explored. Darling Garret proceeds with mapping of terrain near and surrounding Fort Prisom. Immediate territory flat and bounded by lake from northwest to northeast and by creek running from southwest to northeast, as per map.[7] Rocky terrain but severed and smoothened in many areas, perhaps limestone, most useful for building up main fort and two additional cabins started. Creek cuts steeply through soft stone creating deep canyon useful for water supply but not many fish it appears. All men go fishing this afternoon return with few. May need to rely on rations shortly. Additional tents arrive. Wachanas busy around camp in preparation for move.

---

7. Unfortunately, no map as described is extant with this journal. The description of the creek does not accord with the current flow of Wachannabee Creek entirely. Again, the gorge is not acknowledged.

[May] Monday the 8th

Fine weather but rarely clear much rain causing deterioration of chinking on steady basis. Strong eastern wind.

Post spends daily with Wachanas, gathering information and developing favour. Appear to have overcome language difficulties most effectively. Tents do intend to move southwest in weeks after a few injured party are given further time to recover. Source of wounds unclear, perhaps conflict with other Wachanas or Hurons of which they do not wish to discuss. Post develops some trust, supplies them with some brandy and provisions but apparently not enough; concerned that he will lose favour if he is not able to support his kindnesses with goods of value to them. I have asked Post to encourage tribe to stay locally in wait for coming supply of additional goods for trade and gifts, but they do not seem confident in us. Wachanas supply us with cured meat (not deer, but seems like) in return for metalwork.

Garret and Orley continue with mapping out area roughly, complete to borders of creek and edge of lake. Main building of Prisom Factory has been fully prepared for arrival of additional company.[8] Completed repairs to cellar, side cabin and two additional cabins. Men employed with gathering wood for further structures to be built as required. All literature read. Request for supplies and reading sent by Wachanas going to east post for delivery to London. Lack of employment disturbing so men encouraged to continue with mapping and Post with Wachanas.

---

8. The executive of the Hudson's Bay Company would in fact never send additional explorers to Prisom Factory, probably favouring the easier and more popular route further south. Shakely, it appears, was never informed of this decision.

Sunday the 14th

Fine pleasant weather Continues clear Strong eastern wind

Orley takes to circumnavigate and map lake fully with report of possible waterways onward. Garret completing mapping of area around gorge and south lieing area. Wachanas show Post additional stone work extending below the central factory building, consisting of narrow, short passageway leading onto large room, empty save for two kegs and horrible stench. Today Garret gone ahunting all day only kilt four squirrels and one hare Indians claim squirrels are not common in this area

Post has, on my encouragement, moved to living primarily with Wachanas, speaking Wachana fully and participating in day-long hunts, curing of meat and fish for travel, and additionally evening rituals. Continues reporting to me every few days, when possible. Explains conflict with the other tribes as based in ritual of community. During period of weak food supplies, the other tribes not willing to deviate from established ritual but our Wachanas offer and follow alternative process, resulting in their isolation. Post unclear on specifics.

Wednesday the 17

Fine pleasant weather. Continues clear. Strong eastern wind.

Others not arrived. Garret and Orley continue with extensive surveying, suggest possible relocation to site on wider, less turbulent edge of lake. Post believes tribes have chosen this location for a purpose and I agree — suggesting we remain in position seeing as Factory constructed and wood already available. Post discoursing with Wachanas fully, asked to accompanie tribe when it moves southwest, although tribe has agreed to remain local until additional explorers arrive with new supplies for trade and gifts. Post confirms that tribal conflict was rooted in ritual of food consumption starvation tactic requiring consumption of revered meat otherwise only consumed by tribal leaders on certain occasions. Maybe we could supply appropriate meat, still unknown, from England for excellent fur exchange, but information on ritual still missing. Possible that Post is refraining from sharing all his knowledge – when pressed for information, he is silent first before saying he has nothing more to share. He then returns to lisping Wachanas for the night, tribe having now attained its full number of roughly thirty, mostly women and children, some older men.

Tuesday the 23th

Fine pleasant weather. Continues clear. Strong eastern wind.

Orley regularly hunting more squirrels. We joke [choke?][9] him and he says from now on he will go afishing. Orley prefers hunting alone Post also too

---

9. Shakely's use of the word 'joke,' if indeed that is the word here, and not 'choke,' is telling since, in the second half of the eighteenth century this verbal form is rare and generally used by individuals with a higher grasp of English grammar than Shakely suggests, in so many other sections of the manuscript, that he has, and which traders in the New World generally did not have. Shakely no doubt brought some books with him, and he may have come across the high usage in one of these. Alexander Marchinsky cites this passage as one of the possible proofs that John Boswell's *Corsica* was being read in North America before the nineteenth century. It should be noted, however, that Shakely could just as easily have been reading Mrs. Piozzi's *Journal of France* or Mrs. Sherwood's *Brigette of the Manor*, which were first published before Shakely left England and in which this high usage of 'joke' can be found.

often alone with Wachanas who he says are growing impatient with lack of new supplies Post unable to explain to tribe that supplies do not belong to us but to the Hudson's Bay Company. Has taken to eating all meals with them, which I wrongly encouraged at first, thinking to save on our rations but now must work to enforce Post's presence at Prisom Factory. Post, Orley and Garret informed that unnecessary interaction with tribes is to be discouraged for now until supplies arrive and deals with Wachanas completed. Post surly but accepts and remains at factory the next few days. Wachanas most heavily agitated by Post's absence. Refuse communication. Garret continues with surviving [surveying?]. Has located iron deposits as well as supply of limestone if future construction needed Encouraged to record sitings of diverse animals for trapping potential. Extensive supply of beavers and fine weather make this a promising location for a permanent factory. Post goes hunting daily with Orley, unwilling to remain at Factory and, because food is most important at present, I allow him. Post and Orley return often separately but Post always has some catch, having learnt skills from Wachanas. Orley encouraged to discourse with tribe, develop skills. Evenings all employees of your honours returning to factory for meal and sleep. Cohesion of company mostly re-established and will only do so further when additional workers arrive.

27th

Today Sebastian Orley fails to return home. Others have no information on his whereabouts. Wachanas claim no knowledge of his presence.

Beast and boy decided to leave Cora down at the dock when some of her new friends arrived. The two chose to follow the sun as it started its slip in the twilit sky. It was Jem's favourite part of the day, earliest twilight, even though the lengthening shadows signalled his supper shift. Despite an awareness of his own gothic potential, he remained in spirit a lighthearted youth, a child of the sun. He had also retained much of his innocence, even as he had gained awareness of its power. The flip side of *fin-de-siècle* ennui and all its cultural baggage had found a receptacle in young Mr. Waferly, who had turned frustration into an aestheticist complacency, into an adoration for still waters that were not tainted by aggression. Satisfaction had in Jem's era become the dearest quality. It was not akin to contentment; it was an emotion more awake than that. It had been popular at the beginning of the last century, before the First World War, among Edwardians who had deluded themselves into feeling they had escaped the confines of a repressed age.

But there were few who could claim to possess it now, satisfaction. And this, although it was available to most. With the disorganization of the distribution of wealth, the notion of class had dissipated as well, and people moved from slums and back alleys to New York sliver mansions with the ease and inconsequence of angels. Jem didn't realize all this; he only knew that no reason had yet arisen for him to grow older. He could choose to live under the protection of his aunt until he was thirty (if he made it to thirty) and society no longer frowned upon such a decision. It was inevitable that adolescence, having become the most popular of ages, would expand to cover the most years. Like so many others of his age, Jem Waferly had sipped steadily on the pleasures of adulthood without ever having had any intention of defining its realm as his own.

Chappy had avoided sin in much the same way, but this was not as new a phenomenon in the culture of dogs. They had been given a *carte blanche* release from responsibility. Even when a Rottweiler was put down for killing a child, devouring its arms, even if up to the shoulders, the guilty party was not the dog but its owners. 'And me, sir,' the animal always wisely refrained from asking, 'may I not speak?'

It was not that Jem was simple or that he had been protected from an awareness of his aging, but that he had been allowed to cultivate a spirit of youthfulness influenced by a trust of strangers and an appreciation for both easy pleasures and the most complex of tragedies. It would be inaccurate, yet one cannot refrain from recognizing a corollary to opera – the gaudiness of the spectacle and the glitter of cheap jewellery dripping from one hand while honest pain, mystery and death nest comfortably in the other. Love was simultaneously as artificial as the courtly model and as resonant as the conjugality of like minds. And it was all love. This was the emotion to which his soul and body gravitated, to which he directed himself – a gravitation toward the self, a self-gratification. Of course, none of this was ever apparent. The need for the emotional extreme reflected in the pleasure of pain, for example, required a degree of reserve or even subterfuge and, while Jem may have recognized this, most often he himself was unaware of the cautions that secured his sense of joy. It was therefore an image that harmonized with the man's mental state that one appreciated when admiring the black outline fusing the boy and dog as they walked straight on into the sun.

When the two arrived home, Constable Loch was already there, standing stern in a sharp shirt-and-shorts set in two-tone dove grey, tastefully demure. He had changed from the outfit he had been wearing at the bazaar, and now looked more than ever like a model in a department store catalogue, holding a piece of paper in one hand and a bag containing the crushed and bloody evidence in the other. The only ciphers that the constable had been able to make out among the blood stains on the paper were: 'EWES. POSING MA.' Not realizing that some of the letters were part of Giggy's name, he saw nothing in the event except that the community was still harassing Cora. This conclusion was influenced by concerns that she might try to sue him for libel, he being the one who had first accused her. It was this alone that had led him to avoid mentioning Rob on either of his visits to the house this day, and this reason alone that led him to dislike Cora all the more, her wheel of fortune renewing its downward spin.

Before Jem's return, the constable, at a loss for a coherence of clues, had thrice asked Giggy whether she had written the note herself. While making her defensive, this altered her response not one stitch. She and Reg had been getting along so well, she lamented to herself, together checking her wound from earlier in the afternoon, eating the last of the lazy daisy cake right off the plate, prodding the evidence into the semblance of a baby squirrel. She was relieved to see it was too small to be Shirley. Oh, but one of her infants? She would be angry with us indeed, Giggy thought, if that were the case.

The third time he suggested her complicity, she could not keep calm any longer.

'Dear, no offence, but you couldn't solve your way out of that little evidence bag of yours.' This, Constable Loch believed, was not the way to which law enforcers should be spoken. 'I hate myself even for having to consider you a dreadful bore.'

A constable was someone you talked to in a different way because a constable was someone who could make accusations against you as part of the job, could enter your house and eat your food as part of the job, could disrupt a pleasant if over-eventful day by snaking his fat car down your drive and asking you all sorts of questions about a crime that you yourself reported. 'Did I say "bore"? I'm sorry. I should have said "boor."' A constable, at least in the county of Lake Wachannabee, had this advantage.

Giggy, fully aware of these privileges, began regretting her words even as they fell from her lips, but her diatribe had been impregnated with alternative inspirations. Attraction, most forcefully. The snipes were not petty insults so much as a test of the man's affections. If he rose, taken aback, and chose to lecture Giggy on his notions of institutionalized decorum, then she would know that he felt nothing more for her than he would have had her hefty breasts been served to him on a plate like the head of Nero's dog. If he did not stand up when he offered the information, however, then she would know that he was enamoured with her, although it might still have been her breasts that were the prime motivators. To get the ponies trotting, Giggy's mother had made her well aware, required whip as well as wallop.

As it was, the constable remained seated and yet failed to admonish her. The millennium may have arrived but it was still the suburban constable of the late-twentieth century who, beginning to rise, chuckled good naturedly and offered the woman an uninspired 'Now, now.' And it was then that it happened. He could not, she could not, nobody could have foreseen it. The man slipped in blood (a bad omen, no doubt, in any culture). Down he fell, ass first on the splinter-splattered floor. As soon as he stood up, tiny scarlet spots, as many as might fit in Giggy's hand, began to blossom on the right cheek of his shorts. An expression of self-contempt crossed his face. Giggy sighed from the thrill and her body fell softly against the couch.

It's past the time to wilt, she thought, and my boy isn't here and the constable hasn't even loosened his collar let alone torn open his shirt. What is it that does it for him? She gazed at the coat of curls converging about the constable's thighs, as he – unable to sit – licked his little pencil, scratched yet another note as brief as 'butter beans' on his pad, flipped it shut, tucked it back and offered to help clean up.

Giggy was obliged.

It was as the last scraps of glass were being coaxed over the rim of the dustpan that the screen door squeaked open and slammed back. Jem and Chappy stood glowing as if carved from Turkish balsa, the dog still damp but Jem fully sun-dried. The first thing the boy noticed was Auntie's wig, which had twisted forward, creating bangs as long as his own. A pang of recognition that shifted into his first real moment of ageism sprinted through his virtually naked body. Relating the incident of the rodent to her nephew, Giggy was relieved to note that she had not lied to the constable about any of the discovery; her fatigue, she had astutely recognized, would on its own soon threaten the consistency of her narrative. Deciding that she was too tightly wound, too aware of movements to gauge intentions, she excused herself and shuffled off to the kitchen to add 'pane of glass' to the 'sweet yams' and 'soy milk' Jem had written on the scrap of paper affixed to the fridge with a small magnet in the shape of a magnet. 'Sweet yams,' she mumbled fondly as Jem rose yet again in her esteem.

The hip-slim man, meanwhile, had excused himself to check on Rob who, after hearing about the constable's fall and the spots of blood, smiled through cracked lips, albeit not for the first time since his own ordeal had begun. Rob was the first to note that his wounds and those of the squirrel constituted two separate incidents. While he knew who had instigated his own wounds, even knew why they had done so, the news about the squirrel was a mystery to him and, combined with previous information, fostered entertaining speculations. Perhaps, he pondered, they weren't separate crimes. Perhaps somebody had cast the rodent in the hopes of taking credit for Rob's pain, or to draw attention away from those who had really participated. Perhaps Cora had someone do it to clear her name? How he wished he had been in the room when the discovery was made, so that he might have interpreted the faces of the others who'd been present.

Rob's smile was like that of an omnipotent sprite, gentle but sly. Jem realized for the first time that he didn't know everything that his boyfriend knew. In fact, thought Jem, other people also knew what Rob knew and may not want the wounded man to give any of the information away. How was it that Rob had not known of the recent ruckus? Had not heard the glass shatter? Jem put a finger to his own mouth, thinking it best that Rob not try to speak while the constable was still at the villa. Instead, Jem let their lashes entangle momentarily as the men kissed, the Texan tasting the blood brought to his lover's surface by the pain of what Jem thought was his first full smile since he'd regained consciousness. Helping Rob sit up, Jem pressed his lips against the other man's forehead and promised to return soon with a papaya milkshake of love. Rob was thirsty for water – a milkshake seemed too coagulated – but he remained as quiet as the whippet.

Against Giggy's will, Jem helped the constable carry out the pieces of glass. At one point a shard pricked Jem's left bicep but, before Giggy could consternate, Constable Loch squeezed the meat to stop the flow and dabbed away the ruby V. Giggy, still supine, made a vague groan of despair while Chappy licked a mixture of squirrel blood and lazy daisy icing off her calf, a gesture she mistook as condolence. The matriarch mumbled random assurances to the room that she would survive this latest shock. The constable wanted it all, every shard, he claimed, as evidence. Giggy noticed the few pecks of red on the back of his shorts but couldn't establish the etiquette with which she might ask to clean the wounds. Jem stood back for a moment in admiration of the radiant tableau made by Giggy, Reg and the loving whippet. A pair of yellow sheers entangled themselves about the nephew with the vague suggestion of a cotillion gown. Giggy hoped that she and Jem would go to New Orleans one day so that she could become part of his image, but that depended on whether the plans for Helsinki fell through. Just the fantasy of escaping the heat set her body chafing. Excusing herself once more, she carried her torso upstairs to freshen before supper.

Jem and the constable stood silent at the scene of the crime for another half a minute before they agreed that all that could be done had been done. The host saw the constable out. He then hurried into the kitchen to boil podded peas and shuck shrimp and corn for the chilled gumbo. He brought Rob his milkshake, returning to the kitchen with – for his lover's benefit – loose-jointed snippets of 'Zip-a-dee-doo-dah' bursting from his lips. Rob's latest signs of life invigorated Jem more than either could have expected. Through the window above the sink, Jem saw Chappy scamping with the peacocks in the west acre of the veterinarian's alfalfa – an unfair sport, Jem felt, since one of the birds was wearing a splint from a sprain caused by a previous cross-species gambol. He'd have to call Lady Clasp tomorrow to have her check the patient's progress. He could also see that the peacocks' food had become supper for a family of squirrels, or what Jem thought was a family until they started leaping at each other's jugulars, reminding him that sustenance frequently superseded blood relations and religious dogma (his mind looking no further than the writings of Mary Rowlandson for confirmation). The cavorting of the rodents, peacocks and whippet soon moved out of view and into the depths of the Cubist garden.

The peas came to a rolling boil as Jem scaled the trout, laid the fillets in the skillet and placed a quarter cup of unpasteurized milk between the two largest fish, the ones that would be eaten by Auntie and Chappy. The sizzle was loud enough to keep Jem unaware that the constable was still in the driveway changing a flat. The five spots of blood on the man's shorts had spread into a bouquet of zinnias; he would require a change of clothes when he eventually invited himself to stay for dinner.

Giggy filled her tub with cool water and just enough milk bath to make it the same colour as her skin. Once soaking, she unpinned her mop of hair and cast it among the collection dominating one corner of the counter like a pack of feral cats. She could hear the chortling of the grouse and partridges in the garden below and imagined Chappy's slap-happy yips of silence. She soaped her hands and slowly plucked the rings from her swollen fingers, laying the jewels — amber, xanthic, gamboge, ecru — along the edge of the tub where they glittered through the sudsy water like patient turtles. She massaged her fingers and watched the swelling recede in the coolness of the still-fading day.

Something brown flew by the window a-chirp. Giggy mused as to how it might feel for nobody to notice the type of bird you were. 'Birds of a feather,' lectured Giggy to her wigs, 'is a cruel assumption by which to live.' It was obvious to her that she was an individual, but she wasn't so naive as to assume that her individuality was uninfluenced by her social context and its broader supports. She envisioned society as a 3-D diorama, a black forest silhouette enveloping the sharp amber beauty of her character, a fake-fur stole, golden like the tufts of the bird whose limb-thrilled body had just shot past her window yet again.

'It's akin to establishing your social pH balance,' she mused, gazing at her legs as they hovered like well-fed sharks just below the surface of the water. Floundering for the soap which had made its way to the other end of the tub, she considered whether physical traits were as valid as mental traits in defining the individual. The bubbles of a fart skittered like newborn hermit crabs up along her inner thighs. 'A person defines herself by what matters,' Giggy instructed herself, 'not by what matter is.' Here again she found herself trying to make a splashing leap from the wading pool of the analytic into that of the emotional, and here again she knew that at least one mediator between the two was the dolphin hoop of aesthetics.

Eventually, she pried the stopper out of the bottom of the tub with her toe and watched the skin-filthy liquid recede. 'Still,' she continued, rubbing a mint balm along the chafed folds of her belly and crotch, 'we can't throw the analytic out with the bathwater. It's too much a part of the netting that's trapped me into thinking this way. To cast it aside would be to discard the source of my thinking and so, I guess, my self as well.' She considered the poor dolphins tangled in those tuna nets. Then, momentarily, she considered the poor tuna.

'No,' she proceeded, the puff of talc – 'fa fa' – patting her fleshy shoulders, 'what's needed is an aesthetic model that recognizes its own assumptions without getting pretentious about it. Fafaism didn't appear in a void, but that doesn't mean that art cannot be free from the artists.'

'Fa fa fa,' agreed the puff.

This changed everything, but they'd already had their first meeting. Giggy hoped she might get to the notes before Cora had done the transcription; there had been some flaws in their thinking. 'The most important community for aesthetics,' she went on, dabbing into a pot of Egyptian ash, 'is transhistorical, a community through time.' Again something golden-brown dove past the open window and Giggy consciously informed herself that it was that same bird that had passed by before – the one and the same individual, struggling creatively against the assumptive powers of the mind. As the last of the water swirled away with the dingy grey scales of her own used flesh, Giggy heaved her torso out of the tub. She powdered the rest of her body, arranged a towel on her head, and opened the bathroom door to the aroma of trout frying with basil and just a pinch of dill rubbed vigorously along the vertebrae of the fillets. Chappy sat on her bed licking himself intently. A squirrel hovered cautiously on the sill of Giggy's bedroom window like a corrective endnote to her musings.

Shirley!

The realization that she had gotten not only the type of animal wrong but even the species made Giggy lightheaded. She settled onto the edge of the bed to regain her bearings. These sorts of coincidences made her feel sure that she was destined for fame, if not as a philosopher, at least as the county's most renowned clairvoyant. So often she forgot that the mind worked on more than one level simultaneously. It was apparent to her now that, while she'd been formulating her notions of a transhistorical, self-corrective aesthetic, some other part of her brain had been off not only defining all birds as birds but defining even squirrels as birds simply because they flew. 'Even if every bird I ever encounter can fly, flying will not name a bird, just as being netted doesn't name a tuna. Nothing names anybody really, not adequately. How can I incorporate a self-corrective into Fafaism such that it would deny its own superiority, mock its own validity? No, paintings in Canada Dry just won't wash. The new aesthetic will have to be reactive, flagrantly, so that no one will forget our lack of originality.'

Shirley, seeming to understand that Giggy was feeling crushed, crawled onto the bed and hovered about two feet from her ample figure. The animal's eyes swirled in their loose sockets. 'Fa,' her chompy little teeth muttered, 'fa, fa, fa, fa, fa.'

✦

It took Giggy but a moment to realize that, for Shirley to act as brazen as some of the guests at the Ambassador's Arms, she had to be insane. Giggy grabbed Chappy and fled the room while Shirley, startled, made a getaway out the window. Giggy was not even down the stairs before both the whippet and her fears had broken free. She had, she scolded herself, anthropomorphized the little creature. Once she had reached the ground floor, had checked to see that Robert indeed had been fed, bedpanned and turned, and had followed the appetizing scents to the kitchen, she had found her emotional legs again. Jem had been waiting for her patiently, trays lined along the counter, to serve dinner in the dining room because, as Giggy was surprised to discover, they had guests. In what was usually Cora's seat, she found Constable Loch, while Dr. Amicable had taken a place at the far end of the table.

'Oh Jem, look who's here. Reg *and* John. What a pleasant surprise.' She spoke like a character in one of her melodramas. In Giggy's view, everybody had to agree that the professor was handsome, but there were so many opinions regarding his character that she now eyed the man's physique with only a vague conception of his disposition. The glassiness of his eyes and the way his steely grey hair stuck straight up like chives suggested a virility worthy of mention, though in fact nobody had ever commented on it to her. She knew it was illogical, but the stiffness of his hair made his presence seem calculated. His rolled sleeves and bare arms, although scratched with labour, were always so translucently pale that, she imagined, one couldn't cast a shadow on them. Those legs, stretched out and crossed at the ankles – she gazed immodestly at them and the loose threads of his cut-offs as they gathered like down at the substance of his foufoune. (He seemed to wiggle. Did he wiggle?) 'Love, what made you think the wonderful thought of inviting these fine gentlemen?' She sat alone in her giggle. She was doing horribly and the two guests, noting her fluster, offered long and extremely slender smiles in compensation, but neither spoke. After all that had happened this day, Giggy was amazed to find her own mind shift so quickly to the gear of sex, recognizing that she would be willing to sleep with either of them, if it was their wooing that was making them act awkwardly. She was not prepared tonight, however, to play their jealousies off each other; this would not become a triangle of erotics. Her attention shifted to her pate and she was relieved to note that she had indeed put on a wig before descending, although she was unsure which one. While she had no qualms about letting others know that she wore wigs, it seemed gauche to have her hair change too drastically in anybody's eyes – anybody's outside the family, that is. The constable, she consternated, may have seen her go from auburn to black within hours, but hadn't he himself changed his entire wardrobe once already today? And now he'd changed yet again, replacing his shorts with a smart little dish towel synched evocatively around his waist. Had anybody helped with his wounds?

Jem's back was toward them as he continued preparations in the kitchen, his ass shaking vigorously as he stirred the *sauce de lys* for the trout. I would like a wig made from his hair, she realized.

'I didn't,' said Jem.

'Didn't what?'

'Didn't invite these fine gentlemen.'

'No.'

'You asked, Auntie.'

'Yes, of course I did, lovey,' and then, turning to the two men, whose faces hung like opossums over their summer gumbo, 'of course I did.' She winked at the guests playfully, but it meant nothing to either of them. 'Oh, start eating, start eating. You're both such ravenous men.'

'I had a flat tire,' the constable responded to the query in her gaze. 'By the time I'd fixed it, well, I could smell the fish frying and I hadn't eaten all day … the boy was kind enough …' Loch wifled his spoon vaguely in the nephew's direction. And Jem Waferly rose on his wheel of fortune, his skin stretching tauter, basking like a biscuit in the warmth of appreciation that he mistook for admiration.

Jem's 'Think nothing of it, darling' made the constable stiffen. Stiffen his back.

Two small coughs from Dr. Amicable. 'I am here with the honour to tell you that Cora and two of her friends are the first people to have successfully swum across Lake Wachannabee. The assistants asked them to dine there this evening. They will be returned tonight.'

'Has anybody else ever bothered to try? Oh no, don't tell me somebody was chasing them.'

'Not really the point, Auntie.'

'You came all the way across the lake just to inform me? How thoughtful.' Giggy was touched.

'I felt you might be of concern, might be concerned.'

'And did you swim here?' she playfully inquired.

'No, no, I came on my canoe.'

'With no assistants?'

'They're all back at the cabin with the girls. What a heroic young woman, Cora, with all she's had to deal with. And a heroic whippet, I understand. She tells me your dog, he was the one who led you to Robert that fateful afternoon.' The officer volleyed a glance at the professor, who seemed resolute in refusing to return it. Giggy was pleased by Chappy's heroism being recognized, even by the fact that Cora's pleasant evening was pleasing for her to note. She felt her pleasure was a bit contrived but she had been so worried earlier of discovering herself vindictive. To have Cora's exercises move out of the basement of the Winter Garden to some sort of outside endeavours could only be healthy, and not just physically but also with regard to her emotions. Something had to be done to add sinew and flexibility to Cora's mental muscles. The confidence that shored up Cora's belief system, it was all so dangerously brittle. In less kind moments, Giggy imagined the woman as a schoolmistress, a priss. There was nothing wrong with having morals, thought Giggy, but Cora risked sacrificing her self to them. She affirmed them so rigidly, so defensively, that there was no soul left, really, to enjoy the security.

While these concerns formulated in Giggy's mind, one of her mental subchannels had decided to flirt with neither of the men that evening, but to hope for a pleasant evening in the gazebo with both of them, Jem and Chappy cavorting like bear cubs (as she imagined) at her feet, and the insects rattling perhaps a bit less incessantly at the cage which was their world.

'Do tell, Constable, why you bought my chaise longue.'

'It's a beautiful piece of furniture.' Over-aware of elbows, the man gave the impression that he was handling the cutlery with paws.

'Quite so. Except for the seam,' Giggy added with a quickness that to Jem suggested defensiveness.

'The seam? I hadn't noticed.' Though he thought he had stopped his hand in time from its reflex move to his pencil pocket, both John and Jem noticed. The first frowned while the latter – still nurturing an image of himself as an armchair detective – registered the constable's gesture as signalling his interest in the chaise longue as something more than just a place to be seated.

'Oh, you'll see, there's a little tear. It'll be nothing to fix. I was so embarrassed when I discovered it last night. I'll give you the number of my seamstress before you leave. So did you pay a lot for it then?'

'Enough, that's for sure, if the material is torn.'

'Not torn. Cut ... '

'But enough,' pressed Dr. Amicable, 'to fund a summer excursion to some distant stalactites for the children of our community?'

'Yes, oh yes.'

Jem was the only person whose reason for participating in the pregnant silence that followed was his savouring of the trout. His skin flushed at this and he rose and removed the remainder of the course to make way for the Kawartha mousse. He was about to bring out the crystal when somebody suggested they take dessert in the gazebo, and so he switched to some sportier fruit cups. He watched the others leave the room. The breadth of the constable's neck made the young man envision Scotland, highland cattle, parts of Sean Connery. Tonight he felt uncomfortable in the presence of these people, for they not only exuded a sexuality characterized by boldness but all seemed to have surreptitious interests in every topic of conversation. He found it disconcerting to think that he might know less about the crime than anybody else. Sensitive to the surveillant aura of the villa, he felt nevertheless as if he understood little about what took place within its walls. Yet, when he came outside a few minutes later with the desserts, he found the tension he had sensed had dissipated in the smoke of Dr. Amicable's cigarette, the charm of their Muskoka chairs arranged in a tight circle (a fifth left empty for Jem), and the tinkling of conversation that did not hesitate upon his arrival.

The topic was the doctor's manuscript. The constable had read a few pages and wanted more. Dr. Amicable, unable or unwilling to disguise his feeling of flattery, sounded like a seventeen-year-old in his first creative writing class, as he tried to coerce the man into telling those gathered what it was he so admired, what exactly led him on.

'Is it the honesty of an exploration journal?' he asked. 'Or perhaps something in the form itself?' tapping a cigarette against an ashtray and feigning weariness with his own question.

It was Giggy's failure to comment on the dessert that made it obvious to her nephew just how engrossed she was by the visitors. Food had always been to her the Cinderella of the sister arts. She had been especially attentive to his preparation of meats, fowl and fish, but desserts also warranted her attention. For somebody who never cooked, she knew an amazing number of recipes. It was she who had first guided Jem's tapered fingers as they crushed the dill into the nooks of a fish's vertebrae, she who had shown him how to cook grouse without melting the eyes, who had instructed him on slicing veal on a partial countergrain so as to minimize the seepage of the blood. But like Dr. Amicable, she now plunged into the mousse fist first, seemingly mindless of it as art at all.

'The plot,' said the constable.

'The plot? But there is no plot, really; it is life. If that's what interests you most, I fear ... to think what it says about the rest.' The doctor was not truly disappointed; he was only taunting the other man. The constable, he felt, was so driven by production, destination, reward. He, conversely, preferred to relish the moment, to sustain a passing pleasure, to bring it back to the surface through memory and conversation. For the professor, the intensity of a moment rising to an excruciating precision would always be more fulfilling than any long but leaden pleasure. John and Reg had both realized, early on in their acquaintance, that this was their key difference and, despite the intensity of their similarities, it would prevent them from becoming friends.

Giggy would never make such a banal comment, John told himself, gazing off toward his cabin, the sparks of a bonfire just visible while the smoke spread across the darkening sky like incense. Jem ran fingertips down his neck while, with his other hand, he nudged the constable's dessert a bit closer to him. Noting that his nudge had no effect, he demurely rearranged the slice of starfruit on the surface. It pained him a touch to see that his aunt, Dr. Amicable and even Chappy had tossed their slices onto the coffee table. The accent might have been gauche but he felt their disregard was too harsh. He decided to have his body pout. He pulled his shorts a bit lower down and puffed out his belly in an imitation of boyish slovenliness, but to no effect. He knew, from his reflection on the glass in the screen door, that he was offering up a fine Bernini. He would not have been unfair in defining their lack of cupiditas as a second insult, but it was more useful for him to see it as a by-product of their anxieties about other issues.

'Not a plot? But it's an exploration narrative, isn't it? There's stuff that came before and stuff … after.'

'Well, indeed, but who cares for that? It is not the reason people read it. I write it for other reasons.'

'You write it? Isn't it somebody's journal?' asked the constable.

'Don't be an ass. Of course it is, but the beauty of the editing – that is my leeway. It distances, at least I hope it distances, my readers from the everyday. The introduction, it is what first directs the reader on the new adventure; it shoves off the canoe.'

'Oh, I say, indeed,' murmured Giggy, hoping to draw some attention her way. 'The boring everyday lives we all find ourselves leading. I'm not insulting them; all lives are boring eventually. But must everybody pretend that they are getting closer to utopia, that the history of their pleasures is already greater than the pain.' Both older men were at a loss. Jem and

Chappy each had become engrossed with his own image in the glass.

'What pain?' Reg asked.

'What pain what?'

'It's better than whose pain?' persisted Reg.

'Oh, no further pain,' interrupted the professor, 'Mr. Waferly, could you not play something a little on the piano? I refuse any more of this talk.' Agape fell the mouth of the boy. Play us something on the piano? Had he become an extra in a Joan Crawford film? *Above Suspicion*? Was everybody going to start tapping their smoking pipes? Was this what it meant to become older — you somehow went back in time? In a sub-supporting role? Memories gradually dominating over experiences and prospects?

'Now I have begun telling you why I write when the question was what do you find so interesting.' The professor pulled a snack from his pocket and stuffed it between the whippet's eager black lips.

'Point being?' asked Loch.

'I, dear John, say that I like the story,' Giggy offered, 'I can't wait to read more entries. I cannot get enough of them.' John smiled lightly but didn't turn his eyes away from the constable. 'Simply can't. How interesting about the whitefish.'

Jem cast his starfruit into the cluster on the table. 'So too rude,' he whispered to Chappy, scratching the mutt lightly behind his perked ear, 'We must look very sad and then they will recollect their manners.' He wished Rob was not quite so often sleepy, unaware that his lover was awake even now, was in fact alert to their conversation. The dog walked a tight circle, fell on his rump and began licking himself like a cat.

'Please,' said the doctor to the whippet, 'you're challenging the woman's modesty.' The word 'blush' came to Giggy's mind but she didn't know how to act on it, and the constable persisted. 'Somebody must know how to play the piano. Why else would you have it?'

'It's just an heirloom,' Giggy proposed, but nevertheless scowled toyingly at her nephew. Jem dragged his feet inside like sacks of despondency. Soon 'Chopsticks' clattered onto the gazebo with the tempo of a drizzle.

'Oh Auntie,' Jem moaned from offstage.

'I know, dear,' and then, turning to Dr. Amicable with a smile, Giggy leaned back in her chair and scraped clackingly at the bottom of her fruit cup. Jem got the message and stopped his playing to serve her more, while Chappy, on the far side of the gazebo, marched in tight little circles and snapped at his tail. Whippets in general have bushels of energy, but Chappy displayed more this evening than he had all day, not that anybody noticed. The professor sucked his spoon as if coddling a thought. Reg cast his slice of starfruit on the table with the other four. Eventually, like a wounded moth, 'Chopsticks' fluttered again through the summer air. The music warmed Giggy's mood and cast an aestheticizing aura over the pines and sumac she could hear rustling in the darkness. This calm and harmony, she fancied, must be like that which welcomed Robert Shakely and his men each night from their exploring. What she would give for one evening in their lives.

✦

DEATH
IN THE FAMILY

Friday the 30th [June]

It has been four days since Orley's absence and no sign. Wachanas keeping distance, refusing discourse with Post. They refuse to assist in search for body as well.

Sunday July 2nd

Sebastian Orley has returned scratched and bleeding most all over his body even thighs and belly and on from a fall onto some rocks. Found deposited in cellar entry near falls, must be by Wachanas. Left leg especially gashed and requiring bandages and bed-rest. I tend to Orley careful with upper thigh especial need of attention. Recommend medical person at outposts each. My skills perhaps just sufficient. Orley assigned to single bed until sufficiently recovered. Sleep and warm gruel only possible aid at present.[10]

Monday 3rd

Orley's wounds have not been from a fall. Clearly he has suffered from attack from Wachanas They refuse to speak to Post or attend Factory, remaining distant and occupied with preparations for departure to southwestward. When confronted by myself they show only signs of elusion [evasion] or even aggression and no

---

10. The lack of a medical expert at a preliminary factory settlement was not uncommon but the persistence with which Shakely makes recommendations for additional men, here and elsewhere in his journals, suggests not simply a wish to be of assistance to his employers but also his sense of deservedness. It may be, even this early on, that the man suspected that the London office had lost interest in his venture. In this context, the July 2nd entry can be read as chastisement. The irony of this, however, is that Shakely would be chastizing superiors who he felt had already abandoned him. The gesture is controlled and yet it is one he must have recognized as futile.

longer interested in trade in goods. Post and Garret unwilling to go hunting until tribes depart. Post appears to be withholding information still on his encounters with the Wachanas. When pressured he argues he will not discuss it because Orley's wounds are result of distrust of tribe and he will not suffer the same wounds. Reason for trust of tribes over Factory unclear but obviously important concern for myself and your honours. Post strongly encouraged to clarify his claims which he says he will do shortly when Wachanas have left. We have enough food in storage for at least a week and there is also the possibility of being Sneak-Johns out through cellar passage at night if further food required although Indians are probably observing exit regularly. We have been using passageway for fresh water without siting of Wachanas. Myself, Post & Garret have agreed to committee of surveyllance[11] until tribe departs

Friday the 7th

It has become apparent now that Orley's wounds were caused by sharp instruments, that Wachanas do have tools weapons previously not acknowledged. Post refuses to discuss his knowledge of tribe's possessions only restating that he will clarify all he knows only after Wachanas are away from Factory. Is however most helpful in tending to Orley and assisting with surveillance. Garret has made one journey into surrounding area for

---

11. This is the earliest known use of the word 'surveyllance,' the second appearing over two decades later. The French etymology of term offers the possibility that Shakely picked it up from Pedlors. However, a 1799 reference in the *Monthly Register* (xxx.578) to a 'committee of Surveillance' suggests the phrase — the same used here by Shakely — was in circulation among men operating in business.

food and has returned safely. Encounters two indian women at some distance who saw him but did not acknowledge his presence or seem to show any interest in his presence. Nevertheless, I have decided that contact with Wachanas should no longer be attempted and travels into surrounding area only for necessity – food and water. Post proves most helpful with tending to Orley. Has gathered and boiled pine sap and applied it to Orley's wounds, a cure that Orley acknowledges is soothing at first, although somewhat painful when time for removal. Product may be of mercantile value Good for private use. Garret occupied with redrawing survey information. He and I work on repairs of side shed and begin laying out stones for foundation of additions to Factory

Sunday the 16th

Sebastian Orley's body continues to mend. Post has applied sap to the man's torso, belly and parts of his legs as per Wachanas and inflammation of lacerations notably reduced this only being a few days after body discovered. Post manages to attain huge supply of sap from Wachanas. Pay in brandy. If I may recommend though young lads as Sebastian Orley may require training, errors are more than made up for in their eagerness and diligence and dislike for heavy drink of which there is generally a problem with the older men. Brandy has proven most useful for trading – superior to tools, and looking glasses and trinkets, all of which Wachanas seem to have sufficient supply. Night surveillance does not seem necessary.

Monday the 17th

Garret and I have begun surveying and hunting regularly again as Wachanas no longer agitated or sullen.

Post has remained as Orley's main [man?] nurse, having become expert in use of salve and bathing of wounds. Have bottled salve for future use and shipment to shareholders.[12] It is most amazing how quickly the inflammation on Orley's wounds goes down after application of the salve, which makes patient much appreciative. Attack by Wachanas, which Orley has confirmed, has strengthened your workers' support of each other and even spirits of community in general. All eager to meet new arrivals and report experience to date. Especially anxious to begin trade in furs, but lacking in sufficient exchange goods. Orley walking, Post no longer needs to clean his slop, but must remain near Factory due to limited movement in legs and backside. Orley and Post both mute on indians intentions or full role in accident. I suspect cannibalism but game is adequate.

Tuesday the 18th

Fine pleasant weather. Continues clear. Strong eastern wind.

Orley's Leg mending. Allowed Orley to join Post in making check of security of cellar and passage since he is of no other use here he still being mostly beridden. Garret does all hunting and fissing, call him our fish wife. Orley and Post survey the structure and the security of the ceiling in the main room reports that the

---

12. There is no clear record of this salve ever being shipped to the Hudson's Bay Company head office in London. However, a salve made of tree sap was being sold commercially for some decades during the end of the eighteenth and early nineteenth centuries, after which it seems to have been replaced in popularity with a foxglove-based paste. No patent for a sap-based salve has been found. Such patenting was rare at the time.

structure is sturdy, walls being entirely of cut stone type uncertain probably limestone but with some rust stain and the ceiling being laid with solid logs although some rot apparent. Nest of vermin found in corner of passageway. Post and Orley manage to kill or disperse the rodents and have washed the area with lime. Passageway will make a sufficient storage area. Orley's legs mending. I now seeing I have noted that already. Although Orley still also complaining of dizzyness in connection with stomach cramps

Thursday 27th

Fine pleasant weather Continues clear Strong eastern wind. Garret gone ahunting returned with two rabbits. Orley's legs and torso well mended, ass[13] less so with some major scabbing across left buttock but healing with Post's steady application of sap. He has become regular nursemaid Orley chiding. Good spirits generally. Post and I proceed to wash down cellar for winter storage. Corridor and two smaller rooms all made of same stone and wood structuring. One room is empty the other empty save for tools gone dull and rusty from no use. Salvaged two blades, a ore [oar?] and small number of nails also some combs and broken looking glasses obviously intended for trade. Clearly

---

13 Shakely's use of the word 'ass' for 'arse' is notable. The vulgar version arose first among sailors: Cf. 1742: Rigley, *Sailing Rig*: 'The mid-groove, or ass, of the pulley allows the rope to remain set in position during winching.' While there is the possibility of the term entering exploration vernacular through interaction with sailors, there exists no other known record of this word being used in exploration journals, either as a reference to a pulley groove or the buttocks. The more likely explanation seems to be that, for some part of his life, Shakely worked on a ship.

Wachanas not interested in trading for trinkets, recommend tools and liquor be principal commoditie supplied. Corridors continuing from both minor rooms the main corridor having ended here. Glass and mirror proves more effective than limestone in chinking of walls where water shows greatest signs of seeping

Saturday the 29th

This morning Wachanas quickly depart south. One of their's informs us that other tribes have been spotted moving in this direction and they wish to maintain separate rather than risk further confrontation. Weather clear but humid, making travel rather slow but not impossible. They have left nothing of value at their campsite.

Departure of our neighbours has created a sense of isolation among us despite our long term distance from their community. There is some concern regarding arrival of the new tribes which the Wachanas imply are more aggressive and lacking in understanding. Also keen to discover their interest in trading furs. Unfortunately supplies and additional employees have not yet arrived. Waiting has become somewhat disturbing, Garret especially impatient to extend surveying further into territory, which I have permitted in southerly direction, in part to maintain sense of work and to supply additional information to the rest of us regarding the land and its potential for a fur trading site, of which I remain hopeful. Post, Orley, and me keep busy with gathering blueberries for drying and pickling of meat and cucumber-like vegetable for winter stocks. Sufficient supply of salt. All men well disposed, although some anxiety from expectation of new visitors to our territory. Light rain has been falling all evening, hopefully covering somewhat the trail of the departed tribe, God willing, should the others be looking for retribution.

A mildly pinched nerve at the base of her neck, that's all it was, but it was enough to awaken her. Giggy found her head awkwardly nestled upon the minutes of the Fafaists' first meeting, which Cora had crumbled between her bonnet and the lilac brocade of her pillow. Cora, in her bed on the other side of the room, was spooning someone. So too sweet this early in the morning, mused Giggy, the image of fresh love accentuating the taste of tongue in her mouth. Outside the window, she could see the sun bouncing off the vegetation that had been soaked in the storm of the summer night. It was ten a.m. and Giggy could hear Jem brewing coffee. This morning, her usually guiltless rising was tinged by what she saw as her household's growing apathy toward Robert's fate. In penance, she decided to take her bran on the veranda so that she might meditate over the fountain of the *Cristo muerto sostenido por un ángel*. Maybe, she thought, as she went through her morning's ablutions, she could cajole her nephew into speaking more at the boy, unaware of the amount of time they did spend together. They were Rob's closest family, really, she thought, even if some people still believed that Cora was also his murderer. And hadn't Giggy in fact read somewhere that most murderers were usually relations? Indeed, as the crushed squirrel had made apparent, now even she, the matriarch (if somebody must wear the trousers), was suffering from slander.

One might have expected that such peashots of bile would have spurred divisiveness within the walls of the villa, but instead Giggy encouraged herself to do all she could to ensure that the collective alienation strengthened their sense of inter-dependence. Wachannabee had, in a sense, forced a union upon them, made them into a garrison whose validity the community had hoped to undermine. It had given them the rights and expec-tations of a common family.

Oh, not everybody in the community was on the attack, of course. There were people like Lady Clasp, Cora's pack of health-scented women and men, and Constable Loch, thank goodness. He would call today, Giggy reminded herself, after the lab down in Honey Harbour had tried to decipher the note. The realization that the villa's supporters existed beyond the Cubist façade of the Winter Garden diminished Giggy's anxi-eties such that, if at this moment one observed her keenly, one might notice that her corpulence was bouncing ever so lightly on the edge of her unmade bed. She may not have needed the community for a sense of love or family, but even their partial empathy strengthened her affections for the other members of the household – Chappy, Jem, Robert, Cora.

She gazed again at the two heads of dishevelled hair nestled on Cora's pillow like baby hedgehogs sunning on the Ukrainian steppes. Any tinge of infantilization was unintentional and only an extension of the soft love that had begun her musings this morning.

Showered, moisturized, powdered and scented, Giggy carried her body in shifting steps down the stairs to the kitchen where she found Jem's arms plunged, Holly Golightly–like, into elbow-length gloves of refined flour (at least she hoped it was refined). The boy, he was baking a pie and, at the moment, he was consternating over which of the pie birds to have sing the steam. After pecks of affection and pecks at the pecans, Giggy made her way onto the back veranda, eased her weight into a

Muskoka, a couple of Jem's paintings under one arm, the Fafaist minutes in the other. She lightly scratched the soles of her feet on the rough-hewn cedar planks of the flooring. The rash of eczema between her toes cracked familiarly and, while she did not bother to look, she knew that minuscule zags of blood would be rising to the surface and, as quickly, drying. Although the sun was fully exposing itself, drops of moisture still glistened on the moss beneath the willows like the dregs of a party, occasionally building into a roil that carried them toward the house. One might have sensed an eeriness, but one would probably not have deduced its source as the deathly silence of the grouse and partridges. As if picking their moments, only rarely did a peacock give off one of those sorrowful cries that made Giggy feel guilty for keeping them. She had this sense for some reason that peacocks were native only to Eritrea, or perhaps it was Alexandria, and this perception she blamed on being forced, when still a schoolgirl at the gymnasium, to read too much of the French decadents. It was all due to them that her mind made so many false conflations: peacocks with wallpaper, lilies with public toilets.

'Tell me,' ballooed Jem from the kitchen, 'are my geese in line? I've creamed the butter and sugar, and added the salt, syrup and vanilla. Now do I just whip in the eggs, put the pecans on the bottom of the shell and pour the filling over top?'

'You do none of the above, dear, until you've brought me my bran.' The warmth in Giggy's voice hit him as a touch too contrived, even smug, although he would never dare to accuse.

'Yes of course, but do tell me now.'

'The filling goes on top, dearest – 450° for ten minutes, then 350° for thirty-five more. And you call yourself a Louisianer.'

'I have never done anything of the sort, Auntie.' Jem appeared with the bowl of bran curls topped with apple sauce and cinnamon. 'I'm a Texan with a Dixie drawl, and even that's fading, eh?' His lids batted like clamshells in a back current before he returned to his baking. She was indeed pleased that he had begun clipping his 'ing's so often.

'Oh, such a rare bird, sweetie, could you find some cider? Is it not so too hot-feeling already?' But Jem couldn't hear over the whipping of the eggs. Giggy reminded herself that somebody had to call Lady Clasp about the peacock's splint. She watched the bird – an emblem for wounded pride or surquedry – hobble out of the way of Shirley, who was skittering drunkenly down the worn path that rambled past the ha-ha and along the framing hedge of the garden – a garden that had reminded nobody but the original landscaper of the Cubist piece *Nude Descending Staircase*. Regardless, Giggy appreciated the efforts made by the landscape assistants to find bushes that matched the rusty colours of the painting. 'Jem, could it be that somebody is actually in the garden? I think I see a little someone in among the cosmos.' Giggy found no consolation in the fact that, according to the chief gardener, the backyard was stunning when viewed from a helicopter. 'Is it Bella in search of one of her charges? Or maybe a gnome? Either way, it whiffs a touch of trouble. You. Woman! You there in the garden – are you a woman?'

The gardener's original defence had reminded Giggy of the scientific claim that the ovary was not a placid subject waiting to be penetrated by missiles of sperm, but a tactical unit that literally grabbed the dim-witted agnesians by their tails as they waggled past. 'Jem, darling, bring me my sunglasses. Somebody has strayed into the garden. I've lost them now; oh, they're in there somewhere.' Six of one, half a dozen of the other, she concluded, when it came to questions of sperm. 'It's too late for the glasses, dear, call the RCMP. It's like something straight out of Agatha Christie. Oh, but tell them to leave the horses at home this time; what a mess that was. I think you'd best make it a cocktail. Don't call the police. Don't call the police. We don't want them.' The fact of the matter, when it came to ovaries, was that there was no fact of the matter. 'Jem? Darling?' In the case of the garden, the situation was the same, all a matter of perspective. 'Jem?'

'Yes, Auntie?'

'Will you bring me a drink now, dearest? The crisis is over.'

'Oh,' said Jem, who, having missed the string of inquiries and commands, assumed that she was referring to her smugness. 'I'm so glad to hear it. How about a nice cocktail?'

'I think probably that would be best. Very odd thing, that.'

'What, Auntie?'

'The gnome in the garden.'

'The gardener's finally returned then?' They rarely spoke of the Cubist's disappearance. It was a mystery that they preferred remained unsolved.

'Oh, is that who it is? Thank goodness, maybe she'll make some sense out of that mess.'

'Something mauve and Impressionist, perhaps,' said Jem soothingly.

'I didn't mean I'd rehire her. I just thought she might explain what she'd already done.'

Giggy had first upset the old Belgian when she'd told her that few members of the new millennium would find people interested in traversing ten acres of land, and that she herself surely would never do it except perhaps on a Vespa. 'This is not IKEA,' she proposed, 'or Sissinghurst,' knowing full well that many viewed Vita Sackville-West's garden as inappropriately small. The criticism had had the opposite effect to that which Giggy had desired, the older woman demonstratively waving about her Garden Gopher while pointing out that she had in fact improved on Duchamp's work by incorporating into the design a number of self-conducting paths complete with staircases that would lead Giggy back to where she had started. Lot of good that does me, Giggy had thought at the time, since I'm already here. A study in futility – existentialist gardening. 'The Cubists,' the Belgian had shouted, 'were lost, but nobody could get lost in my garden!' She sobbed and flailed her gardening equipment in the air as if brandishing a cutlass. Her nails, Giggy noticed, were filthy and cracked.

'Now are you sure about those temperatures?' hollered Jem from the kitchen.

'Well, I was until you asked me. You'll have to look it up. And sweetie, before I forget, would you spend more time with Robert today? You know how self-pitying convalescents can get. They say that even if they're sleeping, the sick still know you're there. Isn't that fascinating? I guess they're like cats that way. But apparently the sick like being watched. There was something about the peacocks that I'd wanted to tell you too, but I've forgotten now, haven't I? Can I possibly have my cider?' Someone in the brush rustled away, but the matriarch was not about to get excited again.

'It was a cocktail, we'd decided, Auntie.' Jem had chosen not to tell Giggy that he had spent a number of nights since the murder sleeping with Robert. The patient was too inanimate, he felt, to be turned into a topic. How might Robert defend himself? The resultant secrecy gave the men a sliver of privacy, a narrow life but one that was their own. Jem liked being the only one who knew (as he thought) that the tattoo on Rob's shoulder had healed more quickly than the rest of him, or that the patient softly hummed the theme song from *The Poseidon Adventure* in the night. He found pleasure in thinking he was the only one aware that Rob was in fact often happy. Jem liked to feel that he was keeping one step ahead. He didn't know where they were going, but the family had a clear momentum, and he was a step ahead. It was as if they were all in a lumbering caravan being pulled and pushed by others toward some resolution. Celebratory or not, the resolution was inevitable. It would take some effort to arrive a bit before expected, but this remained Jem's intention.

'Yes, a cocktail.' Although she never doubted the garden's functionality, Giggy could not decipher the Belgian's blueprint, save for the fact that little squares signified bricks and loopy swirls signified gravel and not, as she had first thought, smoke. There seemed to be so much brick and gravel for just one garden, and she kept meaning to look up the word in the *Oxford English Dictionary* to see whether she could accuse the woman of not making a garden at all but some sort of surreal parking lot. No matter how vigorously her eyes scoured the blueprint, Giggy could ever only find five of the six fountains that she had commissioned, each marked by a navy asterisk. In the actual garden, she had to date only been able to cool her feet in three, the others not appearing where the map suggested they should be.

'Shall I put it here for you?'

'Won't you join me? I'd appreciate the company.'

'What about Robert? Don't you want me to visit with him?'

'Not just now, dear. He's not going anywhere. Now let's have a look at your paintings. Oh see, that one's good. I can see something happening there.'

'Could be Chappy did that one. I usually use more Canada Dry than that. You see, already it's moving toward having these things mass-produced in sad little puppy farms ... Aren't puppy farms the saddest things? Why are there so many of them here? I remember, in Dallas, seeing entire packs of dogs walking right down Main Street. They had more rights there, I guess.'

'Why don't you bring out some cider? Cider would be so lovely just now.'

'Yes, Auntie, but none for me.'

'Oh, but I can't drink alone. That would look so premature. Why don't you celebrate with me – the gardener's returned.'

'Well, freeze the Mississip, has she?'

'She's somewhere in those bushes.'

'Ah, then there's still a chance she won't make it.'

'Best to bring a bottle along for her. I expect if anybody should be able to find their way through that tangle, it's her. I've never met anyone as determined.'

'All right. I guess we should be hospitable.'

'If we're ever to find all five fountains.' Giggy considered calling the gardener's name, as a beacon, but couldn't remember what it was. The woman had been missing for some time. 'Beyula?' Giggy called feebly into the humidity. 'Oh, that's not it.'

She turned her attention to Jem's latest artworks sunning at her feet. She stared at them as if to scorn them into giving her an answer. Their minimalism seemed appropriately post-humanist, she realized, but the concept was one outside her realm of experience; she hoped it had something to do with Warhol and maybe the silky sheen of computer-generated fabrics. Something hyper-textile. As the sun's buggy plugged across the white-blue sky, she would turn from the Canada Dry works to the minutes of the meeting, which she chose to call the Manifesto, and then back again, and again, but neither offered a breath of inspiration. In both cases, the language seemed too desperate to please, too interested in communicating. And this desire to satisfy turned her attention to her own heart's aims and so she eventually began to call for Chappy.

Giggy was forewarned of the whippet's speed by the familiar clacking of his claws against the hardwood, and so she wasn't surprised at the pressure of his pads when they finally made contact with her belly. But for the wine-dark prints his paws besmirched across her kimono nothing could have prepared her, nor for the bloody maw that he slathered across her expectant lips. The sinuousness of whippets' muscles belies the weight of their bodies when they do choose to pierce the air so smoothly. Chappy's expression was, she dared to suspect, lascivious.

When the dog made contact, Giggy howled and urinated, but slightly. She thought she heard a screech reciprocating from the garden. Perhaps a sympathetic peacock. The sound of Giggy's bellow frightened Chappy, who leapt off her lap and paddled his paw prints spastic over the Canada Dry series and around the west side of the villa. Second to respond to Giggy's calls was Jem, who wrapped one arm around her shoulder as if her flesh were about to fall from the bone. With a dish towel bearing the intricate needlepoint design of two giraffes, necks intertwined and dizzy in love, he fanned her cheeks. Coddling his aunt's bare withers, Jem imagined, must feel much like consoling a listless ox. Or petting Giggy's dog-skin riding boots, if she would one day allow him to do so. 'There there, Auntie. Everything's okay,' he grimaced, language failing him yet again. He couldn't understand exactly what had happened. The blood on his aunt's lips was somehow erotic, and this kept him for the slightest moment from kissing lightly at the awkward hairline of her wig. 'What's gotten into him?' she wondered. 'Does his mind rule his body, or his body rule ... ?'

'Unless the dog has germs,' said Bella who, along with Cora, had come out from the kitchen. 'I mean dangerous germs. We've all got germs.' She gazed intently at the bloody footprints like bursts of fireworks across the canvases. 'I've heard about pigs in China ... ' and her voice faded behind the force of Giggy's thoughts: of course pigs have dangerous germs. In her eyes the suggestion of Chappy's danger tainted not the pup but the vet with an aura of sensationalism, a shadow out of which the other woman would escape soon enough. Sensing the tension, Cora offered to track the prints back to their source to see if Chappy had killed something. Bella, meanwhile, hurried across the field for her supplies. Not about to wait for Cora's report or Bella's return, Giggy, before even washing the blood from her lips (the salt stinging, she would later be quoted in the courtroom as saying, with the bitterness of a mother's tears), marched into the front room intent on calling a veterinarian who'd had a damn bit more sensitivity training. 'So too rude, I think,' she grumbled, 'oh yes, too rude by far,' to the nephew hovering in the middle distance, ready to make gestures that, should she commence swooning, could in retrospect be interpreted as having been a sincere attempt to catch her. The only other local veterinarian was 'in the field' punishing cows with inoculations for a disease on the other side of the country. Giggy would propose inoculating the carnivores, but for her being one of them. All these animal illnesses – one would think it enough to turn everybody off meat, if it weren't for the banality of soy. Giggy was left with no option but to resign Chappy's fate to Bella – a vet, she grumbled, just scouting for trouble.

Jem, instructed to summon his aunt if she was needed, watched the woman's legs stomp upstairs and hoped that she would not lose sight of everybody else in the storms of her own emotions. He could hear Rob mumbling for an explanation of the commotion and rushed in to hush him. Jem cuddled into the scab-stiffened arms of the convalescent, quickly kissed his fuzzy cheeks, and assured the man that he would explain later. Rob knew Jem was confident that he alone knew that Rob was verging on speech, but Rob was not aware that it was this fact alone that at present made Jem feel one step ahead. The Texan believed it best if Rob not get entwined with these latest developments, as if he might see himself as in part to blame for this pain, as if simply the reappearance of blood would associate the confined man with the morning's events. Jem was glad that Giggy at least was innocent. She had been victimized twice now – the crushed squirrel, the bloody dog. During his stay at the Winter Garden, he had grown to love his aunt deeply, her respect for his intelligence and beauty making up for the subservience she expected him to adopt during the crises that she fostered in order to encase herself in an armour of passivity like others used an aura of philanthropy. He hugged one of Robert's hands and, as he left the room, cast a glance that the victim was not mistaken in interpreting as patronizing. Rob's earlier desire to refrain from telling Jem of his part in the murder had been rooted in love, but now he could sense – his immobility giving him much time for such sensitivity – that

Jem's affection had begun to be lost amid his pleasure in silence as a form of power.

'I found it,' said Cora, entering the kitchen where Jem now stood shaking crumbs from the toaster. There was an edge to her voice, as if others had threatened her to perform some one-legged task on a remote but beautifully lit island. Of course, Jem acknowledged to himself, she had been threatened – hunted, isolated, ever since she'd decided to sleep with Robert. He had been fooling himself in thinking that at least he had nothing but sympathy for her. The paper bag that she held dripped five petals of oozy red that splattered on the parquet like a fresh Jackson Pollock. Even I have threatened her, he realized, and that bag is a symbol of her damaged heart. It was second nature now for him to reach for the Pledge.

✦

Gazing toward Cora and her paper bag, left bang hanging Veronica Lake–like across his forehead, he wondered whether she exuded that disconcerting eagerness even in her sleep. He let his own lithe figure accentuate its whiplash curve as an example of an alternative. The poor dear, Jem thought with a trace of spite so mild he did not sense it himself, could use a weekend at the Hotel Relaxo.

'So, what should I do?'

'I don't think some sort of course on inner harmony would be out of the question, darling. Or Pilates. I've heard good things about Pilates. We could all do it. In the garden. It could be a family event.'

'About Chappy's squirrel.'

'Chappy killed a squirrel?' The pride Jem felt was not diluted by the fact that he realized the dog's act was self-indulgent. Possibly, his pride was rooted in this very narcissism. 'Well, take it out on the back porch and show Auntie. There's no good letting it drip on the floor. Grits?'

'Toast. Tea for me, and a cappuccino for Bella — I saw her coming — if you know how to make one.' There was no malice in her voice. There didn't have to be; the animosity had begun to culture its pearl within Jem's mind without Cora's contribution. The fact that it reflected the duplicity she felt for having slept with Robert before discussing it with Jem and that she spoke

155

with the victim in the early dawn of every day without her friend knowing might have been an initial catalyst in Cora's self-alienation but now it need not be recognized as anything more than a coincidence. Rob made sure to tell her no more than he had told Jem, but he had not adequately factored in that the two had different sets of knowledge to begin with.

'Sure I do. That's the stronger one, right?' Cora understood that he was joking. Soon, what Giggy would later tell the lawyers was the most harrowing morning of her North American life had the potential of becoming for Cora, Jem, Rob and even Bella little more than a pleasant day. Oh, a bit more blood than usual but still a day full of promise and potential, hope and aspirations, dreaming and eating. Cora left to retrieve Chappy while Jem prepared Bella's cappuccino and then went off to update Robert who, surprisingly, giggled. In the meantime, Lady Clasp noticed the blood-soaked paper bag. She laid a clean sheet of plastic on the floor of the veranda and dumped the mangled, breathing mess upon it, briskly crushing its head with the sturdy heel of her left pump. She then took a popsicle stick out of her breast pocket and scooped a few dollops of foam from the rodent's split lips. The froth was transferred to a vial, corked and packed into her supply case just as Jem returned.

'Treating the creature like that,' mumbled Jem when he spied the scene, 'it's asking for the poor thing to be diseased.' Jem and Bella went to help Cora find the whippet and thus, when Giggy, unattended and unbeckoned, ventured for the second time that fateful day onto the veranda, she was met by nothing but the bloody rodent stretched like the victim of suburban Satanists across a sheet of Cling Wrap. The woman found herself with no choice but to collapse on the stoop in the gentlest of heaps. 'Life,' she sighed, 'it always dries darker,' and resigned herself to pleasant mornings leading to traumatic days. Here she waited, breathing, for the inevitable end. Clouds eventually did begin to shift spastic in the wind and yet, despite the apocalyptic inevitabilities, they seemed unable to cover the sun.

When the others finally returned, Chappy and the wounded peacock were with them and appeared to be arguing agitatedly about who should be treated first. Despite the painful charley horse along the length of one of her arches, Giggy managed to hold her pose. She was rather pleased to discover that she still had arches at all, but nevertheless lamented, 'Oh, when will this day end?' Lady Clasp held an angry pet in each arm, as Jem and Cora helped Giggy to her powdered feet. The matriarch tested her legs as if she'd been in a skiing accident while Bella began somewhat too officiously to offer a report on Chappy's well-being. She confirmed that the canine was unhurt and that the blood on his mouth was probably that of the squirrel. 'Shirley,' sneered Giggy. Bella was worried, however, that the squirrel was rabid and that the dog, despite the innocence of his romp, may have bitten into something fatal. This would become the metaphor for illness in the new millennium, Jem prophesied in silence — species, communities turning on each other as a way of garrisoning themselves, ultimately setting themselves up for their own starvation of pleasure. And as if this trajectory weren't tragic enough, Cora was quick to point out that the dog had kissed Giggy, who had since been kissed by Jem. Jem didn't mention having kissed Rob's scarred lips and shoulders, oh so many times, but it didn't matter; it was the fear, not the fluids, that would spread the disease.

'Oh there, Chappy, cupcake. It was that vindictive little squirrel. Come here, don't scratch,' pleaded Giggy, 'don't you know who I am?' She coddled the head of the uppish whippet and tucked the blanket, interwoven with the belly hairs of domesticated buffalo, tighter around his mannerist neck as if he suffered from the flu. 'You know you can't be in the sun. You're becoming so dry all over.' Chappy gave her a look of impatience. There was far too much blood about for him to sit there silent in her gelatinous lap.

All bound with a kiss, each participant seemed a-swoon, but the practiced Giggy did it most convincingly. Her already being seated in repose did nothing to keep her from exuding the essence of falling. Everybody motioned mildly toward catching her while she hung, she hoped, in a resemblance of Bernini's *Saint Teresa*. Following a brief silence that Giggy interpreted as an appreciation of her art, Lady Clasp assured the family that any transference from canine to human was unlikely. She then unbound the peacock's splint and the bird began to walk about as stately as a general, the mild limp giving him a mysterious elegance suggestive of espionage in Havana.

Giggy sat to one side humbly mumbling a prayer she had learnt during her pilgrimages to the town of Sainte Anne de Beaupré in the province of Québec: 'Sainte Anne, render fruitful my misery. I unite it to the sufferings of Jesus, a man of sorrows, despised and rejected by all ... ' Jem thought this might be a prayer for the deceased squirrel and hung his head respectfully. The peacock cast a furtive eye but continued to exercise his limbs. Giggy had never considered whether the prayer really meant anything, or whether it had a narrative. 'One day, he will wipe away all tears from our eyes. I offer Him my grief. May He be glorified and shower graces on us ... ' She liked the fruit and, in this heat, the showering graces. What with this latest threat against her, she did feel an affinity with the notion of being rejected, though she didn't see it as applicable to the little baby Jesus. Who wouldn't have loved the little baby Jesus? He seemed never to cry or whine. She couldn't even recall him ever soiling himself. Who wouldn't love a baby like that? She had always seen the crucifixion as the result of an unfortunate combination of circumstances and misunderstandings that at any moment could coincide upon any undeserving mortal. Herself, for example. Today, for example. It was perhaps, she acknowledged, more likely to happen to Robert – so many metaphors mingling with the blood, the water, the pus of his miraculous murder. People seemed to get irritated with Jesus only once he'd begun to expostulate, and Robert was wonderfully silent.

It was as Jem assisted the peacock down the stairs of the veranda that Chappy made the soon-to-be scandalous lunge at the youth's throat. Bella leapt to knock the dog aside and the four of them tumbled – flesh, feathers and fur – into a rose bush whose petals showered down about the limb-filled gyre like drops of mango juice. Chappy, it was now clear to Lady Clasp, had been rabid for some time and, as she stuffed the whippet into a sack she'd yanked from her supply case, she instructed the family to come to her place to have themselves checked for infection. The peacock – never one to enter easily into the histrionics of the household – took the opportunity to blend chameleon-like into the depths of the *Nude Descending*, her plaintive call trilling like good news from among the golden leaves. Giggy adopted a visage of glazed rapture and fondled her collar as she would a string of rosary beads.

'Shower graces on us ... ' For a moment she thought that she saw a ray of silver stars pass through the faded blue sky. But it was only the tears that she shed. 'Shower graces, please.' She admired Lady Clasp, admired because she feared her, as she feared anybody licenced to inoculate. But it seemed ludicrous to trust an animal doctor with one's potentially fatal illnesses. Too harried to take charge, she tried to get her nephew to act by communicating through the pained look in her eyes. Ah, but everybody was too worn out to challenge the specialist now. Only Chappy's acquiescence had to be induced. The gaggle proceeded across the honey-tinted field to the office attached to the back of Bella's house – everybody except Giggy, who was too distraught to walk and instead drove over in the Bricklin. Through a tear in the burlap, Chappy could see the peacock and her companion watching their departure with the malicious grins, he thought, of morticians.

The sterility of the office was uninspiring. Satisfaction warmed Lady Clasp's body when she noticed that, while Giggy, her nephew and the dog fussed so much in deciding where the prick of the injection would least sacrifice their fleshly consistency, Cora had simply laid her head against her sun-kissed arm and gazed out the window at the field of grain. Her stolidness — that stolidness that so many mistook for reserve or conservatism — was, in the context of this group, refreshing. Even now, Bella thought, the woman's expression is admirably controlled. What could she see in this sun-hazed landscape of alfalfa, bushes and hills? In fact, Cora didn't really see anything. Rather, the fields reminded her of Las Vegas — the home she had left years ago. It may have been known to others for its casinos and immoral heterosexual bonds but, as any Las Vegan knew, the corpus of the city was satiated in tradition and a righteous moderation that, in its bondage, was what gave the location its shine and the nights their beauty.

Most of North America had found itself at one time or other beneath her shimmering shadow, and Cora could say — not with the fear of the tourist but with a confident efficiency — that she had never found a beauty that compared with that of the valley on a clear night as one's convertible wove through the mountains from the Hoover Dam. Dark and silent, yet humming with the expectation brought on by the occasional casinos marking the highway like token promises, the drive was more spectacular than that to the Grand Canyon, which had nothing to heighten one's senses before experiencing that once, and never again, sublime moment. Las Vegas alone seemed to capture the sublime and hold it in its stars. The string of roadside casinos ended midway through the mountain pass but the flat blackness stretched on and on, weakening the car lights, inducing a chilling sense of isolation until, suddenly, the night burst apart with the solid lights of the city. They shimmered thick and constant, like a swath of gold lamé borne aloft on the fresh countercurrent of a roiling runoff – the amber lights glittering as if just submerged under some clean, shallow body of water, glittering like starfish cast chaotically over a galactic ocean floor bordered only by the suggestion of the black-soaked ridges of atmospheric infinity. Cora could remember taking her mother's car to the hills on the outskirts of town well before she was of legal driving age and, while her mess of peers leered at each other, shutting their eyes and opening their maws to explore that familiar part of each other's bodies, Cora would gaze down through the undulating Las Vegas at the stars sliding together and apart on the floor of this electric lake, connecting, multiplying and dividing, thickening over the night's watery blackness until the darkness itself was lost in their glitter like gold dust at the base of a waterfall.

'What are you thinking of?' Bella asked, no longer able to accept the woman's disregard. She recalled how she herself had once carried the same distant look like a burden, the same apparent desire to be somewhere, anywhere else but where she was. It wasn't until she had reached her early thirties that she'd realized that her desire to always be somewhere else was really a desire to not be with herself, a self-loathing manifesting itself as a dislike of those around her. She'd realized then that there was always some model of society that presupposed the view of human intercourse that she imposed on it. She realized, too, that this probably wasn't what Cora was thinking about at all, but what Bella herself had transposed onto her. And yet, just because it made Bella recall her own musings, Cora seemed to her to be more profound than she had been before the doctor had injected her.

The subordination of the role of the individual within this model didn't frighten Bella, though it did make her realize that her feelings for Cora, like anybody's affections for anybody, were already accommodated by the institutions of love before the two women had even stroked their eyes across each other's bodies. Sometimes this deterministic realization lead her to spend entire days drinking camomile infusions and listening to Joan Baez's 'Diamonds and Rust.' Just now it led her to a melancholic realm of the mind, a realm closed to others. It was a dim, dank space almost entirely void of the senses, of the elements, of the notion of space itself.

'That stone cellar next to the gym,' said Cora. The needle quivered and Jem said 'ow' and Giggy screamed and Chappy mimed the crazy howl of his inner wolf as he finally managed to tear through the sack that had been holding him and started running circles about the office, his mind rapidly growing more and more agitated even as he noted to himself that the order of things would have to ultimately return to its previous state of normalcy.

'What about it?' asked Giggy, one eye glued to the randy whippet and two fingers methodically rolling the tobacco out of a cigarette that the vet hadn't let her smoke. 'What are you doing in my cellar?'

'That's where I found it.'

'Found what?'

'The rabid squirrel. Bella asked. That's what you asked about, isn't it?' Cora was tired of fending off the accusations she saw as too eagerly lobbed in her direction.

'No, I asked what you were thinking of.'

'Well, I was thinking of where I found the squirrel – that dank space beside the exercise room. The paw prints led me there. It looked like a hallway to some cellar, all those glass jars, that space almost entirely void ...'

'Yes, okay,' scuttled Bella, not having intended to make anybody more agitated, let alone Cora. She prepared to pierce Jem's limp limb once again. He couldn't care less now where she thrust the needle. She could stab him in the eye, for all the pain he might feel. The lower lid of his left coddled a tear as thick and clear as jelly. His arm had already developed a plum bruise where the vet had pressed her thumb. Plum like the slippers of the Prince of Cinque Stelle, he mused, plum like the irises of Lady Elizabeth Taylor, plums as rare and sweet as the honeyed figs eaten by the Czar's lost nephew, Ivan. He just knew this veterinarian's office was not his place on earth. Jem Waferly, of all people, to die rabid without ever having drunk absinthe, without ever having to answer questions about his sexuality put forward by the popular press. Giggy saw the agony her nephew was going through as sufficient excuse to push open a window and light her Cameo. She smoked with her head craned over the sill and thrust into a blast of azaleas and tiger lilies. 'Can you do Auntie first? Auntie is strong willed.'

'Should that dog be running around rampant?' asked Cora.

Giggy sneezed. 'Is that a sign,' she squeaked, 'of rabidity?'

'I don't think that's the correct use of that word — "rampant,"' said Jem. Giggy began to cry. She was sure it was — a sign, that is, of rabidity. Cora rolled her eyes. Even the glittering strips of Las Vegas were not powerful enough to withstand the harsh agonies of Wachannabee daylight. Jem, overwhelmed, began to lose consciousness, realizing that many members of his family might soon not be alive (except probably Rob, who had ironically now become the one most likely to survive). It struck him that the time he had spent worrying that he might start growing muscles had been wasted. And then he thought once more of Rob, whom he'd seen but once that day, and Jem asked to use the phone, the vet concluding he was dazed. And then he felt the short, sharp pang, and then his nerves ran free, and then he saw her draw the needle as he fell upon his knees. And somewhere the boys sing praises, and somewhere the peacocks sneer, but silence ruled in Wachannabee, save the ringing in Jem's ears.

Giggy clasped her nephew's head between her scented palms and shouted for Cora to check the matriarch's purse for some sort of birch-bark balm known to cure even paralytics in frozen stupors of ten years. The balm was not to be found but Jem came around regardless, Bella having splashed cold water on his wrist.

Giggy had had enough. 'The colonel has returned from his rounds,' she declared. 'Everybody into the Bricklin. We're going home.' She agreed to let Bella keep Chappy for observation but, as she left, she didn't hesitate to kiss him. Nor did Jem.

The Bricklin eased its curves into the driveway of the Winter Garden with the familiarity of a cow sidling into its milking stall. Giggy, exasperated and uncomfortable in the heat, was erratic in her motions and thought it best to convalesce for the remainder of the day. Jem begging off joining her she did not mind, for his intention was to visit with Rob. It seemed to her somehow rude to stand there in the driveway and show empathy with the murdered so soon after feeling the needle-prick of one's own mortality, but the nuance was too subtle to massage into an actual concern. Instead, she suggested he wait before visiting Robert just in case the nephew's emotions were still too raw, perhaps as long as it would take him to go into town to buy groceries and restock the kitchen cupboards. She and Jem had both been taping additions to the list on the fridge, and it had begun to resemble tickertape. The boy, so co-operative, was not averse to the idea of lowering himself into the driver's seat of the Bricklin, lowering his sunglasses over his eyes, lowering the wing doors of the vehicle and sliding out of the driveway with a resolve that might evoke a Bond-like sexuality. Jem, Jem Bond. Giggy cast a glance lethargic in the direction of Cora, who was making her way decisively across the lawn toward the house. The tears spangling Giggy's eyelids combined with the mist of the sprinkler that someone had set up over the tomato plants to cast chaotic prisms of colour across Cora's shoulders.

Giggy followed only slowly. It was a while before she found the other woman, though she hadn't been looking for her, upstairs with a carton of lime sherbet in a champagne bucket full of ice. Cora knew her presence was unexpected and so smiled shyly. The matriarch, while not taken with the idea of being alone with Cora, found herself swayed by the two Louis

XIV sherbet dishes and the parfait shovelettes (which Giggy chose to recognize as a charming faux pas) askance in the chilling bucket. With the sun filtering light rays into the ice cubes as it shifted behind the clouds, Giggy began to relish the prospects of an afternoon out back overlooking her property and playing Find the *Nude*. The reduction of Giggy's anxiety was visible. Her growing appreciation for Lady Clasp's concern for the family's health was not.

Her body snugged into the canvas recliner with the ease of a sack of flour, as the coy sun took licks off the corner of the wrap-around balcony that extended from their bedroom. Giggy hiked her dress up above her thighs and let the breeze enliven the ice cube that she rubbed along the underside of her knees. Cora, wearing nothing but cotton boxers, dolloped out sherbet.

'I wish I could take my top off,' said Giggy, removing her wig.

'Why don't you?'

'My skin is too sensitive, dear. Like Michael Jackson's. Even my hair suffers.'

'What *is* your natural hair colour?'

'Oh some sort of brown, I think. With a bit of leeway, I can probably get away with calling it burnt umber, but then who but some artist would know what the hell I was talking about?'

Cora laughed. 'Chafing has nothing to do with sensitive skin. You know what you should be using?' she asked as she ran the side of a finger along the edge of her dish before leaning over to serve herself again. Oh damn, there, thought Giggy, now she did it. One of Cora's nipples had begun to harden from the cold of the champagne bucket, to harden as if it had been touched by Midas's wife herself. Giggy glanced a second time to check for any change and, yes, it had tightened further and grown darker, even extending a bit as well, it seemed. What, no shame?

'And what's that, dear?' asked Giggy as she leaned over and looked into the bucket to see if there was more sherbet.

'What?' Cora crossed her arms.

'You were going to tell me what to use for my chafing.'

'Oh, once again the humble cucumber fulfills an unexpected domestic need.'

'And here I've been putting it on my eyes each night before going to sleep. Mind you, they never chap.'

'Did you see the minutes of the meeting I put on your bed?'

'Yes, they were fine, weren't they ... for a first go. Somewhat embarrassing, though. I can't imagine when you found the time to type them up.' It amazed Giggy that so much had gone on already today. She recalled waking up on the Fafaist minutes as if it had happened weeks ago. What made the day seem all the longer was that it wasn't over. There was still supper and dessert and hopefully a relaxing evening of beer and cocktails. She felt the wind across her chest and remembered to be grateful that she'd managed to shift the topic away from her taking her top off, but then had to wonder why Cora wasn't answering her question. The other woman leaned against the railing, one hand shielding her eyes.

'Somebody's coming up the road.'

'Not that gnome again.' Giggy arched her palm along her brow and pivoted her head back and forth waiting for Cora to give directions. 'Gnomes, I had been led to understand, will rarely show themselves in broad daylight, but this one is something else.'

'I don't know who they are.'

'They? Are they driving or walking, dear?'

'Driving, but slowly, a small pickup.'

'Oh, that's Lady Clasp.'

'I've never seen that truck.' With her second sneeze of the day, Giggy lifted an unextended telescope to one eye and began to search out the vehicle. Her lens eventually caught the gaze of a million eyes on the peacocks' tails as the birds cowered conspiratorially on the ledge of the black fountain with the engraving of twenty Sapphos bailing.

'She's got a subterranean garage. Very early eighties, very now. Wave so that she knows we're up here. Is there sherbet enough for her as well?' Cora waved, Bella honked, Giggy farted, but silently. Lady Clasp knew her way around the villa, having administered to Giggy's pets for years, and made her way to the balcony with the stalwart assurance that, as Giggy would later tell the jury, was the foundation of the woman's character. Sherbet awaited her. Cora had even managed to pluck three silver leaves from the willow wisps bannering by the balcony and to arrange them on the dish in a design reminiscent of Rennie Mackintosh's early period, when nouveau was influential but not so 'nouveau.'

'My my, that's showy,' complimented Giggy, while Bella pulled up a chair and took the dish being offered. She let her hand hover around Cora's for more than a moment.

'So, what are the test results? How is he? How are we all?' Always in threes, it seemed, either calculated or habitual. Giggy's easy panics reminded the veterinarian of the whippet himself, the same circular waste of energy, the same forcefulness in the face of ignorance that she found mystical in other animals but simply dense in humans. But she had enough of an education in the humanities to be able to admire Giggy's eclecticism. We each coddle our own social sicknesses, she thought, sucking her shov-elette as she looked out over the tufty orange brush. The word 'coddle' made her envision a porcelain table piece of Noel Coward lounging, eyes directed upward in patient ennui, each hand out and cupping a few Scotch mints.

'So?' insisted Giggy.

'Oh, I'm sure you're fine. The test results won't be available until tomorrow.' Eyes shifting about in the middle distance, Bella noticed an especially golden tuft, triangular and dense. 'Chappy is still a dervish but I'm not sure whether that's because he's rabid or because his nerves are shot.'

'If Shirley had something to do with this ... '

'Or perhaps he's inbred.'

167

'No, no, no. He comes from the line of the Meander Kennels. Their reputation precedes them. Did you not notice the balance and solidity of his brisket? And you can't find a whippet whose eyes are a darker hazel. Did you know blue eyes are marked as a fault in whippets? Isn't that interesting?'

Blue-eyed Bella ignored this. 'I'll know if he's rabid by tomorrow. For now, I've given him a sedative.' It wasn't this information but Bella's nonchalance that ultimately proved most comforting. 'I think I see it.'

'What?'

'The *Nude Descending*.' Giggy guffawed at the possibility. Bella had played the game before, many times, but always only half-heartedly. She had never really believed that somebody could design a garden along the lines of a Cubist painting, though it was easy to accept that Giggy would have requested such a scheme. 'I've been assuming that we were at its feet. But what if it's upside down? Or we are? What if the nude's feet are way over there, descending into Wachannabee Gorge? It sort of makes sense, geographically.'

'I still don't see it,' said Giggy, not really wanting to. 'Do you, Cora?' but without waiting for an answer, 'Explain it to us again, dear. Thank goodness somebody's got some fun out of it.' Giggy didn't care to believe that anybody had figured out the figure before she had, though she was ready to acknowledge that, if anybody could, it would be Bella, queen of the night classes. Giggy didn't think there was anybody in Lake Wachannabee whom she respected more than Bella, not that she would admit it until she was forced to by the authorities.

'I don't know what the *Nude Descending Staircase* is supposed to look like,' said Cora, standing up in a lacklustre performance of *Woman Showing Interest*.

'It doesn't matter,' said Lady Clasp. 'The gardener seems to have made a lot of it up as she went along. The starting point is that especially dense bush in the distance.'

'I'm sorry, sweetie. Those instructions don't help at all. Why do I always find nature so uncooperative. Is it something to do with my values? Wasn't it nature that taught us where north is, after all? Maybe I should burn the whole thing down.'

'Oh, don't do that. I think it's divine now. If only you could get the perspective. I can't wait to see it in winter.'

'I'm not serious, really,' returned Giggy in a raspy whisper, 'I'm just trying to scare the shrubbery into co-operating.'

Cora tried to see the *Nude* one last time, gave up and mumbled, 'Oh, I think I see it.'

'Is it something quite awful, dear?'

'No, no,' she replied, regretting having lied now that it meant she'd have to prove herself. 'The way I have it, it would have no thighs at all. You can't descend without thighs.' From this angle, she could see Jem meandering down the road. He'd never driven before. Dust enveloped the boy as the summer wind sped past him. The car threatened to careen but the dust lifted just in time. The sun cast those peculiar rays of light onto the landscape, like aluminum siding extending from the sky to earth. Cora's grandmother used to tell her that these shafts of light were stairways to heaven, but the young woman had always expected that, when the time came, she would find only escalators. It is heaven, after all.

Cora stretched, tired but happy, here on the balcony with Giggy and Bella. Other than the sex she'd had with Bella the night before, Cora really knew nothing about the veterinarian. Still, the physical love had proven enough to make her feel that at least Lady Clasp had never questioned her involvement in the murder. This support had been enough to loosen Cora's usually rigid self-restraint. A community of two was enough for her. Such a long day it was, too, with the garden stretching out before her and shimmering away into the summer haze and up, up into the rays, into the clouds; with the peacocks' theatrical *kree, kree, kree, kreeee, kreeee* splashing over the dim echo of water cascading

169

into the gorge; and her friend Jem almost home now, surrounded again in a cloud of dust as he accidentally sped the Bricklin off the road, over the ditch and down the bank toward the lake. His head and hands were flailing excitedly out the driver's window. If not for Cora's scream, the scene might have seemed comical in its silence.

✦

Only days had passed since the death. Nobody had dressed any less appropriately than anybody else for the funeral, but they each felt that at least one of the others had. Everybody wore black, even though the main mourners had forewarned each other that somebody might appear in a print or a floral pattern under the pretentious claim that it symbolized the randomness of death – as if wearing black symbolized evil rather than simply good taste. They had prepared each other for the fact that, for most of the community, the private lives of the household were tantalizing. At the same time, Robert's wounds had been enough to define the group as a family unto itself, with its own secrets, rules and punishments. And this, even though he smiled openly now without bleeding. More of them than any of them realized also knew that the victim could speak. The village gossips had made sure that from the innocence of chaise longues and squirrels had sprung forth accusations of murder, druidism, lesbianism, cannibalism, hermaphroditism, vampirism, veganism, atavism, philately, arrogance. And now, at the funeral, the throng itself had sprung forth prepared to gawk if the opportunity presented itself. So far, however, the event had been staid and the key participants, thanks to a combination of melancholy and codeine, had remained remorseless and well-dressed.

Next to the coffin, one was met by the vision of a taut off-the-shoulder number that had the effect of lengthening the hipless body and paling the flesh. A sharp uniform of black crepe de Chine with a crisp, pleated skirt wandered agitated back and forth across the foyer of the community centre wringing kid gloves or stopping to yank at flesh-toned nylons. Next to the samovar one found a somewhat excessive summer gown with a ribbon motif that barely managed aesthetic coordination, languid and undisturbed thanks only to a heavy intake of *Carum carvi* prior to arrival. Among the plethora of darkest moda, however, the most striking of the outfits was unquestionably the three-piece. The pants were a coarse rayon pleated boldly along the front and tapered not too finely to an Alsatian cuff at the ankles, which flashed just a hint of doe-grey socks slipping into taps that, special for the funeral, were lined with chamois so as not to tap. The vest and pea jacket – one fashion columnist's discerning eye recognized that it sported a modified sailor cut – were also made of rayon, the cuffs trimmed, as the writer put it, 'to a whisper.' If given the honour of peaking beneath the vest, one would find a Sir Humphrey plate, thin yet appearing full because of the starch on the ruff cascading down the front. Even Giggy had to admit that Cora was the belle of the funeral.

'First one assumption is dashed,' Lady Clasp was explaining to Constable Loch, 'and before you know it … ' In search of lemonade and hors d'oeuvres, the pair had found their way to the basement where Bella was indulging in shrimp kebabs. Giggy, swaying lightly from the apparent fight the *Carum carvi* was having with the cucumber paste she had applied to her temples earlier in the morning, eavesdropped while admiring how the constable's legs filled his pants. The image was so absorbing that it resulted in her own thighs chafing and she made her way back to the coffin.

'That's the charm of this novel … the charm of this novel existence of ours,' returned the constable, who felt funerals demanded a refinement of speech. 'I could only imagine, of course, but what is this I hear about it being successfully argued as a cause of temporary insanity?' The subject was menopause. Aware of being out of his realm, the officer simply hoped to keep the veterinarian talking so that he might have a chance at some of the seafood.

'It wouldn't stand, Reginald. Menopause – too amorphic.'

'But isn't that exactly why it would stand?' The constable tipped forward slightly, realizing only now that the lemonade was spiked. Bella assumed he was admiring her cleavage and pulled her damask shawl further forward over her shoulders.

'No, I think it's reasonable to doubt that they'd let someone commit murder just because we don't know that menopause didn't make her crazy. Is that a double negative?'

'No, no, I understood. You're right. Then if menopause were legally seen as justification for murder, I bet it would be only days before men admitted to experiencing it themselves.' The alcohol made it difficult for Constable Loch to hide his pleasure in having displayed sensitivity. 'I wonder what the root of that word is,' he mumbled as an afterthought.

'It'd be tight, wouldn't it? They'd have to weigh the benefits of the loophole against the benefits of women being officially redefined as lunatics.' Lady Clasp switched from tigers to Arctics. She had absent-mindedly stacked her used toothpicks in a small circular pile modelled on nomadic dwellings she remembered from a childhood trip to Eastern Turkey.

'But the most interesting thing, I think,' ventured the constable, 'would be that insanity would be considered normal. Every woman would be expected to go crazy for a while at some point. If crazy can become normal, what does that say ... ?'

'Oh my god, Reginald, I've eaten all the shrimp,' and she broke into a brief cackle. 'Let's move to another part of the room.' She wove her way through the crowd, her red hair glowing like a pumpkin in the burnt field of funereal clothing. One huge barrette glittered like Lake Winnipegosis in the tangle of her 'do. 'Let's go talk to Cora and Dr. Amicable,' she said.

Reg, however, stayed back, having concluded, since the awkward discussion of the exploration narratives that evening at the Winter Garden, that it was best not to speak to the archeologist while drunk. 'Cora is the beauty, isn't she?' continued the veterinarian, now out of Reg's hearing. He made his way outside, enjoying the liberating sway that inebriation had cajoled into his hocks.

'And so he is asking me for a copy of my manuscript immediately, but it isn't finished. So why does he want it?' The professor was only somewhat irritated but his accent added an earnestness to the argument. He offered Bella only a glance. He was dressed respectfully enough in a pair of black jeans and a grey government-issue shirt. His tie was, unfortunately, tartan, but then everybody knew he lived in a cabin. His translucent, toned assistants, who had all come to the funeral though none of them paid their sympathies, were dressed similarly. Their cheap ties flashed like tropical fish amid sun-deprived kelp.

'I couldn't tell you. It does seem strange.' Since Cora's visit to his camp, she and the professor had made public displays not of friendship exactly, but of respect for each other's individuality and stolidness. From Cora's standpoint, it had been the doctor's cabin and the keenness of his assistant that had lifted her out at least to the lip of the despondency into which she had submerged. She had been most appreciative then that none of them doubted her innocence or even showed the usual small-town interest in the murder. Now, with the support of Giggy and Bella giving her a position from which to critique others, she began to re-evaluate what she had earlier categorized as their kind disregard. Her sense of agency was enhanced even further by the recent conclusion by the laboratory that the blood-soaked missile identified the latest victim of community libel not as Cora. 'TO MISS ANDREWES,' the bloody note read, 'POSING MATRIARCH.' Giggy had figured this out some time ago. Bella suspected her father, who had never liked the

Winter Gardeners and tolerated them even less now that Bella had become close to them.

'What's this, what's this?' squawked the vet, interrupting Cora and John's conversation. The professor, concluding from this gregariousness that Lady Clasp was flirting with him, acknowledged each of her breasts with a nod and a curve of the left eyebrow that he hoped would be all she wanted.

'Loch has asked the doctor to hand in the Shakely manuscript as evidence,' Cora explained.

'Evidence for what?' asked Bella, quickly looking around to locate the constable.

'Well, isn't that exactly it?' returned Cora.

'Well, that is it. I have nothing to do with the death. Sometimes these things happen as some people might wish, but that's all speculation.'

'Dear professor, I don't think anybody was suggesting your involvement. Has the death even been proven a murder?'

'No,' said Bella, 'It was too late when we'd finally recognized that it would be worth checking.'

'Yes, yes,' blustered the professor, 'that's my point. You see, he doesn't tell me what he wants it for except evidence. He thinks we're all a bunch of crazy carpets, don't you think? How am I supposed to know what he's looking for? He says he doesn't have to tell me evidence for what, that he's the constable and he could just demand it. Is this true? He knows, he knows there is nobody now who could incriminate me but myself.' The intensity of John's ire seemed over-determined. Between a scientist, an Asian-American and a veterinarian, he argued, somebody should know what the invasion-of-privacy laws were, but this turned out not to be the case.

'How indescribably rude he is,' Bella cooed.

'Yes, that's the word,' reinforced the doctor, using his cavernous lungs to rumble the sound forward.

'I,' someone added in passing, 'could only agree.'

'I bet he can take whatever he wants for evidence,' sighed Bella, sucking on a toothpick she'd eventually add to another of her nomadic dwellings, 'but he's got to tell you what it's for.'

'I ask him, am I accused of something? And he says no, just that he needs to look at my manuscript. You know, I think he has the chaise longue in his office as evidence, too.'

'I thought he said it was for catnaps.'

'So, did you give the manuscript to him?' Bella asked, her eyes torn between admiring Cora and scanning for seafood.

'Ha ha, the joke is on him. I told him it's not finished, and gave him only one bit more of transcriptions. That is that for his evidence.' All laughed sportively. The doctor himself smiled proudly and splashed the rest of his lemonade against the back of his throat – like a character, Cora thought, in a Mexican musical. There, amid the swarm of sympathizers and those who came simply to stare, the man began to stand out for her as a sort of aesthetic ideal. Wanting to reinforce his bravado, Cora followed suit with her drink and, although some of the liquid hit her teeth and sprinkled onto her chest, the effect was not diminished.

It wasn't his appearance that caught Cora's imagination but the thoughts she felt fit comfortably into the mind of one with such gestures of defiance. She knew that she herself could never stand with such authority upon her own morals, but that did not mean she could not hold them as strongly, nor admire the physical manifestation of masculine virtue when she saw it. He was, she realized then, her kin in this masculinity. Somehow, the stiff Berber carpeting of the room, the efficient panelling on the walls, and the sunlight pouring through the stained glass and washing over him all cohered in this image of beautiful, resilient masculinity – a masculinity that was her own made flesh. She suddenly felt self-conscious.

'Well, you know your business. I think I'll go upstairs and sit with Giggy. She's no doubt feeling lonely.'

'I'll join you,' said Bella, intentionally too quickly. It was as Cora had expected; Lady Clasp had felt it too – the younger woman's blossoming masculinity. Cora was even more pleased now with the suit she'd found in Jem's bedroom. The pair made its way through the crowd, Cora savouring the newly fanned embers of her own beauty, and Bella feeling beautiful simply by being near Cora. Giggy sat alone. They took the two chairs to her left, the coffin itself on Giggy's right. The women smiled consolingly and Giggy returned the gesture through her dew-lily veil. The pamphlet Bella had given her regarding a pet-loss support group trembled in one hand. The sheet offered various validating statistics. Among the splay of thick fingers, Cora could make out four:

• Pet grief has been officially recognized as a valid medical illness in 8 provinces and 38 states.
• 90% of all pet owners consciously recognize a period of mourning upon pet demise.
• 85% of all pet owners feel that replacing a dead pet too soon is disrespectful.
• 30% of all pet owners experience physical illness upon pet demise.

We know they're more than pets; they're family.

Cora sat back in her chair and let Bella take charge of the consoling.

The entire arrangement of principal mourners now took on a profound symmetry, accentuated by the slight disruptions of Bella's bright red hair on the right of the coffin and the shiny aluminum wheelchair on the left. Meanwhile, Giggy's mournful sobs seemed to be met, one for one, by those of Jem, who had taken up the mirror position to his aunt. The band-aid Jem wore over his right cheek was all that remained to remind people of his recent incident in the Bricklin. Robert sat semi-upright with a gossamer black sheet covering his body, naked save for the gauze and a black pair of Calvin Klein underwear that Jem had bought especially for the occasion. The two men rubbed each other's palms throughout the ceremony. Jem's accident had welded the relationship together again, its purpose enhanced through the sharing of pain and recovery. Two lips of tremulous joy now hovered below each man's nose. Neither of them spoke, though it was clear to all the onlookers, including a somewhat insulted Giggy, that the men's primary interest was not Chappy's corpse as it lay on its side tastefully a-frisk, fawn fur aglow on the creamy satin surrounding it, forepaws caught mid-action with his favourite Georgian pillow. Five rubies glittered like pigeons' eyes across his collar.

The storm of the whippet's final days had passed and he rested in peace. For her suffering, Giggy found respite in solitude. Not the family-packed dramas of the Russian novels for her, but the honesty of Shakely's record of his struggles and growing alienation. The journal entries embodied a guileless poignancy that proffered to Giggy companionship, even perhaps friendship, across time.

✦

Thursday the 2nd [January][14]

Storm has finally ended. Major damage to sections of secondary buildings. Indians have put up tent nearby and taken to steady wailing, two of theirs having died in the storm, one being an old man for whom Post informs us little care is directed but the other being a young man seeming about thirteen years of age just beginning to serve the group and therefore a great loss to them no other young men in the group. Men also surprisingly effected especialy Post but also Orley. In poor spirits and unwilling to go to work, displeased with ongoing labour on buildings. May I humblie report sense of displeasure appears to be arising from lack of news or supplies from London. Difficulty in almost full year of labouring at Prisom Factory with no communications. Passing trappers information inconstant but imply stronger Hudson's Bay traffic further south of Prisom Factory. Clear previous missive not received at London. Conclusion shared with Garret, Post, Orley — all seeming unsurprised and disgruntled. I urge patience and understanding that message may be

---

14. No single explanation for the absence of records from July 1775 to January 1776 has been established. It is unlikely that Shakely failed to write any records for this time, especially because he makes no comment in this regard when the entries pick up on 2 January 1776. The original document, however, lacks any suggestion of missing pages. There are, for example, no incomplete entries that would suggest this. Dr. Wilcox's earnest desire for establishing an explanation for the gap in the narrative has resulted in some speculation that materials may have been removed while the manuscript was in New York State, perhaps because they were seen as historically relevant regarding the Third New York regiment's invasion of Canada in August to November of 1775 and the capture of Montréal and Fort St. Johns in the Lake Champlain region. Perhaps Shakely recorded information on this encounter and, because his extant records make no mention of the regiment's string of failures in 1776, this material was not removed.

mislaid but passing Pedlors continue to deny any communication from Hudson's Bay for us. Post and Orley most surly with news. Post has returned to new Wachanas, has sharing [?] tent with Wachana woman.

Mon the 6th

Has been ten months since arrival and no word from main office since. This record may not find its way to London office, who voice no interest in our progress or well-being. Others have become silent and ornery. Orley well healed and continuing with glass chinking. Have sent Post and Garret hunting. Post fails to return Garret returns with three rabbits. Little to report

the 24th

Post has not returned and assuming will not return. Is living fully with Wachanas and not aggressive to us but unwilling to continue with our waiting—as he says. Has taken Wachana woman and settled with them. He tells us he has told them that supplies will be coming and he will give all to them. Wachanas eager for further supplies, appear to be setting up somewhat more permanent camp than previous group. Post invites Orley to join him, as Orley reports, but refuses to leave Factory for which we thank him. Supplies sufficient for remainder of winter but no goods remaining for trade with natives, who refuse to accept we have nothing to offer and often request either brandy or tools.

February 2

Weather has preceded calm. Post discoursing rarely now with Orley, fully satisfied with Wachanas. Has travelled twice south to second post, notes supplies from Hudson's Bay Company there aplenty and asked for some diverted up to Prisom. Southern post says they wish to comply shortly. However with no communication or supplies to Prisom Factory, I am prepared to conclude that your honours have chosen not to continue with this site. Must decide wether to proceed further westward or join with Oshawa Factory southward. Work on additional buildings stopped. Post has now invited me to become more friendly with tribe.

13

Wounds caused, Orley reports, by Wachanas and Post as part of ritual for request for communion with the strength of the young. I am not of the words to explain or even understand what Orley has reported, but it seems he was used in a ceremony of strength or youth. Says through Post that young warrior lost in January was lost in a raid by previous tribe. Process unclear and Post's allegiances unclear, but not to your honours is clear. Previous tribe feared not dispersed but in hiding. Wachanas tense for further attack. Orley and Garret also impatient, strongly encourage moving either further west or preferred to Oshawa.

Men occupied in hunting. Orley fully mended. Post presses his invitation to me.

March

We have not heard from your honours and do not expect so. The number of traders, esp. Pedlors, increasing as weather proves more accommodating. Trappers from Eels Factory arrive and set up base for trapping at Prisom Factory, but have no word to us from London. Say surprised to find us, but pleased. Garret eager to work with trappers. Orley says he will follow route south to Eels, leave Prisom to trappers and Wachanas.

I am inclined to accept Post's invite for communion with Wachanas, I no longer eager to remain at Factory with no purpose on hand.

Full clear day. Snow quickly melting, but insects already intense.

TENDERNESS

The tender sublimity of the tableau vivant didn't go unnoticed by the others assembled there that day, but the Wachannabee community quickly rebounded from their lapse into sympathy during the family's loss. Soon after the funeral, townsfolk began to buzz with an indignation greater than they had before. Giggy deduced that Robert was the cause: his esoteric garment of bandages, his sustained, overt display of affection for Jem, but above all the speculations going about the town that the role of murder victim that he had invited upon himself was in fact a fabrication that he had had the strength to cast aside long ago, had he chosen to do so. There was something disconcerting, even tasteless, about a victim with agency. He is the type of boy, conjectured Giggy, who refrains from opening his bottle of pop early in the journey. Giggy was herself not unconvinced by the rumours, and the possibility of his subterfuge made it seem all the more inappropriate, to her, that Robert was the main draw of concern and conjecture so soon after Chappy's funeral.

Giggy herself, ever since the rabid pup had been put to sleep, lacked the mental energy to sympathize much with anything other than herself. Notwithstanding the fact that the dog had been an expert at only soundless yapping, the Winter Garden seemed somehow to have gone silent since the canine's lethal injection. It had finally become, to Giggy's ears, appropriate to describe the peacocks' cries with an adjective that others had worn thin from overuse – 'plaintive.' They too, she thought, were mourning Chappy's passing. Jem meanwhile had appropriately toned down the food for an autumnal palette and now somnambulated about the house like the moribund, his only moments of joy coming when Robert called him over. But Rob's memory of events appeared still to be patchy. Jem spent hours sitting on the ottoman next to the bed, patiently tossing a rambutan from one hand to the other, knowing that some day it would have to be cut open, letting loose the sweet stench which he imagined was already seeping through its smooth, dry flesh.

'I feel, with all this death and sickness, Robert, I feel so hopelessly alive, as if I were in a state of perennial decay. There's nothing pleasurable about being the only youth in such a house of pain.' He groaned as if suffering from a case of dyspepsia that only three weeks in Ghana's Labadi Pleasure Beach and a diet of coconuts could cure, but he sounded as sincere as a pop band signalling angst on cue.

'This isn't the island of Dr. Moreau,' said Robert, managing a twinkle along the reddened laugh-lines of his face.

'You don't know how good you've had it. It's disturbing everything so, all this commotion about your murder. Sorry – incident. The constable and the manuscript and Cora being threatened – you're really quite lucky not to have gone through all this with the rest of us. Though I know your pain has been horrible. Please don't think I'm making light of it.'

'But Jem, if I hadn't been skinned, none of this would have happened.'

'Well, of course not, dear. Don't feel guilty.'

'According to what you're saying, if I hadn't been skinned, I wouldn't be lucky right now.'

'That's it, lovey. That's all right, then. You're going a touch delirious. Now best to let your mind rest before you strain something. Don't get me wrong, I want you to talk, I want you to talk until the cows come home, but it's all so depressing now. What could have driven you to this? Was there something about your flesh you didn't like, despite what you say?' and Jem glanced affectionately at his own slender legs as they sunned themselves across the regal blue of the ottoman.

'It was what I'd asked for, it really was.' Rob tried to sit up but he could feel the tender skin pull across his abdomen. 'It's the only way I knew how to get myself to remember ... ' He slumped back down as half a tear snuck out from the corner of an eye and lightly stung his face. 'Our only hope for utopia,' sighed Robert, 'is in things we only imagine.'

'Oh, I say. Keep it for the Gigster; she might have patience for it.' Jem smiled like a nun who'd just stopped singing as he crawled onto the bed, lay down beside the patient and, with two marble-pure fingers, coaxed shut his lover's lids. 'Our only hope for utopia, dear, is that there are things we can't imagine,' he whispered and then moved his hand over the victim's mouth.

The two men had for some days now shared the conservatory next to the kitchen. Their bed, a cumbersome Victorian number with oak drawers lining the base, had centred itself beneath the window, from where it now intimidated the only other piece of furniture – a spindle-legged end table balancing a fishbowl that somebody now forgotten had hand-blown at a Renaissance summer camp many years ago. The blue-tinged vessel itself contained a few choice pieces of amber and a small green frog that Bella and Cora had found during a recent picnic at the lake. 'But it's every new imagining,' Robert said, continuing Jem's thought as he stared down the burping frog, 'that confirms the possibility of the unimaginable.'

The frog was in the conservatory because Giggy believed that only a body preparing to die required complete rest. What a body aimed at recovery needed was stimulation just beyond the realm of ease. In addition to the frog, therefore, the room also contained six *Urtica urens* in unseasonal bloom and two large clay pots bursting with black pepper fruit with a scent so heavy it was almost visible. Indeed, the room was more of a conservatory than it had ever been. The frog sprawled on its back across the pebbles, struggling to digest a fly that hadn't gone down right.

'Can one satirize something,' asked Jem, 'that never originated in culture? Can an animal satirize itself?'

Giggy continued to tend to Robert's well-being, despite what she saw as his bed-ridden grandstanding. She would never realize that her skepticism of others was more than mildly tinted by her affection for her nephew, which had become stained with desperation ever since the community had added a sense of foreboding to her life. Though she had always led a private existence, the Lake Wachannabee community had clearly affected her. Now the collective persona, though physically absent from the Winter Garden, weighed down upon her spirit like pound cake. To keep both her and Robert's minds occupied, Giggy had initiated an ongoing game of Go, telling herself that she would let him win as soon as he became good enough not to make it obvious. Every day, immediately after breakfast, Giggy had Jem bring the game down from her bedroom, the man taking it away again at 11:30 when it was time for brunch. Somewhat insulted by this new task, Jem proffered a silent protest by wearing a needlepoint apron, but his new-found maturity made the gesture seem, to Robert, rather silly. Giggy thought the garb a touch large but otherwise becoming.

Once the *Wachannabee Orderly* had reported that an anonymous someone had informed them that Robert had stripped the flesh off his own body, threats against Cora had ended. However, the animosity toward Giggy, as the matriarch of this collection of peculiar residents, had begun to rise. Constable Loch said that he was sure that Robert was lying but seemed unwilling to try and prove it. Dr. Amicable, conversely, came forward in bold support of the wounded youth, although there would later surface an ambivalence of interpretation as to whether he had supported the other man's honesty or his actions. The professor had framed his defence as a plea for Giggy's peace, but the matriarch thought he had chosen to contradict the constable as a means of differentiating himself as he vied for her attention. Robert, meanwhile, had yet to confess publicly to anything.

As Bella had suspected, her father, a swarthy man with sideburns that connected under his chin like the ribbons of a bonnet, had proudly confessed to having thrown the bag through the window those weeks ago, and nobody, save for Giggy's friends and family, seemed to think the less of him for it. He had been silent then, Sir Clasp claimed in the *Wachannabee Orderly*, for the sake of his family's good name, but he spoke out now, he argued in the next issue of the paper, for the sake of the same. He was sure that his daughter had been coerced by Giggy into becoming not only a lesbian but also a part-time gardener. Sir Clasp then published a personal request to his daughter, in what was becoming a regular column, that she abstain from communicating with anybody from that family. Upon reading the piece, Bella rushed over to the Winter Garden to apologize for her father's actions, a move that the man witnessed from his stakeout among a grove of sumac across the road from the villa, his bone-white car adequately camouflaged by the wild oats growing along the roadside. What nobody in the ensuing litigations seemed to question was whether Clasp's claim of familial defence was sincere. What his column did establish was that the attack on Giggy was distinct in motivation from Robert's carniphilic stripping. Meanwhile, the veterinarian's father denied even knowing that the Winter Garden housed a dog, which seemed valid since he'd never been there.

Giggy struggled to remind herself that the man was not lucid, but her tolerance weakened with every fresh corpse that found its way onto her property. Sacrificed vermin had become the community's symbol of disrespect for Giggy. It was, of course, all the more painful than they knew, because every gnarled squirrel on her doorstep, every maggot-infested rat among the rhodos, every disembowelled mole smashed against the limestone of her Cubist gazebo and left there purple and bleeding, brought to Giggy's mind Chappy's death. It was like a Promethean wound never allowed to heal, the frail scab being pulled off fresh each morning.

Robert in his own right was a model of appreciation, not that anybody noticed. Rarely rung was the crystal bell that sat beside the fishbowl as patiently as a Taoist at the dentist's. He was embarrassed for not having explained sooner how he had come to be skinned, but the ultimate release of his efforts, the return of ecstasy to pain, the itchy layers of flesh that grew over his image of himself exposed, led to a mingling of wisdom and normalcy that he was not predisposed to discuss. The rush of mediocrity was nothing like a balm. But his improved physical state also affected his mental health until finally he was able to conclude that his actions, being self-directed, were not a crime.

And Giggy, she suffered on. She made weak efforts to return to the lighthearted days when she believed that Robert had indeed been the victim of a murder attempt. It was hard for her to accept the fact that Bella was the daughter of the man who was the well-spring of anguish at the Winter Garden. It was sure something, the way in which the intensity of grief brought an intensity to all her emotions. And now, disquietude had lifted Giggy's feelings to the level of the aestheticist. To sustain the pleasures of our painful days beyond their moments, she concluded, this was success in life. In a sense, it might even be said that our greatest pain arises from the habit of its emulation, for, after all, habit is relative to the stereotypes of living. But it is the roughness of the eye that causes callousness and thus the roughness of the eye that promises new, subtler flames of pleasure.

✦

Giggy wished she could more easily turn for support to Bella, a woman at least sympathetic to her generation. Awkwardly, almost on the wrong feet, the two women had begun their relationship. The veterinarian had introduced herself – 'But folks usually call me Bella' – and then added, in a stilted syntax that to Giggy exposed classicism, 'And in what way would you like to be referred?' Finding garish the question (not to mention the gangly profusion of elephant ears that Lady Clasp clearly intended to offer as a gift), Giggy responded acidly, although the vitriol proved unable to burn Bella's altruism. Instead, in response, the woman offered to tend the border of Giggy's garden. The purple-black ears in the calloused hands convinced Giggy to do the veterinarian this favour.

'Derek, honey,' – Derek being the cook/musician who had preceded Jem and then left his band (and Giggy) to pursue his own projects (why, Giggy had mused, did a musician always *pursue* a project, as if the latter were a fox in the coop?) – 'come and get these beautiful leaves from Lady Clasp. Would you like some wine, my dear? Perhaps Pernod?' A cup of lime sherbet she agreed to and a pattern of affection was thus initiated, Giggy reciprocating with a cool treat for whatever bounty Bella bore. In strawberry season she bore a basket of berries; with the first crop of grain, a loaf of bread; peaches, peaches; plums, plums. And on each of these neighbourly visits, Giggy reciprocated with an offer of Pernod (to which she had always given preference during the summer, until Jem introduced her to beer), which Bella would always kindly refuse in favour of sherbet. Perched in the gazebo or on one of the balconies that clung to the sides of the villa like swallows' nests, they discussed Bella's garden, or Giggy's, or how Bella's tending of Giggy's was going. They would go on about Giggy's young cousins in Israel or Bella's two daughters in the archeological heights of Oaxaca. Eventually, Giggy would become uncomfortable, wanting to burp or to scratch or to sing, and she would excuse herself, saying she had to take a nap or a compress or whatever came to mind. She would then sneak off to an east window and watch Bella navigate the path that meandered across the field to her own home, the woman's rust-coloured hair flashing erratic in the sunlight as the grains splayed away from her swaying hips.

'You don't think I was rude, Derek?' Giggy would ask, hurrying into the kitchen where the British boy with thin blond hair would be washing the perishables or snogging a harmonica, 'I hope she didn't think so.' Sometimes he would grind the plums into a pasty compress for Giggy's chafing, though the effects never suggested any urgency with regard to the patent.

'No, no. You weren't rude. Why do you think she keeps coming?'

'Maybe I'm supposed to drive to her place someday. Or maybe I'm expected to offer vodka. Could that be it?'

'I understand vodka isn't being offered this season due to an influx of the "coolers."' He'd picked the word off an advertisement in the *Orderly* and didn't think he was using it quite correctly, but Giggy would feel reassured by his comments regardless and make her way back to the recliner, looking forward to tasting a bit of whatever it was that Bella had brought.

Today, perched on the southern balcony alone with Robert Shakely and his isolating woes, Giggy thought that she could see her neighbour even now coming toward the Winter Garden.

'Is that Bella, sweetie?' she asked Jem, who had just walked out waving a postcard from the Belgian landscapist who, it turned out, was happily ensconced on a yacht off the coast of Belize, apparently unaware that she and Giggy had been in an aesthetic conflict so intense as to verge at times on the juridical.

'Well, it isn't the gardener, thank goodness; look at this lovely postcard. I think it's the constable. I just saw him park at the top of the drive. Are you sure we all can hear Robert's peal from here?' Giggy patted Jem's knee, spritzing his devotion with a light mist of mockery.

'Don't worry about that, dear. We don't want him ringing it too often,' and then, after a pause that led Jem to consider his aunt's hesitation, 'Carpal Tunnel Syndrome, sweetie.' Giggy leaned back in her chair and poured some crème de cassis into her teacup. The scent of wild penny roses carried over on the wheeziest of breezes.

'It couldn't be that nosy man. I've already given him the juiciest of my stories. It must be Lady Clasp,' she sighed, 'and it must be peaches. He's up to something, you know. There are so many plots afoot that one can't keep track of them all, but this one, this one I really would like to know.' Had she been honest at that moment, she would have confessed that her mind had just shifted from plots entirely. She was imagining instead soft, succumbing peaches, their loose skin begging to be peeled back to let loose the moist insides, thick as the depth of a half-blown rose in the shade of autumn, thick as the clouds that she now saw rising over the distant ridge, perfect as a second glass of crème de cassis and the smoothness of its strong sweetness after the first had accustomed one's throat to the initial tang.

It was this sort of sureness that Giggy appreciated most these last weeks, for Chappy's death had made her lose faith in those elements of existence that one was taught to assume were fortified, such as life and love and time. Now she found herself falling back on minor verities, such as taste, endearment, affectation — seemingly slighter sources of faith, but all the stronger because they were more personal. Giggy's taste, Giggy's endearment, Giggy's affectation, shrouded about her like the skins of peaches which she liked to imagine had been coddled by the baby Jesus himself.

'No, not the constable.' The figure in the field was clearly not attempting subterfuge, as it waded about in the alfalfa like a victim in a flash flood. The stick the person carried suggested to Jem someone trying to catch grasshoppers for fish bait, but the zigging and zagging and crouching implied an intention more sinister or more confused. The nephew was relieved to hear the ping of Robert's bell because it pulled him so purposefully from the stranger's antics. Something had indeed made a noise, thought Giggy, but it came from the field and the clouds out there churning slate grey and ready to pour.

The change in air pressure seemed remarkably like a mani-festation of the pressure she had begun to feel again from the community. It had sustained its distrust not despite but because of Robert's statement that he had agreed to have his skin peeled away, because he had encouraged it, had enjoyed it as something larger than his own physicality. What Giggy, alone on the balcony there beneath the storm of clouds like the victim in an opera, was on the verge of realizing was that murder was no longer a crime of import and that, more specifically, Robert's 'murder' was never the crime in which the community had been waiting to revel. The crime in fact had been her own, although she herself could not articulate what it was. She had never teetered closer than she did at this moment, as the first pocks of rain slapped against her cheek, to clarifying the reason for their vilification. The change in the weather and the rise in the volume of the rain's tattoo could not have prepared her for the sudden, sharp crack whose magnitude literally cast her back before it rebounded again and again down the valley before rounding out into the thunder's rumble.

But for the briefest moment the birds stopped singing and one could imagine all the deer within a thousand metres of Giggy's villa lifting their heads and twitching their ears nerv-ously, much as Giggy herself now did. For that long, brief moment, everybody – Giggy, Cora, Jem, Robert, Lady Clasp, the constable, Sir Clasp, even Dr. Amicable, whose canoe had just docked a few minutes earlier — everybody was in a part of the estate. And each of them felt that his or her individual position in relation to the sound was notable.

A gunshot, and no doubt. Giggy had seen the figure in the field fall down among the shafts of alfalfa glittering in the first spatterings of rain. The victim? Or the attacker? She could see the stick make circular gestures like the top mast of a ship before it sank into the ocean of grass. Giggy eased into action.

Cora, assuming the crack was thunder, rushed to bring her bicycle into the gazebo and then scurried about letting down the mosquito netting, purpose hanging from her shoulders with the weightiness of a medieval shawl. A spectrum of pests had already taken shelter on the porch. She opened the gazebo door for the rain-spattered Dr. Amicable, who was running down the driveway. He had arrived to give Cora her canoe lesson. Now that the taunts against her had subsided, she was no longer as confined to the equipment in the basement, though she still appreciated the intensity of stationary exercise.

This was the first storm since Robert had been able to sit comfortably in a chair again. Jem, relieved to see that his love was calm, sat at the man's feet and watched the summer rain through an open window. 'Sugar, it might be time for you to let the rest of them know the whole truth,' suggested Jem, unaware that he himself knew so little of his lover's complicity. Robert turned his head and gazed out at the asphalt sky. Today he would write his confession. He could see the constable, caught in the rain, running up the drive toward the house. Perhaps his car had stalled.

Giggy was alone in seeing the figure in the field fall and she alone had concluded that the crack was that of a rifle. She rushed in her way down the stairs, out the back door and into the open landscape of the *Nude*. She noted the sensuality of the rain as it poured down her shoulders, chest, thighs. She chruned through the grass, casting off her itchy wig as she went, forsaking her loose sandals when they got stuck in the thickening mud. Though at first she moved forward with a sense of purpose, the drive soon gave way to a feeling of liberty which carried her forward almost buoyantly as she plunged deeper into the waves of grain. Three, six, nine steps she waded onward before she let herself sink into the soil like a wasted calf, her tears like the raindrops seemingly unwilling to let go of her heavy, shaking face. They weren't tears of sorrow that poured forth from Giggy's eyes but tears of frustration.

The storm of her catharsis had finally broken and bled its brazen orange glow. In front of her, the light shattered through the unspun coils of grey hair hanging before her eyes like a waterfall. The clearing eastern sky shone down and began to wipe in gentle swirls the wet from her mottled cheeks. Looking back, Giggy could see the rain tearing over the town of Lake Wachannabee, pouring down unselectively on each and every façade glimmering in the distance. The town glowed in the new light. She felt revived by the rain, steeled against the catcalls of the community. But there was nowhere to go with this new commitment. So she sat there in the mud, torn between the fickle warmth of the sun on one side and the liberty of the rain on the other, gradually realizing that she herself was probably positioned at the base of somebody else's rainbow.

It was Lady Clasp, mud smudging one side of her body, who found Giggy floundering but mesmerized among the broken shafts of grain. 'You were caught by the lightning, too? What a day you've chosen to come into the garden. Oh, just look at me. I thought I'd never get out of the mud. Here now, lean on me, dear.' The two women made their way back to the house, where they found everybody running about in search of the missing matriarch. Even the frog, seemingly taking his cue from Robert, lifted his baggy torso and craned his head to conduct a search of the conservatory.

To Robert, as to everybody in the villa in fact, Giggy's disappearance was not a complete surprise. They had all realized to varying degrees that it was she who remained the centre of the narrative that had shaped itself around their lives. Robert's wounds, Cora's defensiveness, Chappy's death had only been reasons for those residents of Lake Wachannabee already convinced that criminality marked Giggy's household to push their curiosity to a state of accusation. The aura of guilt had been lobbed into the house like a bomb intended to smoke out the matriarch and force the public perusal of her lifestyle. And now those who had thought themselves most sympathetic to Giggy's views suddenly found themselves alone together in the Winter Garden, almost making manifest the woman's guilt through their exchange of questioning glances. All along, they came to recognize, the crimes and accusations that had seemed most obvious — even appropriate — had not in fact been so important; they were not seen by the townsfolk as the root of crime, only as the offshoots. Giggy was the root.

Jem was the first to feel guilty for doubting his aunt's intentions. Perhaps he over-compensated, however, when he offered to prepare a meal of Chicken Lambertini in celebration of her return. Hours later, having all calmed themselves and showered, they feasted in the dining room. Only Robert was absent, having pleaded fatigue, although his true reason was a growing need, almost a palpable itch to write his own history. He needed to publish his story now, while it was still a topic of interest, so that others would have the opportunity to understand. The story would be above all convincing, he promised himself, in its sincerity, so convincing that nobody could doubt it.

Giggy held court in an especially confident tone, asking for compliments on her jewellery and criticisms of her denouncers. Lady Clasp was most strongly supportive of Giggy's comments, in part because of their muddy bonding, but also because she wished to distance herself from the actions of her father.

Indeed, by the time Jem set out the Baked Alaska, Giggy's accusations had become too vindictive for everybody but the veterinarian.

'I have a right mind,' proclaimed Giggy, 'to take Sir Clasp to court for libel.' Most assumed that she spoke more for effect than from conviction, but twitch-wiggles of discomfort nevertheless made their way around the table. Perhaps, some hoped, it was just too much of the crème de framboise, and all of this would dissipate.

'Oh, that wouldn't hold, Giggy,' coaxed Constable Loch, twirling his butter knife. He wore one of Jem's too-tight T-shirts across his expansive chest while a beach towel hung about his waist like the arm of a drunk lover. His own clothes were drying.

'I believe it would,' said Bella, nurturing the new affections that the recent encounter in the grass had encouraged, 'I know you don't need it, but I'd be happy to stand as a character witness against that man. The stories I could tell, you wouldn't believe.' Such devotion could suggest complicity, thought Dr. Amicable, looking askance first at the constable and then at the darkening skies.

'Oh, that doesn't sound necessary,' interjected Cora, offering the hostess more pureed yams. Giggy held the dish while Jem cleared a space near her plate to set it down.

'I wouldn't want to become a cat's-paw between father and daughter,' she said lightly, but with a tone that silenced Lady Clasp. Had the conversation ended here, nothing would have been lost in the storm.

'To accuse you of posing ... posing as a matriarch, Giggy,' mused Dr. Amicable on what he thought was a change in subject, 'never struck me as an insult. Unless you are that strongly against the notion of family, which I know you are not.' Could he steer her toward acquiescence? 'Clasp, he could not have known this.' He glanced downward for Chappy's support, a habit unfortunately still being triggered.

'No, of course not, of course not,' said Giggy. 'It's the word "posing" that's libellous. Am I not a mother? Is it wrong for me to love like a mother? The barb is in Sir Clasp's claim that I am a *false* matriarch. It's an insult hard to bear.'

Semantics, thought the constable – this should be safe. 'Well, technically,' hemmed Loch, 'you aren't a mother. Now, I know that truly you are, I'm not contesting that, but suing Clasp for libel would get you nowhere. They've different definitions than you, the courts. And you don't want to start him digging about for . . . well, for anything. Do not incriminate yourself, and deal appropriately with those who might.' Glances ricocheted about the room like light from a prism. 'It's a Moldavian saying, that is all.'

'You're Moldavian now?'

'Even if you won,' added Cora, her joy in having recently been moved out of the ring of community gossip emboldening her toward a harshness of enthusiasm, 'that doesn't mean anybody would believe you. This is a bad time to take on the town.' Enthusiastic, and so also less reserved in voicing her opinion.

Bella rose. On this turbulent evening, Jem would later try to explain to the jury with a shrillness put down to nerves, Lady Clasp's 'toggle switch of friendship' stuck for a moment in the lock of defensiveness. She pushed back her chair, stormed to the door and turned to them with the precision of a general. 'I can't believe what you're all saying. This isn't the way to treat your friend, someone you claim to love. Why don't you support her? It's a cruel thing you're doing, this after-dinner flagellation.' With these words, Bella left the Winter Garden for her home, this time choosing to make the journey via the side of the road.

Enlivened by the woman's defence, Giggy likewise rose to huff, 'No, it's not a nice thing to do, not a nice thing at all.' She herself retired to her bedroom, where the breeze cooled her kindled emotions. From the open window, she could hear the tapping of Robert's keyboard. Eventually, one by one, candles on Bella's windowsills began to glow. From below came the sound of chairs scraping against the floor and then, soon after, the constable's car starting and driving off.

Jem went to sleep in the gazebo, leaving Robert alone to write. But Dr. Amicable and Cora stayed in the dining room sipping on port. At times their conversation carried up to Giggy's ears, but she could make neither heads nor tails from their ribbons of speech.

'It is important to remember complicity ... '

'Complicity or merely acquiescence?'

'I cannot imagine condoning ... '

' ... has to be done, you see. He knows. It's only a matter of time before he informs others.'

'I can't. Don't ask me ... '

'Why not speak to him tonight?'

When the young woman finally came to bed, Giggy asked for gossip, but Cora denied there was any. The matriarch saw no subtle way of pressing the point and so let her attention drift to the glint of the moon on her left thumbnail. Looking out the window, she could just make out Dr. Amicable's canoe tenderly slicing across the soft-lit face of the lake. She wanted back that peace that she had so recently taken for granted. The matriarch was realizing that she currently had less agency in the household than she'd ever expected. Bella was right. She would have to clear her name. And she would have to do it now, while she still held some sway.

✦

I offer this not as a confession but as an explanation of my involvement in the events that have led to the vilification of those associated with the Winter Garden. It is not that such an explanation is required and I recognize the risk of sensationalism attached to my publication of the story. I present it here as a personal statement motivated primarily by my hopes that others with sensitivities akin to mine, those with their own carniphilia, may have a chance to see their feelings described in a public forum. It is, I believe, one of the only means we have at present to reach out to each other and, as my story makes clear, I know that I am not alone in my feelings.

Stretched half-skinned on a slab of slick stone, leather tongs tied tenderly about ankles and wrists through which my crushed veins were pushing to pulse, I could not, at first, explain my own position. When I flexed my ass to scratch an itch, the archeologist laughed, not entirely misinterpreting the gesture. I could just make out the man, his hairy legs planted firmly. The word 'plumb-bob' kept coming to mind, but I couldn't remember what it really meant: plumb-bob, plumb-bob, interspersed with both the man's hearty guffaws and my own pulses of pleasure so sublime that I knew this ecstasy had been bestowed upon me because of the intensity of my faith. The mirror-encrusted ceiling with its white-to-golden stalactites glistened with the interior solemnity of a Greek cathedral. I could see a few flowing channels of brilliant orange mixed in with the creamed gold and, as the ecstasy of my experience consumed the experience itself, the orange streams grew bolder and blurred into a scratchy softness which reminded me of the blanket that Giggy had been clutching about Chappy's throat when she'd shown me the way through the forest.

She had seemed worried more about getting mud on the undubbined leather of her boots than about helping me. I had been staying at her place no more than a week and she had agreed to lead me only to the footpath that would take me to Dr. Amicable's gorge (Wachannabee Gorge, actually, but, ever since he had discovered the Wachana wintering bower under the falls, it had become nobody's but his). Now that I think about it, I'm not even sure whether Wachannabee is a person or just a Wachana word. Perhaps it simply means 'gorge.' Giggy had no answer. It was, she assured me, only a fear of getting lost in her own back yard that kept her from venturing any further into the wilderness than the start of the path leading into the gorge. She and Chappy began discreetly letting go their irritating sneezes to inform me that they wished to turn back now. I knew something was making them nervous because of how their ears twitched, the bite-sized glass that hung from Giggy's lobes clinking like little cowbells. She was finding it difficult to hold both the dog and the train of the rainbow-hued raincoat that she had insisted on wearing.

'Maybe you should take the dog back to the villa,' I offered, 'he seems to be getting cold.' Chappy shook as if with epilepsy and a transparent drop of mucus glistened on the tip of his black nose like a satellite. This meant he was happy, it turns out, but I didn't know this at the time. I hadn't been introduced to the family that long before. It was Dr. Amicable who had first suggested I might be able to board at the Winter Garden. I had only just met the man myself and I remember thinking at the time that his aura of virility seemed rudely permanent. And I recall the erotic scent of starter fluid. But now, in July, it was the smell of black pine that seemed an aphrodisiac – that and what I think was the castor oil of Dr. Amicable's canoe, an aroma that physically stimulated my nates.

While the bower was definitely of interest to a historian who is as highly respected as the professor, it was the stories of Wachana youths who had been stripped of their flesh by their own tribe that took most of the man's attention. That first evening on which we had stopped by the Winter Garden, we had found Giggy sitting in the gazebo, her plump pale leg hanging like a content calf over the arm of the recumbent kitchen helper – Derek, I think his name was. She had offered us chicory, which Derek prepared, and then we had settled down for a peaceful evening.

Nobody had asked the doctor for his story, but neither did anybody mind when he began to tell it, his deep voice sluicing into the warm, dark evening as if it were rising from some gorge of its own. His narrative was derived from bits of past writing on the indigenes of the Wachannabee region. As he told us, there were – in addition to the Shakely journal – fifteen extant tales, recorded primarily by Jesuits and, while most of them claimed that the tribe had simply eaten the flesh of boys' thighs due to starvation and that the tribe itself was not Wachana, three versions claimed that the boys were stripped of their flesh because of their pulchritude. One in particular was so beautiful and healthy, the claims went, that the other members of the kinship group felt driven to participate in his bodily experiences, not just touch him but expose the workings of his unveiled musculature to their own senses. Or, as one of the Jesuits explained it, the indigenes believed that they themselves could become engorged with the pleasures of having the boy's body, a single body thereby becoming the sensory fulcrum of an entire collective.

This transmutation through the tender flesh clearly fascinated the professor. His voice sharpened as he spoke of it. He was even preparing an anthology of these tales and writing a substantial introduction that explained the transition from simple infatuation to sensory immersion without slipping into the ductility of the mythical. Everybody in the room had swooned that evening when the professor had pronounced such words. *Pulchritude. Ductility.* I imagine they reminded not only me of the rainforest, although, to my knowledge, none of us has ever been. It was his accent – every letter pronounced as if his mind took on its articulation individually, each sound filled to bursting with mystery.

It was this sense of being engorged, satiated, that I recalled as I made my way along the path to the gorge, stopping only to pick occasionally from the wild raspberries dripping from their branches. Amazingly early for them to be so juicy, I recall. My flesh and hair were soon sheened and glistening from the moist and dripping leaves which hung out before me like the open palms of beggars. A pungent and thorny bush of Rose-Nasturtiums (Latin: to twist the nose) clawed my flesh, exclamations of blood rising up to the scratches on my skin. I touched my tongue tentatively to the markings. I have always been surprised to find that the fluid moves so close to the surface of my flesh, which otherwise appears as thick and white as wood. The sight of my own blood gave me a giddy sort of pleasure, not really an ecstasy, but I was nevertheless grateful that I hadn't been cut deeper by the branches, for fear of fainting.

After a short walk, ten minutes, I entered the plunging depths of the gorge, and it was no short moment more before I found the professor's canoe. I knew it was the professor's because it was covered in tar and castor oil, with the edges lined in beaver fur, the professor explaining that this made for a smoother ride in the tight spots. The remains of Robert Shakely were apparently buried somewhere here in the gorge, he having never made it out of Prisom Factory, buried somewhere beneath these layers of moss, cool and green and shimmering from the mist of the Wachannabee Falls which splattered into the canyon and funnelled off in spastic whirls through the unmarked and unattainable underground churns.

I was awakened from my reverie by the chuckle that Dr. Amicable volleyed from the other side of the brook, which, to my amazement, had at some point widened into a thrashing creek, the gorge having expanded into a sort of ceilingless cavern. There didn't seem to be anything to laugh about. It was the same chuckle with which the straight-backed professor had introduced himself the evening that I had arrived in town to research Prisom Factory. The man reminded me of the professor from *Gilligan's Island*, dressed entirely in silvery beige and oozing a misdirected sexuality.

'Robert. I'm glad you are here. How goes your little dig?' Guffaw. I had been exploring some stone work on Giggy's property.

'Oh, there you are.' I waded across the water, marble-eyed rainbow trout bannering about my legs as the lower half of my body numbed from the frigid roils.

'But you don't tell me, how is your little dig?' It was clear to me that the doctor liked the word 'little' more than a small amount.

'I haven't really been digging. There's a series of damaged foundations that I've been mapping out. Two spots with signs of broken crockery and rust. The channels all seem rather random so far. I haven't figured it out yet.'

'So how then did you find my bower?'

'Giggy.'

'I knew you would make it eventually.' While Giggy generally seemed to speak too much and yet at no one in particular, it often felt that Dr. Amicable was saying more than I could take in – not because of the noise but because of the ambiguities. The professor brought me to a waterfall that poured over the entrance of a cave like strings of coloured beads, glittering amber and red when the light caught them at the right angle. The image was Parrishic but, once inside the cave, my eyelids began to flicker distractedly from the flashes of sunlight entering through the liquid curtain.

The cave was more a room – huge, almost square. The walls and ceiling were covered in pieces of mirror or glass the size of irregular dominos. Everything was dripping with water and there was no hope of my sopping clothes becoming any drier. Imagine my surprise to see Chappy here. He cast me one stern glance before returning to guarding a back entryway. Five assistants that I had met a few times before stood dressed only in shorts and working intently on a central stone platform. What they were doing wasn't apparent. Their bodies glowed a milky tangerine like the stone itself. I could see their muscles and veins shifting distinctly, as if they had been making the same movements for hours, days.

Catching my gaze, the professor said, 'You've met the other assistants.'

'What are they doing?'

'If you're interested, I could use you as well.' This, although the professor couldn't have known it, had always been a flattering if somewhat coercive line in my mind. To hear it again made me smile wistfully for an innocence I wasn't sure I had not maintained. But the thought was brief, for my efforts at recollection were soon joined by an immense pain along my neck, as if it were being twisted or pushed downward into memory. I recalled J. C., the manager of the A&P down in L.A., using the same line – 'I could use you' – when I'd applied for a job in the deli section. And the professor at UCLA had used these words when she'd asked me to be her research assistant – 'I could use you.' The fact that I knew nothing about the civilizations that had populated the Arcoiris Valley turned out to be unimportant because all I did as an assistant was lie face up on a shallow underground riverbed, day after day, taking rubbings of pictographs (clusters of swirls, triangles and stick people). After making a rubbing, I would slip it into the waterproof pouch strapped to my chest.

The position was painless enough, the steady stream sliding beneath and around me, drenching my T-shirt and shorts, stroking my bare skin. My soaked head, it seemed, was being slowly, gently shorn of its hairs. Pools of liquid cockled my ears and stimulated my cheeks and neck, rubbing them clean as the nerve endings dulled from the cold until the steady pull numbed my shoulders and chest, glistening in the minimal light, my sides also being rubbed as moist as fresh papier mâché. The shallow basin of my stomach succumbed to the gurgling persistence of the flow and swirled with water as the flesh seemed to slide gently away, as if I were river rock and my belly a basin of stone.

Gradually I realized that the affectionate strokes could also be felt as strokes of pain, entering through ecstasy but balancing on the threshold of both. It all depended on how I bent my mind, so that even as I felt myself being rubbed bare, I also felt myself being steeled, my final willing submission arising from my greatest moment of erotic command. I could feel myself battling for control of an orgasm, until at last I chose to lose myself to pleasure and my cock shot semen that almost immediately became one with the larger flow of liquids. I faded into a half-sleep, the frail flashes of sunlight reflecting off the water like trout scales, the mixture of liquids streaming by me like the comforting hands of someone familiar with my body, the colours taking the shapes of pools of luminescent tangerine.

You could imagine how my ecstasy escalated when I realized that, this time, I had not given up consciousness while rubbing pictographs but had lost myself in Dr. Amicable's gorge, that I was no longer the man with the tools but that it was I who was on the stone being scaled, rubbed raw, embalmed alive in my own fluids. Others were skinning me but I had given consent, encouragement, had initiated the process. On the periphery of my vision, I could see Dr. Amicable reclining on a chaise longue and slowly twirling a scalpel. It was on this day that he accidentally made the cut of which Giggy would later be so embarrassed. The assistants' sturdy hands were just now working near my waist and thighs, taking their pleasurable time in stripping my body, one or two layers of skin at a time in strips thinner than a dragonfly's skeleton, watching the blood and water mingle on the new surface before slipping down onto the stone. The assistants, the sturdy musculature of their own bodies exposed, seemed to feel no pain, and my own flesh tingled with a sensitivity like that of a warm chinook.

Though aware of my risky position in the experience, I saw myself as in control, even in authority. I understood that the pleasure felt by Dr. Amicable and the assistants rose from my own body. I could tell by the intense joy emanating from my chest and stomach that my comparatively insensitive ass and back had not yet been skinned, unlike the melon-rusty flesh of the professor's aides. Their surfaces had been stripped strategically, so that no marks would be visible when they were fully clothed, like Giggy with her discreet tattoo. Feeling the surge of our collective orgasm, I nevertheless maintained control of the energy. I tried to remember what 'each taut muscle perfectly defined' could have meant to me before I had seen the vision of these five muscle-clad men and women arching their backs and shooting miraculous starbursts into the glistening air, what it had meant before the five words had started rolling around in my head like the last five stars in an orange dawn, before the always silent Chappy leapt off the chaise longue and onto the stone slab to which I was strapped and began his happy lapping.

It was on seeing that dog that I first realized the subterranean channels of the Winter Garden were connected to the gorge. This, I concluded, was why Giggy wished to keep the children of Wachannabee off her property. I think now she may very well have been concerned for their safety, although I know there was no reason to be. Giggy really had no idea what was going on; she's just sensitive to pain, I think. It may be she knows nothing of these goings-on even now. Perhaps this has been in part why I've kept silent – fear that even those nearest to me would not understand. But, primarily, none of us who took part have spoken yet because the experience had been consensual.

Clearly we had taken it too far with me. I don't know how my body made it into the basement; somebody – more than one person surely – had carried me there, I imagine. Had I not fainted, I would have acted afterward as had the assistants and who knows how many others who have been stripped before me – keeping silent, taking pleasure in the hint of pain hidden beneath my clothing. You see, my silence has been necessary in order for everybody's ecstasy to remain complete. I have chosen to give up that pleasure now, in order to clear away the accusations. Cora had pleaded with me to do so. Dr. Amicable had pleaded with me not to. Until recently. Cora must have convinced him to change his mind. Unfortunately, as this pleasure is rooted in a single collective, my explanation here will diminish or destroy not only my experience but everybody's. Clarity. What a sacrifice for clarity.

✦

Sir Clasp had declared himself not guilty, claiming that his accusations were true and were made public for the benefit of the community and his Bella. And so there was to be a trial. The judge was fifteen minutes late that day and, upon his entrance, Giggy surprised everybody, including herself, by leaping to attention; it was something she had been taught to do as a child, on those occasions when her father joined the family for dinner. The courtroom tittered and Jem hung his head. Robert muzzled into his boyfriend's cowlick and rolled his fingers affectionately, as if they were cigarillos. Mr. Umbridge, Giggy's lawyer and the Lake's most established of prosecutors, offered the first of the opening statements. He was a moderate-sized man with clean definition and no excess fat on the postern. His head was appropriately lean, albeit not as wide between the ears as is generally desirable, and his eyes were not as dark as Chappy's had been. A stricter judge might say his jaw was undershot and he himself tried to make up for this by growing a goatee, which only drew attention to the weakness.

The prosecution began by arguing that it was 'a matter of serious moment that such a libel as that which Sir Clasp wrote upon that paper should in any way be connected with someone who has borne such a high reputation in this country.' Nobody knew what Giggy's reputation in any country was but, upon hearing that she had one, they were quick to speculate. Had they been given a moment to confer, they would have agreed that she must have a clean reputation, being a charitable woman (recall the children's summer camp) and from a family of pedigree (she clearly lacked the stamina to have gained financial comfort on her own). Unfortunately, the notion that she came from such a family also worked against her, suggesting as it did that she may be the inbred progeny of a spindly ancestry. Giggy realized this and sighed over the influence that clichés seemed to have on the masses.

The prosecution clarified that the defence need not prove simply that Clasp's intentions weren't public but, as Clasp had openly accused, that Giggy was only 'posing' as a matriarch. The woman, casting her soggy eyes downward, thought that she was now further from posing even than when she performed her toilet. Dr. Amicable also looked downward for, once again, he found it difficult not to imagine Giggy as edible. The prosecution noted that, though the missive was delivered privately, Sir Clasp had already admitted his public intent and that the method of delivery — being tied to a squirrel he'd caught on the premises and then cast through a window — ensured an audience to some degree, simply through the *Wachannabee Orderly*'s reference to the incident the following day.

As Umbridge went on, Cora, Bella, Jem and Robert watched the matriarch's shoulders heave and knew that, if she started crying, each of them would have to leave. They knew her mind was active but that her body lacked the go, and if they asked permission to support her, doubtless it would start a row, for all the people in the courtroom were laying gazes at her feet — some with pity, some with sorrow, some nerve-dancing in their seats. But just as many glanced to wound her, driving lances through her sides, driving pins and driving needles, driving anything their minds could dare create, lest the red-iron curves of their precious smiles reveal an element of hate.

Umbridge tried to interrupt the sway of eyes toward Giggy by making a plea to the jury's 'moral lucidity' and then shifted to a clarification of Giggy's relations with her nephew, Robert, Cora, Derek and other people whom she had invited to stay at her home as family members. It was Umbridge's aim to discuss all the elements that the defendant's lawyer would want to use as ammunition. Anything the other might construe as vile, he would foreshadow with amnesty. Umbridge read a passage of the Fafaist Manifesto where Giggy referred to Jem, a passage that might to naive minds suggest that her sexual attractions contradicted her claims to familial affection. 'Giggy is an authoress,' noted the lawyer, 'and the passage is a piece of fiction. Moreover, since so many elements in this particular work – the claims to artistic subtlety, the suggestion of talent – do not reflect the plaintiff, it cannot be argued that she describes her own emotions toward her nephew either. Don't get me wrong; Giggy is in no way ashamed of this work and she should not be, as it is an expression of her aesthetic sensibility. It is the origin indeed of a new aesthetic school, Fafaism, which Giggy assures me will have great influence in New York's West Side, on Hastings Street in Vancouver, even in Moldavia.'

His language, thought Jem, is so stilted, so chalk dry, as if drawn from tabloids over a hundred years old and then stuffed into the mouths of lawyers to let longevity stand as credence. It all came down to time. Should one lawyer bring out the Constitution, this could be usurped by *Paradise Lost*, which could be tossed by *The Tempest*, pilloried by 'The Pardoner's Tale,' and finally bonked blind by anything from the Koran, the writings of Lao Tzu or the Bible (save for the Song of Solomon). Umbridge was winding up his statement by noting Sir Clasp's rude and illegal actions. He then disassociated Giggy from the *Orderly* which, he argued, showed poor judgement in publishing both Sir Clasp's bloody slander and Robert's confession, and had itself recently attained national attention for a string of legal battles due to an editorial arguing that excessive charity was counterproductive to the virility of the nation. He threw in a passage of Shakespeare quoting the Bible, so gorgeous that Jem, appearing as pious as St. Piotus during his famous genuflection to the *Pietà*, sighed audibly, turning heads and gaining sympathy for the entire household of the Winter Garden. It had all come together after all.

The defence would now make its opening statement. Sir Clasp's lawyer was a wan pup with a last name that nobody ever pronounced correctly – Boiant. He was an acquaintance of Jem's that Giggy had once even entertained at her home. His suit did much to disguise his slender body but one could still recognize that his thighs were weak and his hocks were probably not well let-down. His steep croup and short coupling were most unfortunate, but he did display an adequate length of loin. So much attention is placed upon the head and, in this regard, Boiant displayed admirably, having virtually no stop. Some might judge his neck as verging on ewe-like, but 'Verging is not being,' as the standards note. His hands were well-knuckled as well and rather long, as was in fashion.

'Nobody wants to drag this out more than is necessary,' said Mr. Boiant, trolling one elegant finger along the timeworn top of the judge's desk and then back and yet once more until everybody was unawares rubbing their own fingers along pieces of the courtroom furniture as if in an effort to remove the suggested filth of the proceedings. 'The description of Dr. Amicable's gorge, recently published in the *Orderly*, has revealed much of value to these proceedings. I apologize for having spent some of this sunny morning reading it to the jury. I imagine only a person who gets some perverse pleasure from the work could have read it through on their own.' Rob sniffed defiantly and Boiant – not wishing to be upstaged – returned the gesture. The implicated crowd, meanwhile, shuffled like an Off–Lake Wachannabee Community Centre dance troupe, slouching its shoulders forward in what Giggy saw as a dispirited imitation of the sewer scene in *West Side Story*.

214

'We are not,' he continued, 'members of academia.' How gauche, thought Giggy, to rhyme it with 'macadamia.' 'Nor are we here to judge the text by its compliance to censorship laws. No,' and here Boiant drew his middle finger along the judge's desk yet again. The judge began to experience a rare instance of guilt, but the janitor, who was peering in from a side entryway, remained confident of his work. Like a god did Boiant roll the cosmic dust he'd gathered off the furniture between the pads of two of his fingers, like a god did he flick the tips to cast off any mortal debris and then, like a god did he wipe them once, lightly, across the back of his pant leg.

Oh, oh, oh. Too late, too late. How right they were, whoever said, 'Time in a courtroom, it shifts along as slow as a snail only suddenly to spring forward like a mamba snake.' With that last, minute gesture, all the judgement on the scales instantly, instantly turned on the lawyer himself. Too late he recalled that the first rule of courtroom drama was never to touch oneself in public – not one's face, not one's hair, not even one's pant leg. At first, only Giggy caught the faux pas, but she well knew that it was only a matter of time. Sure enough, mid-sentence, Boiant began to redden and soon everybody in the room realized what he had done. As the light trail of dust on his pants proved, he was human after all. Imperfect. Who was he to judge? Sir Clasp screwed up his face and sucked back spit. A tinny murmur filled the air.

'No,' Boiant continued, somewhat wilder, now overconscious of his digits, weaving them together behind his back, stuffing first one hand, then the other, into his loose pockets ... reddening, reddening ... crossing his arms over his chest, those guilty fingers dangling from his sides like the clipped wings of a naughty angel, 'No,' and his voice rose to take attention away from the digits. 'Surprisingly, we are not being asked to judge the text at all. Remember who the accused is. Remarkably, I say remarkably, it is Ms. Giggy Andrewes who is the plaintiff in this case.' With that he drew forward just one of his fingers and, like a magician casting a spell or a setter on its mark, held it at point on her. He had succeeded in reverting the crowd's attention to the woman sitting in the front pew like a lump of polished amber. Giggy held hope that Boiant's use of the passive voice would work in her favour.

'Honoured jury, it is because of the extended ramifications of the decision you are soon to make that I felt that every bit of information offered by this veritable confession be put forward. Now, having heard this pitiable piece,' the man went on, staring at Giggy as if she and not Robert were the author of it, 'and keeping in mind the social context in which it was created, I would like you to ask yourself, "Can I still find the accused, Sir Clasp, guilty for wanting to protect his daughter from that individual? Is Sir Clasp guilty of criminally libelling that woman?"'

The man accused sat in front of the dock holding his hat in one of his palms as he darted his eyes about the room with the caution of a nutria. He wiped sporadically at the corners of his mouth or smoothed back the saddlebag cheeks that framed it. Occasionally he would make a light stab into the floorboards with the point of his cane. A tie with his family crest hung outside his suit jacket like the tongue of a St. Bernard. His portly stomach and hunched back accentuated the notion of arrogance that much of the community had placed on Giggy's shoulders, which, powdered and cloaked in a humble fawn smock, were at the other end of the room from her accuser. Some would later suggest that it was because her hat, with its rim of canary feathers, accented her blouse too well that certain audience members failed even to consider her innocence. The Earl of Abingdon veil that hung over her face did little to cover her upraised eyes and down-turned lips which, appearing to tremble, were actually reciting, as if it were a catechism, Jem's Sweet Yam recipe. The words now held for Giggy a profundity that quotidian existence rarely allowed — the fusion of Jem and Chappy, for example, in phrases like 'sweet yam' and 'whip until fluffy.' The ethereal purity of salt, of eggs, of vanilla — vanilla as deep, vanilla as pure, vanilla as dusky, she imagined, as Robert's love-gasping eyes, as dark as the ebony cane twisting in the palm of her accuser's fist, as rich as the desk that seemed to entrap the judge and crush him behind its weight as he pawed softly the stacks of papers spread before him like tarot cards.

Giggy gazed toward the window where the sunlight spilled like icing sugar into the dry and dusty room. A small illegal market in soft drinks, Rainbow Rockets and Revellos had opened up outside the courthouse and the din of business wafted into the building like catcalls or the voices of milkmaids begging their cows to come home. Eventually, Giggy was asked to take the stand, which she did with the calm of a heifer who has eaten a few too many apples. She was collected enough, however, Jem was relieved to note, even to lie about her age, though only by a few years. Umbridge, anxious that the woman's language would alienate the jury, asked simple questions that highlighted her love of animals, her support of the children's summer program, and her charitable contributions. The exchange felt more like an amicable conversation on a downtown street than any sort of interrogation, which is as Umbridge had intended. He sensed the jury's gratefulness for this respite from boredom.

'Is there more?' Giggy asked.

'No, that will do fine,' replied Umbridge kindly, at which point the judge adjourned the trial for lunch. Umbridge held out his hand to the plaintiff, which she used willingly in her climb down from the stand.

Bella thought it best if Giggy were not seen with her until after the case was over, and so she and Cora spent the hour alone drinking claret and planning Giggy's escape, should it be necessary, through the gorge and across the lake to the Huntsville docks where they would have Jem waiting in the Bricklin to speed her off to Toronto. They had little confidence in the matriarch's success. Giggy, meanwhile, had turkey salad with dijon on Polish rye and shared a bottle of Chablis with Jem and Robert. The two men tried to convince her to drop the case, but Giggy seemed not to be there, seemed to be thinking *en Français*. They'd found a secluded booth in a restaurant just down the street from the courtroom. She held her hat on her lap, not wanting it to fall into the dirt, and fought against tears, knowing there would always be plenty of time for them later. The sandwich was dry, and more Chablis was ordered. When Jem finally told Giggy that it was time to return to the trial, she was sufficiently revived. Still she hesitated, tired of having Boiant and the rest drag her along like a pull-toy through their system of justice. She would wait a moment more. Maybe she would arrive late, maybe not — that wasn't the point. She would arrive when she was ready. Jem and Rob each kissed her on the cheek, gently so as not to mar the powders. Giggy bowed her head to avoid the glare of sunlight shooting off her nephew's bangs and recited a snippet of the yam recipe. The words, paced quickly but solemnly, hummed from her lips. All the salt seemed appropriate to her. Inside the courtroom, they parted.

Giggy quite liked Clasp's lawyer's description of her having lived a life of appetizers, but things became wearisome when he began reciting her relationships to the people at the Winter Garden, none of which were news. He pointed his sharpened tongue to a few passages of the confession in which Robert's objectivity had been derailed by the pleasures of the baroque, and then asked whether the sexual relations intimated in the work and by Sir Clasp reflected her own actual relations. His leer caused chuckles, but nobody felt implicated. Giggy folded her hands on her lap demurely and tilted a stern gaze, as if to say, 'Need you ask? Look at me.' The strategy was not effective and Giggy, suddenly nervous, concluded that it had something to do with her hat. She took it off and placed it on the sweat-worn arm of the chair, from which it fell. She bent to retrieve it, changed her mind when she realized her dress didn't allow for such movement and, distracted and exasperated, replied, 'There is no connection whatever between these relations. Oh, this is so too distressing. Am I foolish-looking? Can we do another take?'

'You're doing fine, Ms. Andrewes. Now, just to clarify one point. Is the dog named Chappy who is referred to in the piece read out today your dog?'

'I haven't a dog.'

'But you did previously have a dog named Chappy, isn't that so?'

'Yes. I once had a dog named Chappy — Chappy of Meander. I've a private notion you're hoping to tangle me in words; it won't work, you know.'

'Is this the same dog described in the *Orderly* recently?'

'Well, Chappy was a whippet, but utterly unique in the species. I got him through the humane society. His ears weren't right for a show dog, it seems, despite the pedigree and the perfect colouring.'

'But my point is that you did have a dog by the name of the dog in the confession just read out.'

'It was a non-confession,' offered Rob from the sidelines.

'Don't feel badly, dear,' the woman offered the lawyer. 'Fiction is meant to be misleading. Listen now.' Giggy was so pleased with the ease of these questions and the depth of her knowledge. 'Just because your parents name your dog Lassie doesn't mean it will grow up to be a collie. Or altruistic, for that matter. Chappy was a whippet in real life, which is different from being a whippet character named Chappy. Now, terrier blood is considered most advantageous in a hunting whippet, but you must all know that. Still, that doesn't make a terrier a whippet. There. There's no other reason to get confused.

'No, it's all fiction, the stuff about the dog. A terrier doesn't look at a whippet and see another terrier, Mr. Boiant (she pronounced it 'Bwah,' as if sensitive to the French). This is important; you see, I once saw a flying squirrel and thought it was a bird – I felt bad about it then, upon realizing my mistake,' then to the audience, 'as you could imagine.'

'Just answer the question, Ms. Andrewes. Yes or no?'

'I was responding to a question?'

'Right. In his piece, Robert refers to Dr. Amicable's gorge. Is that referring to our Dr. Amicable?' Boiant cracked his knuckles and the professor knew exactly what he was about.

'Yours possibly, though he's never said so to me.'

'Can you point out Dr. Amicable in the audience?' Giggy did so and he grinned as if he had just been singled out during a talk show. Even his smile seemed to have a slight accent. He waved to those who might not have found him otherwise.

'Is this the same man in the confession?'

'Non-confession,' but half-heartedly by now.

'Well no, the other doesn't exist except ... '

'Enough games. Is the piece referring to that Dr. Amicable over there?'

'You should ask Robert.'

'The piece describes a man who enjoys having his flesh removed. Do you think that is an enjoyable thing?' Shivers all around, some of pleasure.

'I did have an in-depth peel once, thanks to the gentle skills of Agnes Burnes-Primley. Agnes?' and the woman stood sheepishly, although her smile registered pride, before sinking back into the crowd. 'Remember? You recommended her to me. I've never heard of anyone except salespeople refer to it as enjoyable. Sorry, Agnes.' This was a lie, for Robert had described it as such.

'So do you think it blasphemous to claim to enjoy such an experience?'

'The argument would not convince me.'

'But do you think it's blasphemous?'

'I think it may be a poor choice of topic, if that's all there was to it. Is that what you mean?'

'Answer the question, ma'am. Do you or do you not consider the notion blasphemous?' The natural light had begun to wane, shifting from its warm hue to something less complementary, like butterscotch. During the questioning, the green room had taken on a cavernous air, the corners rounding into darkness, the floral design of the moulding along the edge of the ceiling beginning to ooze shadows across their own petals, across the walls, across those members of the jury sitting in the highest row of seats. Yet nobody turned on any lights and, indeed, since the stifling heat had not subsided (the windows only minimally ajar), it did not feel as if dusk were upon them at all. It seemed more as if the sun were tired, although the day itself was far from spent. A remnant of summer still hung from the gauze laced limply around the yellow hat that once seemed so symbolic and now lay forgotten in the dust shifting thick as amoebas about everybody's feet.

'Is self-mutilation blasphemous?'

'I don't use the word "blasphemous." I think hurting one's self is frightening and dangerous and a sign perhaps, oh yes, of desperation, and I think to address the issue is to show interest. Think of tattoos; they aren't a passing fancy.' Giggy had begun to slump in her seat, but the lawyer persisted.

'Is it not horrible to show interest in such acts?'

'You're showing very much interest in it yourself, Mr. Bwah.'

'My interest is in the truth, Ms. Andrewes.'

'And my interest is in the humane. Are you enjoying this?'

'Will you admit that anyone who would approve of Robert's confession would thereby pose as guilty of improper practices?'

'Not at all. Tattoos, Mr. Bwah, I remind you again of tattoos. Or collagen or exercise and all those other forms of masochism. Such pleasures, or stories of such pleasures — carry no aesthetic weight.'

'But moral weight?'

'Oh, that sort of impropriety. I never realized your questions were prurient. It depends on how the story is read. But I do suspect a spiritual reading would offer the only explanation.'

'So the author isn't responsible for the story, then? Do you see a person as generally free of responsibility for the things he or she writes?'

'Not responsible for the uses to which the story is put.'

'But isn't an author responsible for the truth encouraged by a story.'

'Is truth truth, or do you think it can be "encouraged"?' Giggy was feeling somewhat more on solid ground again. 'I've found it wise, Mr. Bwah, to make it a habit to distrust people who claim to tell the truth, especially those who appear sincere.'

'I don't think it's necessary to go through a wild analysis of the passages in this text to see if you agree with them. You appear to have subsumed the entire work within a notion of art that is apparently separable from the real world and its responsibilities. Is that so?'

'No, no, quite the inverse. I believe that all of the world and its responsibilities are subsumed by a notion of art. It's simply a matter of articulating rules of fair play.' This response didn't satisfy the members of the jury, most of whom — ready for a nap — were unwilling to follow past the notion that life was art. Jem had begun a silent sobbing some minutes ago and Cora finally had to lead him outside for air. Bella sat prim and eager to speak. The witness box was to be her ring, if they would only let her put on the gloves. The defence tried to focus the interrogation once more.

'For the sake of argument, let me ask if you think it is fair play to present people who you know in a manner that suggests that they are immoral?'

'If you wish. It's your fantasy.'

'Would you represent a person you know if you were an artist?'

'It's inevitable that an artist represents what she has known and so, yes, I would surely represent everybody who has ever been at the Winter Garden, Mr. Bwah ... everybody.' And two hundred and eighty eyebrows rose and hovered like mosquitoes avoiding a sudden whiff of smoke from a bonfire. 'People of minor consequence, of course, couldn't all be conceived of as individuals. More as strains in the background, a hum in the summer's heat.'

Mr. Boiant's efforts to lead Giggy to articulating her culpability in the lifestyles of the Winter Garden had failed precisely because Giggy did not see herself as the author of the lifestyle. They had reached a stalemate which meant that the lawyer for the defence had no choice but to continue his questioning. Just then, as Cora and Jem re-entered, the sound of Canada geese drifted into the stifling courtroom and everybody, keen to let their imaginations take wing, murmured satisfaction with Giggy's later rebuttal.

'I see. Let's try another avenue. You're accusing Sir Clasp of libel for stating that you pose as a matriarch.'

'That's correct.' Bella's father wiped the saliva from his lower lip nervously.

'And it is the notion of posing that offends you?' Jem hated this questioning. Every word, it seemed to him, needed definition. How he wished his aunt could gather her brood together in a little bundle and take them back to the Winter Garden.

'As Sir Clasp used the term, yes.'

'Is it correct to assume that one of the people toward whom you feel motherly is your nephew, Jem.'

'Oh, definitely. I love him.'

'He was also your cook, right? Although he wasn't trained as one.'

'I don't know that it matters. Artists need leeway for their imaginations.'

'Another art? Is everything art?'

'Mayakovsky, the poet, once wore a carrot for a tie. He once turned a bowl upside down and asked that his borscht be served in that. But then, borscht ... His point was that anything can be art, though many things are done artlessly. Now everything Jem does is pleasantly artful.'

'Is he an artist?'

'Not in the sense of creating anything. He's intellectual and clever, and I love him very much.' Well yes, I do create, thought Jem, as he admired the copper veins meandering up the back of his hands. But to be bothered now by his aunt's choice of words would be a misapplication of energy; it was, no doubt, part of her strategy, and he could always brood later.

'How do you love him exactly?' This was a question for which many had been waiting, although they might have worded it differently. The distinction between a matriarch and a poseur was in the way they loved or, more precisely, in the way they saw themselves loving. The language Giggy had employed thus far, the jury felt, suggested that her love was not that of a mother. And yet, they could be swayed by the slightest shift in rhetoric.

'I love him tenderly, Mr. Bwah.' This courtroom experience, Giggy felt, had become almost unbearable. Jem could tell that she wasn't enjoying herself any longer, if she had ever been.

'In what way?'

'I love him enough to allow him to live with me as he wishes. I encouraged him to bring his friend with him from New Orleans. When he and Robert became boyfriends, I let my love for Robert grow and, when Robert hurt himself, I tended to him with as much affection and attention as I believed he wanted. It was I who thought of putting the frog in the fishbowl by his bedside, Mr. Bwah.'

'Indeed.'

'Yes, and I let Jem drive the Bricklin. He had his own room, until he moved into Robert's. He drinks and eats and smokes whatever he wants and I don't even consider charging him for it like some mothers might. I've had long conversations with him on the gazebo, some of which have lasted entire days. Jem has become my greatest and dearest friend. He's intelligent, artistic and thoughtful. And you need only glance in the stalls, oh, where has he gone? Well, you know very well what a beautiful and handsome man he is.'

'Why do you say that?'

'What?'

'That he's handsome.'

'Well, because he has fine skin, and slender, boyish legs and deep, intelligent eyes that … Oh Jem, stand up and remind Mr. Bwah what you look like.' But the man remained seated, unprepared to confront the disturbance in the ambience.

'No, Giggy. Why did you tell us of his physical appearance at all? Do you love your nephew because he's physically attractive?' Some in the jury and audience interpreted Giggy's description as non-maternal because she spoke of her nephew as if he were an acquaintance, a close friend, another adult with whom she enjoyed spending time, even leisure time. They could see now where Mr. Boiant had been leading them, but they were more disconcerted by the realization that they had all along been led. So each waited like a crop-duster to sense the direction of the moral breeze.

'Do you find your nephew sexually attractive?'

'Exasperation, Mr. Bwah. Jem's simply a beautiful human being.'

'In what way? Physically? Is that why you described him physically?'

'Indeed, I can tell when somebody is good-looking even if they are related to me. I can find them sexually attractive. We all can.'

'And would you have sex with your nephew?'

'Why should I say that I wouldn't?'

'Are you speaking flippantly now, Miss?'

'No. This isn't a flippant answer, but you need to understand ... '

'I've no more questions.'

'And me, sir? I have so many. May I not speak?' It seemed a fair request, and not only to Giggy, but the option was not considered.

Sir Clasp, though he was the defendant, was questioned for less time than Giggy. The others of the Winter Garden got off with relative ease as well, although Jem tried to make the most of it. The next day, the defence presented a conclusion that reiterated the words that whizzed with effrontery over the town. He stated that from the beginning to the end, Sir Clasp, in his dealings with Giggy, was influenced by one hope alone, 'that of saving his daughter.' Boiant then read a letter from Bella to Sir Clasp in which she threatened to inject him with genetically modified bovine fertility serum if he continued to interfere in her life. The jury drew back in collective surprise; she was *their* veterinarian, too. Paradoxically, Bella's acknowledgement the previous day that her alliance with Giggy's family was greater than that with her father – what the man had aimed to prove all along – now made the entire Clasp family suspect, especially the patriarch himself. He sighed in frustration. Giggy wiped a tear across the side of her face. Jem doubled over crying. His stomach was beginning to cramp with anxiety. He needed the breeze. Everybody did. It all seemed so practiced, purgatorial, a rehearsal after the show had ended its run. Giggy placed her left hand lightly over her right like the Emperor at the Coliseum signalling ennui. She was posing reserve, because fortunately reserve was so hard to see through. Heaven, she thought, can be such a long way from home.

The defence reminded the jury that the question to be debated was whether Giggy had posed as a matriarch. 'Posing,' they wondered in a fresh attempt at attention, their backs straightening and eyes deglazing to demonstrate that they were in earnest. The jury must decide whether Sir Clasp's statement was true in fact and substance, and whether it was made for the public good. 'The public good,' they wondered, as some of their heads began to tilt as if in thought and their faces began to nod as if heavy with knowledge, all for the sake of the audience. What good could come of insinuating intrafamilial passions on which nobody had ever acted? Like most members of the jury, Giggy was plucking lightly at her clothing. New stains of perspiration formed on her dress whenever another section of the material happened to touch her flesh. She held a palm to one side of her brow just as three members of the jury did the same. She was going to faint.

Jem, foreseeing the crisis, rose and strode through the silence to the entrance. If he leaves, more than one person thought to herself, I can perhaps shortly follow. The public humiliation had lost its entertainment value. The spectacle had trailed off to its gaudy end. The final verdict didn't matter much any longer; for most of those present, it never had. But Jem had never forsaken the suffering and he would not now. He pushed open the heavy, dark doors as if he alone knew that the breeze from the lake had been waiting to saunter in. He wedged the doors open with the toes of his sneakers and returned barefoot to the stalls. And the winds, the winds drew everybody together as they questioned, without a word, why they were gathered there at all when the breeze was strong and the geese were call-ing and the lake waved like a silk sarong wrapped loosely about the evening.

The cool air had accepted the man's escort inside and now swung the hem of its robe about the corners of the courtroom, reviving the crowd and raising the jury from its performance. Giggy felt the balmy strokes of the breeze as if they were made by the fingers of her nephew himself. She was going to faint regardless. She swigged the air desperately, turned toward the window and – along with the judge, the jury and everybody else – imagined what the room must look like from aloft, from above the buildings, body naked in the cool, dark night. She imagined the air and its moment's respite from the chafing that had occurred throughout the court case, throughout her inter-rogation and that of Clasp, and still now. It was only those who have retained some innocence, she mused, who can seriously consider the imaginary as an avenue of escape. This had been the point all along – of the summer, Fafaism, and now this trial.

She envisioned her body being borne by the breeze above the other members of the community and out of the building, the satin of her lemon dress flowing sleek about her in the dewy air as barn swallows and yellow larks swam past with waving wings and, yes, oh yes, Dr. Amicable's long and extremely slen-der canoe slivered beneath her like a slip of cantaloupe. A-glisten would be the slip and brightest amber would be the lake as her body hovered like a dew-gemmed dragonfly, just keeping itself from shifting down toward the stillness of the water.

Slowly she passed over the city, the lake, the stately pines, until she reached her Winter Garden. Circling there, she could see her family settling calm and cool among the weeping willows, Chappy and the peacocks managing somehow to stay out of each other's way. Bella and Cora were sharing sherbet, the silver leaves of the willows whipping against their golden limbs and tangling their thick, messy hair. The men reclined nearby drinking ginger ale and Pernod, counting perhaps, out of sheer curiosity, the blades of grass encompassed by a peacock's foot-print or the drops of moisture that balanced on a single blade, like the pearls on the tiara of the exiled Princess of Grozny. Jem, rising onto his haunches, placed two slips of grass between the sides of his thumbs and pressed the cutting edge of the blades against his lips. And he blew then, letting off a thin but pierc-ing bellow into the garden where it rumbled like the trumpeting of alpine shepherds. The amber skin of the apple from which they were cutting slices glistened against the milky white of its inner meat. And the family's own flesh glowed in the shade of the *Nude Descending Staircase* into which the two always excitable peacocks had fled. Giggy, hovering above, could see all the fountains, shooting forth the cool, crisp liquid that bubbled up from the many cavernous tunnels of Dr. Amicable's Gorge.

Circling higher and higher toward the sun, she could at last make out the *Nude* herself, golden, tawny and auburn – gigantic in the evening light, solid and heavy, her lines clearly delineated from the flaming bush at her crotch to the soft, sure curves of her forehead, shoulders, breasts and thighs, free of the straps and stays that had confined Giggy for so long. She smiled to see that the fountains did not mark her nipples, her vagina, her lips. Instead they were scattered as loosely as the stars of a constellation offering no real outline for what they adorned. She could just make out the peacocks' cries – *kree, kreee, kreeee* – as the birds fanned out their tails and drew them in again before scurrying, so far below her, from one fountain to the next, first at the *Nude*'s earlobe, then leaping to a shoulder, her side, a spot on the outer edge of her left hip, and so on among the erogenous zones of the golden body, all the way down to her dark, bare feet which proceeded, as Bella had claimed, scarred but confident through the wild grasses and muddy banks leading into the moist darkness of the gorge.

✦

ACKNOWLEDGEMENTS

Morgan Holmes has been selfless and devoted in his sacrifices to the creation of this novel. Unfathomable remains the reservoir from which Alana Wilcox has taken her persistence and patience in making the final product as clear and polished as it has become. And thanks to Jason McBride for his insight, energy and support, and to Ian McInnis for inventing stained glass. To this amicable team, I would like to add those librarians and archivists who have helped with my research at the National Library in Ottawa, the McLennan Library at McGill University, the Ryerson University Library, Robarts Library at the University of Toronto, the British Portrait Gallery and the British Library.

ABOUT THE AUTHOR

Dennis Denisoff began writing as a teenager at the David Thompson University Centre in Nelson, BC, the origins of the Kootenay School of Writing, of which he was a member. In addition to *The Winter Gardeners*, he has published another novel, *Dog Years* (Arsenal Pulp, 1991); a book of poetry, *Tender Agencies* (Arsenal Pulp, 1994); and a monograph on the Canadian poet Erin Mouré (ECW, 1995). His most recent publications include the scholarly study *Aestheticism and Sexual Parody: 1840–1940* (Cambridge, 2002) and the forthcoming *Sexual Visuality from Literature to Film: 1850–1950* (Palgrave-MacMillan, 2004).

In addition to his own work, he has also edited the first-ever collection of Canadian gay male prose, *Queeries* (Arsenal Pulp, 1993) and an anthology, *The Victorian Short Story* (Broadview, 2004), and is the managing editor of the literary journal *The White Wall Review*. He teaches literature, culture and creative writing at Ryerson University.

Typeset in Centaur and Mason and printed and bound at the
Coach House on bpNichol Lane, 2003

Edited and designed by Alana Wilcox
Cover design by Ian McInnis

Coach House Books
401 Huron Street (rear) on bpNichol Lane
Toronto, Ontario
M5S 2G5

416 979 2217
1 800 367 6360

mail@chbooks.com
www.chbooks.com